A Wager with the Matchmaker

Books by Jody Hedlund

A SHANAHAN MATCH

Calling on the Matchmaker
Saved by the Matchmaker
A Wager with the Matchmaker

COLORADO COWBOYS

A Cowboy for Keeps
The Heart of a Cowboy
To Tame a Cowboy
Falling for the Cowgirl
The Last Chance Cowboy

The Preacher's Bride
The Doctor's Lady
Unending Devotion
A Noble Groom
Rebellious Heart
Captured by Love

BEACONS OF HOPE

Out of the Storm: A BEACONS OF HOPE *Novella*
Love Unexpected
Hearts Made Whole
Undaunted Hope

ORPHAN TRAIN

An Awakened Heart: An ORPHAN TRAIN *Novella*
With You Always
Together Forever
Searching for You

THE BRIDE SHIPS

A Reluctant Bride
The Runaway Bride
A Bride of Convenience

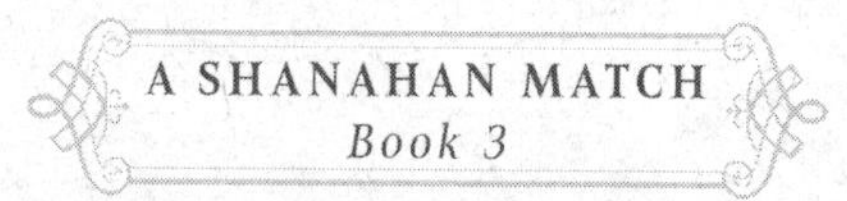

A Wager with the Matchmaker

Jody Hedlund

BETHANYHOUSE
a division of Baker Publishing Group
Minneapolis, Minnesota

Published by Bethany House Publishers
Minneapolis, Minnesota
BethanyHouse.com

Bethany House Publishers is a division of
Baker Publishing Group, Grand Rapids, Michigan

Printed in the United States of America

Library of Congress Cataloging-in-Publication Data
Names: Hedlund, Jody, author.
Title: A wager with the matchmaker / Jody Hedlund.
Description: Minneapolis, Minnesota : Bethany House Publishers, a division of Baker Publishing Group, 2025. | Series: A Shanahan Match ; 3
Identifiers: LCCN 2024041940 | ISBN 9780764241987 (paperback) | ISBN 9780764245060 (casebound) | ISBN 9781493450831 (ebook)
Subjects: LCGFT: Christian fiction. | Romance fiction. | Novels.
Classification: LCC PS3608.E333 W34 2025 | DDC 813/.6—dc23/eng/20240906
LC record available at https://lccn.loc.gov/2024041940

Scripture quotations are from the King James Version of the Bible.

Cover design by Jennifer Parker
Cover image by Lee Avison / Arcangel

Baker Publishing Group publications use paper produced from sustainable forestry practices and postconsumer waste whenever possible.

25 26 27 28 29 30 31 7 6 5 4 3 2 1

1

ST. LOUIS, MISSOURI
JUNE 1849

She had no work and no place to live. Again.

Alannah Darragh rubbed the rag vigorously over the grand piano that took up the center of the parlor. It didn't need dusting or polishing. The dark reddish wood was already so shiny she could see her reflection in it. But she had to stay busy, or worry would rise and strangle her.

Mrs. Christy's humming filtered into the parlor from the front hallway where she was boxing up the final items that would be shipped to New Orleans. The housekeeper didn't have a care in the world since she hadn't been dismissed. She'd been asked to stay and maintain the home while the O'Briens were gone—however long that might be, perhaps months. The coachman, Mr. Dunlop, was also staying.

Mrs. Christy expected that Captain O'Brien would keep his wife out of St. Louis and away from the fearsome cholera until it was no longer a threat. Maybe Mrs. O'Brien would even reside in New Orleans until after her wee babe was born in the autumn.

Whatever the case, the O'Briens no longer needed an extra domestic servant, not when the future was so uncertain.

Alannah paused and pressed a hand to her throat, as if that could somehow ward off the tightening and the feeling of suffocating. A breeze floated in through the open side window, fluttering the loose strands of her pale hair that weren't tucked under her maid's cap. For early June, the warmth of summer had already descended, turning the O'Briens' home into a sweltering oven.

'Twas only in the early morn—like now—or late in the night that the air was tolerable and more like that of her native Tralee in County Kerry.

She closed her eyes and envisioned the rugged rocky coastline, the warm sand on the beach squishing between her toes, the salty ocean breeze caressing her face, the rhythmic waves crashing onto the shore.

Heat stung behind her eyes. Ach, if only she'd never come to America . . . maybe then her younger brother would still be living. Maybe she'd still be with her cousin Hugh, who'd been her closest friend. Maybe she would have eventually been hired as an editor at the newspaper with him.

But there was no sense in crying now, so there wasn't. What was done was done.

She opened her eyes to the beauty of the parlor with the all-new furniture, elegant in the upholstered cream color that contrasted the cherry wood. The damask draperies were a pretty pale blue Mrs. Christy had said matched Alannah's eyes. With exquisite lantern globes, pure silver candleholders, and vases of freshly cut flowers, the parlor was lovely—

just as lovely as all the other rooms Mrs. O'Brien had recently redecorated.

To be sure, it was the nicest home Alannah had ever stepped foot in. 'Twas a shame the job hadn't lasted more than six weeks.

Of course, Mrs. O'Brien was a kind lady and had told Alannah she could stay as long as she needed until she could secure other employment. Mrs. Christy had assured her of the same.

But after just one day since the captain and Mrs. O'Brien had left, there was already nothing to do.

Besides, Alannah couldn't live on charity. She'd had to do that enough over the past couple of years before leaving Ireland, and she loathed the prospect of being beholden to anyone ever again.

The simple fact was, she had to find another job right away, preferably one as a domestic. Then she'd have a new place to live and plenty to keep her busy.

But how could she even begin to go about finding a position? She had no connections, no friends, no relatives—other than Torin. Even though she'd told her older brother yesterday of her need for another job, he wasn't a miracle worker.

With a sigh, Alannah moved from the piano to the cream-colored mantel above the fireplace. She dusted a lovely silver-framed painting of a steamboat on the river before she moved to the ornate clock.

At a firm knocking at the front door, she stilled, her rag growing idle. Who would be calling now that the O'Briens had left the city?

Her pulse ticked a faster beat in time with the mantel

clock. After two months since the incident with Shaw Farrell, surely she didn't need to be afraid of being captured.

Regardless, she sidled next to the bay window overlooking the front of the house. She peeked past the drapery but couldn't see the stoop at the top of the entry stairs. Only the short-trimmed grass of the front yard was visible and the gravel drive leading to the carriage house and stable at the back of the property.

Mrs. Christy ceased her humming and opened the front door. "May I help you?"

"Oh, aye." The response belonged to a young man, a voice Alannah didn't recognize. "I'd like to speak to Alannah."

Alannah froze, and her heart switched to double time. Someone was here to see her? Why? Had Shaw Farrell finally discovered her whereabouts?

The notorious gang leader couldn't have. She'd been so careful to stay hidden, to remain invisible, to never go anywhere.

Maybe someone in the Farrell gang had spotted her leaving St. Louis two weeks ago during the fire, when scores of people had fled to the countryside and away from the inferno. Even though it had been night and she'd been in the carriage with Mrs. Christy and Mrs. O'Brien, 'twas still possible she'd been seen.

Or maybe one of Shaw's men had glimpsed her returning to St. Louis a couple of days after the devastation. She'd ridden back in the same carriage, again with Mrs. Christy and Mrs. O'Brien. It had been daylight then, and she'd stayed as far from the carriage windows as possible.

"Alannah is working at the moment." Mrs. Christy's tone turned firm in an obvious attempt to send the visitor on his way. 'Twas kind of Mrs. Christy to be looking out for her. Alannah had never shared the details that had forced her into hiding. But Mrs. Christy was a right sharp woman, so she was, and had likely drawn her own conclusions.

Panic began to make a trail through Alannah. Her gaze darted around the room. Was there a place she could hide? In a closet? Behind a piece of furniture?

The sofa was too close to the wall, the piano was too out in the open, the chairs in front of the fireplace wouldn't provide enough cover.

"I only need to speak with her for a few minutes," the man persisted, his voice calm and kindly.

Shaw had been calm and kindly enough during their first encounter too. She'd only been in St. Louis a week back in March, had no employment, had nothing to do, and had wanted to explore—even though Torin had warned against going out of the tenement.

But the apartment and the entire tenement where he'd arranged for her to stay had been crowded and dirty and falling apart. She should have been grateful for a place at all when others were living in shacks in alleys or sleeping in hallways or even setting up tents along the river.

She'd tried to stay inside, tried to be content with her corner spot and one of her books. But her Tralee blood had pulsed with the need to see the sky and the river and anything that would remind her of home.

During her exploring, she hadn't been able to view the sky through the permanent haze of coal smoke. The riverfront had been crowded with steamboats, and the Mississippi River had been muddy. So she'd walked the two miles to the glass factory where Torin worked. There the city was less crowded, trees and grass and flowers grew in abundance, and she could see the sky clearly.

She hadn't heeded Torin's pleas not to come again. Instead, she'd walked the distance every afternoon, having located a park where she could read and pretend she was back in Ireland just for a short while. Then when the glass factory whistle signaled the end of the workday, she waited for Torin outside the factory, and he accompanied her back to her tenement.

It wasn't until the end of the week of her routine that Shaw approached her, once at the park and then while she waited outside the factory the following day. Both times he'd made it clear he thought she was beautiful and was interested in her. And both times she'd tried to make it clear that she wasn't interested in return.

When Shaw had stopped her again the next week, she'd ignored him, but he wasn't the type of man to tolerate that. "Hey, beautiful." He'd sauntered toward where she stood near the entrance of the glass factory. "It's your lucky day."

She pretended to keep reading. But when he stopped just inches from where she'd perched on the steps, she was left with no choice but to acknowledge him. He had a boxy head with light brown hair and was clean-shaven with a thin scar above his lips. As he peered down at her, his eyes were filled with only one thing—lust. She'd seen it enough to know.

"Sorry, mister. I don't believe in luck."

"Well you will now." He chortled, and several of his big, burly friends laughed. "Lots of women want me and would marry me. But I'm gonna let you have the honor."

Indignation stiffened her spine. She'd had proposals of marriage before, but none quite like this. "No, thank you—"

He reached for her, and his massive hand circled her upper arm. Before she knew what was happening, he jerked her to her feet and pressed his mouth to hers.

She was so taken aback that she stood frozen in place for a moment while his lips plied against hers. She felt nothing in response, not even an ounce of attraction.

At a roar, from the corner of her eyes she could see Torin exiting the factory. He was shouting curses and careening toward Shaw. His blue eyes that matched Alannah's radiated with murder, his face was flushed with rage, and he already had both of his knives out.

With a strength she'd had to cultivate over the years, she wrenched herself free, raised a hand, and slapped Shaw across his cheek.

Shaw was no longer paying attention to her, however. Instead, he unsheathed a knife of his own, along with a revolver.

"No!" she screamed, grabbing on to Shaw's arm.

He shoved her, and she stumbled away, far enough to see that the factory owner, Kiernan Shanahan, had exited and was glowering almost as much as Torin.

Several of Torin's friends and fellow factory workers latched on to his body and held him back. At the same time, Shaw's bodyguards jerked him backward too.

"You owe me," Shaw shouted, as he wrestled to free himself from those restraining him.

"I paid off my debts," Torin called.

"No one ever walks away from the Farrell gang." Shaw's

expression turned lethal. "Not unless they pay the right price."

Torin had joined the Farrell gang when he'd first arrived in St. Louis last summer because Shaw had promised him employment, steady food, and safe housing. In a place so far away from home and family, Torin had been hungry and sick and vulnerable. He'd needed friends, and Shaw and his gang had made him feel wanted.

Too late he'd realized the Farrells were involved in crimes and illegal activities that had nothing to do with making a better life for anyone but themselves. Torin's conscience hadn't allowed him to be a part of their crimes any longer. Finally, he'd broken away from the Farrells and joined the Saints Alley gang instead.

He'd known that severing his connection with the Farrells would put him in danger—maybe eventually cost him his life—but he'd been willing to sacrifice to live more honorably.

"There is no right price." Torin spat the words at Shaw.

"Oh, there's always a right price." Shaw cocked his head at Alannah. "I want to marry your sister. That's the only payment I'll accept."

"No!" Torin thundered.

Shaw's lips had curled up into a grin. "Give her to me, or you're a dead man."

Torin had spewed more curses as Shaw and his men left. Once they were gone, Torin had asked his boss for help in hiding Alannah. Much to their surprise, Kiernan had made arrangements for her to work as a maid for his sister Enya, Mrs. O'Brien. Alannah had come to the O'Briens the next day, and she'd been in hiding there ever since.

She wanted no part of Shaw's plan, not only because she wanted to protect herself but because if she fell into Shaw's clutches, it would kill Torin.

With her heart pounding out a fresh urgency, she studied the parlor again, her gaze snagging upon the draperies. Could she hide within the folds? They were thick enough that if anyone glanced into the room—and didn't look too closely—she might be able to remain undetected.

Another breeze rushed in the window and fluttered the elegant material.

The window. Maybe she ought to sneak out the side window. Then she could race around the back and hide in the carriage house. Mr. Dunlop would surely do his best to keep her safe.

"I'm sorry," Mrs. Christy said, "but I cannot allow Alannah to be away from her duties for even a moment."

Alannah started across the room toward the window. The kindly housekeeper was buying her time, and Alannah couldn't squander it.

"Her brother sent me."

Alannah halted midstride beside the piano. If Torin had sent this fellow, he'd be safe. Maybe he'd even relay news of another employment opportunity.

"I'm Bellamy McKenna. My da is Oscar McKenna, the matchmaker."

Bellamy McKenna? She hadn't met him before, but she'd heard about him through Mrs. O'Brien. As the next in line to take over for his da's matchmaker role, Bellamy had recently started forming matches. He'd brought together Captain and Mrs. O'Brien's earlier in the year. Alannah had never seen a couple as in love as those two.

Apparently, Bellamy had also found a lovely match for Mrs. O'Brien's older sister, Finola, and Riley Rafferty. Soon Bellamy would be tasked—if he wasn't already—with finding Kiernan a match. Not that Kiernan needed a matchmaker. His auburn hair and dark blue eyes were fetching, to be sure. With his chiseled features, brawny build, and the dimple in his chin . . .

Alannah stifled a dreamy sigh. He was the most perfectly handsome man she'd ever laid her eyes on, so he was.

In addition, he was kind and fair and decent. He paid his employees well, and he also took an interest in them beyond just their work for him. When one of the men feared he'd lose his apartment and his family would be homeless, Kiernan had found him a place in one of the Shanahan tenements. When another fellow had been sliced by glass at the factory and required stitches, Kiernan had paid the doctor's fee.

When Torin had needed help, Kiernan hadn't hesitated. He'd not only found her the maid position, but he'd stopped by on occasion to check on her. Even the night of the fire a couple of weeks ago when he'd raced into the neighborhood to see how his sister was faring, he sought her out and made sure she was safe.

Kiernan Shanahan would make some lucky lass a good husband. And Bellamy's job of finding that lucky lass would be easy.

"I know who you are, Bellamy McKenna," Mrs. Christy said, her tone still unyielding. "If you give me your message, I'll pass it along to Alannah."

Alannah straightened and resituated her lacy maid's cap.

There was no harm in meeting with Bellamy for a few moments, especially if he had news from Torin.

She crossed to the door, her leather half boots tapping a hard rhythm, even against the plush rug. She exited into the entryway painted a fresh bright cream and that contained more of the same pretty blue accents as the parlor.

Bellamy, standing in the doorway and holding his tweed flat cap, shifted his attention to her. With swarthy skin, dark hair, and dark brown eyes, he was much more good-looking than she'd pictured. Even attired in simple, worn garb—wool trousers, white shirt, with a vest and coat—he had an enigmatic and charming aura about him.

"Top of the morn to you, Alannah." He was taking her in too—not lustfully but in a more calculated way, as if he was intending to find a match for her, which was a silly notion altogether.

Torin wouldn't do that without asking her first, would he? For that matter, how did Bellamy know she was Alannah and not some other maid?

Mrs. Christy's sweetly rounded face was wreathed with concern. Twenty if not thirty years older than Alannah, the housekeeper had wispy, grayish hair in a loose topknot and brown aging spots on her cheeks and nose. She wore the same style of dark frock and white apron as Alannah, with a similar starched white collar and cuffs.

She planted her hands on her ample hips and frowned at Bellamy. "I'm doing my best to send the fellow on his way."

"'Tis alright, Mrs. Christy." Alannah gave the woman what she hoped was a reassuring smile. "I'll meet with him."

Bellamy didn't wait for Mrs. Christy to agree. He stepped into the hallway and closed the front door behind him.

"You're sure?" Mrs. Christy raised her brows, clearly not understanding why Alannah would visit with a fellow after the past weeks of shunning all interactions.

"Rightly so." At least as sure as she could be.

"Shall I stay?"

"I'll only visit a wee minute." Alannah said it as much for Bellamy as Mrs. Christy.

He didn't respond as he watched the exchange. Instead, he leaned back against the door and crossed his arms over his broad chest.

Mrs. Christy began to walk toward the rear of the house, leaving the trunks open with the remaining items beside them still needing to be packed. As she reached the dining room door, she paused and lifted her brows again at Alannah to ask if everything was okay.

Alannah gave her a quick nod, hoping to convey reassurance.

Once the housekeeper's footsteps faded into the dining room, Alannah tucked her hands into her apron pockets. Her fingers brushed against the hard cover of a small book, a collection of short stories by Edgar Allan Poe.

She traced the embossed lettering along the spine and waited for Bellamy to say something.

He studied her as if he was trying to see right into her mind. He couldn't do that, could he?

She plunged her hands deeper into her pockets to keep them from trembling. "You said you had a message for me from Torin?"

"No, not a message."

"Then whyever did Torin send you? Surely not to set up a match for me." A scoffing laugh slipped out.

Something glimmered in Bellamy's eyes. "Oh aye, your brother came to me secretly last night and is wanting to marry you off."

2

Marry off Alannah?

Kiernan Shanahan halted in the breakfast room, his hand against the door to the hallway where Bellamy and Alannah were talking.

He'd been near the carriage house handing over his mount to Mr. Dunlop and conversing with the fellow when he'd spotted Bellamy walking down the street toward the house.

Something about Bellamy's hasty pace and stealthy glances had set off warning bells inside Kiernan. Although Bellamy had never given him a reason for mistrust, Kiernan couldn't keep caution from racing through him.

He'd snuck inside Enya's home through the back door and managed to make it through the house without being seen or heard. He wasn't sure if that was a good thing or bad. What if he'd been someone more disreputable, like Shaw Farrell?

Kiernan's blood turned cold just like it always did whenever he thought about the way Shaw Farrell had kissed Alannah. At that time, he hadn't known Alannah, since she'd just moved to St. Louis. He'd only heard the men teasing

Torin about how beautiful his sister was and Torin telling them not to go anywhere near her if they valued their lives. From the lethality in his voice and face, it had been clear he hadn't been teasing in return. And from the way the men had immediately stopped talking about her, it was also clear why Torin was a leader of the Saints Alley gang. He was more dangerous than he appeared, and they knew it.

When Kiernan had first seen Alannah outside the factory, he'd realized she was just as beautiful as the men had claimed, if not more so. With her blond hair and soft blue eyes, everything about her—her graceful neck, her full rounded eyes, the high sweeping cheekbones, and even the tiny pucker of her upper lip—was so tantalizing. As if that wasn't enough, even though she'd still been thin as a result of the Great Hunger and the hardships of the passage over to America, she had a womanly figure that her clothing couldn't hide.

Kiernan could admit he'd found her attractive from the start and still did. A man would have to be completely daft not to notice her. Unfortunately, Shaw had noticed her, too, and the gang leader was as dangerous as Torin, if not more so.

Kiernan didn't understand all that had happened between the two men, but apparently Torin had made an enemy of Shaw. With the Saints Alley and Farrells already rival gangs, the hostility between the two men had only made things worse.

Normally, Kiernan stayed well away from involvement in gang problems and didn't tolerate any gang fighting in his factory. But after witnessing the threats that day Shaw had kissed Alannah, Kiernan hadn't been able to say no when Torin pleaded for help in hiding her.

Kiernan usually swung past Enya's once or twice a week to

reassure himself that everything was still alright with Alannah. Now that Enya and Sullivan had left for New Orleans, Kiernan would have to cut back on his visits, or he'd risk the neighbors gossiping and assuming he was having illicit relations with one of the servants.

On the other hand, if Torin had asked Bellamy to find Alannah a match, maybe he wouldn't need to come much longer at all.

"Torin doesn't need to be marrying me off," Alannah said. "I'll be just fine, so I will."

"Naturally." Bellamy sounded as though he hadn't a care in the world. But underneath it all, Kiernan suspected more was going on than met the eye.

"I'll find another job soon enough."

"Another job?" Kiernan couldn't keep the question from slipping out.

At the silence from the hallway on the other side of the door, he guessed he'd given his presence away. Not that he'd been trying to hide.

With a curt tug on the lapels of his cutaway morning coat that matched his light trousers, he shoved the door open and stalked down the hallway.

Bellamy was leaning against the front door and had been watching Alannah with an unsettling intensity. Was the matchmaker interested in Alannah for himself? Was that why he was here?

Kiernan narrowed his eyes upon the fellow. "Bellamy McKenna. What are you doing here?" He didn't care that his question came out partly as an accusation.

Bellamy opened his mouth as though to defend himself, then his brows rose.

Alannah was attired in her maid's uniform. As plain and simple as the garb was, it only seemed to make her beauty all the more startling every time he saw her. Over the weeks of employment for Enya, Alannah had filled out so that she looked healthier and less likely to blow away in a gust of wind.

Her pretty blue eyes had shifted to him, but the moment he looked at her, she dropped her sights to the floor, showing deference.

She was only behaving as most maids did. Mrs. Christy had likely trained her on the protocol around those above her station, around the family, and especially around the men. The fact was, the maids and the men of the family weren't to mingle—at least in the Shanahan house. His da had strict policies about chastity. That included chastity regarding the hired help.

"Kiernan Shanahan." Bellamy's gaze was bouncing back and forth between him and Alannah. He was clearly trying to make sense of their relationship.

Well, Bellamy's gaze would have a lot of bouncing to do because Kiernan didn't have a relationship with Alannah and never would. He talked to her during his visits, but never for long. Mostly their conversations centered on Torin and his involvement with the gangs and how worried she was. Kiernan had offered to try to help Torin more, but he also knew that once involved in the Kerry Patch gangs, there was usually only one way out—death. But he didn't tell her that.

"What brings you out on this lovely morn?" Bellamy's dark eyes started to twinkle.

Kiernan had nothing to hide from Bellamy. Nothing at all. And he wouldn't scramble or cower or pretend otherwise.

Instead, he drew himself up to all of his brawny six-feet-three inches. "I came to check on Alannah."

"Oh aye. 'Tis a fact if I ever did see one."

"It's a blessed good thing I came when I did." From the corner of his eye, he could see Alannah watching him again, her eyes wide and surrounded by long, thick lashes.

"I agree." A smile tugged at Bellamy's lips. "Truly 'tis a most fortunate occasion."

What did that mean? And why was Bellamy smiling? Kiernan gave an irritated shake of his head before turning to Alannah and gentling his voice. "What's this I hear about you needing another job?"

"With the mistress away now, there's nothing for me to do here." She had her hands in her pockets, the outline of a book evident in one.

He'd learned over the past weeks that she liked to read. He'd caught her in the act on a couple of occasions, and she'd made no pretense about what she was doing.

"Enya won't mind if you keep the position."

"She's a kind mistress and said I could stay until I find something else."

Kiernan could feel a storm gathering inside him. "She can't fire you from your job every time she leaves town."

"She said she's not sure when she's returning. It could be months, likely after the babe is born."

With the death count from cholera mounting higher with every passing week, Sullivan had talked of moving Enya out of the city. Doing so made sense, and Kiernan didn't blame Sullivan for taking her away. But for so long?

Kiernan doffed his hat made of fine black felt, then raked his fingers through his hair, ruffling away any hat marks.

Bellamy's lips twitched with a smirk.

Kiernan palmed the back of his neck. "Listen, Bellamy. I don't know what Torin told you. But I'm putting an end to this nonsense. Alannah doesn't need to get married. She needs another job."

Bellamy shrugged. "'Tis what Torin wants. He came to me last night. And he asked me to find a nice fellow."

"I'll find a nice fellow on my own, so I will." Alannah jutted her chin, her lips set stubbornly.

The angle gave Kiernan a better view of her neck and the long, elegant lines of her jaw. It was too bad she had to wear the collar.

Bellamy gave him a pointed look.

Kiernan glared back. The young matchmaker needed to stop the insinuations. Kiernan had no interest in Alannah. He was simply trying to help both her and Torin during this difficult time.

"I agree with Mr. Shanahan." Alannah spoke again, her tone firm. "I need a job, not marriage."

Whenever she called him Mr. Shanahan, he felt middle-aged like his da instead of twenty-two. He'd been tempted to tell her to call him Kiernan, but that would be inappropriate, especially around other people.

Bellamy was still leaning against the door, and his expression grew serious. "Your brother thinks marriage will keep you safe, out of danger."

Kiernan's ready protest died. Alannah didn't respond either, studying Bellamy.

Was Torin right? If she was married, would Shaw drop his threats? Shaw might be a scoundrel, but he wouldn't pursue a married woman, would he?

How much did Bellamy know about Alannah's predicament? About Shaw's threats? About the rivalry between the two gangs? Torin must have explained some of it to Bellamy.

Kiernan nodded at the matchmaker. "I see Torin's point."

"No." Alannah's chin rose higher. "I'm not marrying someone I don't know. What if I trade one unhappy situation for another?"

"That's why your brother came to me." Bellamy offered a slow smile. "Because then I can be finding just the right husband for you."

"And how will you know who is right for me when you don't know me at all?"

"Good question." Kiernan let himself meet her gaze.

She rarely looked at him squarely. But this time her eyes rounded, clearly not expecting him to agree with her, and they held a curiosity, almost as if she wanted to know more about him.

He could usually tell when women were interested. He'd learned to read the signals. But with Alannah, he'd never been certain. And it didn't matter. It really didn't matter in the least. He'd been reminding himself of that every time he wondered.

Just as he'd been reminding himself that it didn't matter if Shelia had shown some interest in him recently. . . . The fact was, Liam was madly in love with her. As a best friend and business partner, Liam deserved to have Shelia all to himself, even if she had once been the woman Kiernan thought he'd marry.

Kiernan's stomach knotted again as it had whenever he thought about how beautiful Shelia had looked last night. He shouldn't have stopped by her family's country home in the first place. But the Douglases lived next door to Oakland, the Shanahans' country estate. And she'd been outside as he was passing by and called out to him. It would have been rude not to stop, and he'd only visited for a short while.

He shifted his attention to Bellamy. "I suppose you already have some candidates in mind for Alannah?"

"Oh aye. That I do."

Kiernan didn't know what to say at Bellamy's quick—certain—response. Obviously, Bellamy did know most of the single men looking for wives. Apparently, he'd already narrowed down those he thought could provide Alannah with a good life. He might have even consulted with his da, Oscar, who had been the matchmaker in the St. Louis Irish community for as long as Kiernan could remember. The older fellow probably had all kinds of possibilities.

"I thank you, Bellamy." Alannah took a step away from him as though wanting to put an end to their conversation. "You're kind to offer your help, to be sure. But marriage is such a big step, and I'm not ready to take it."

"It doesn't have to be today." Bellamy's voice held a chiding, almost teasing note.

Kiernan wasn't so sure that Bellamy would refrain from whisking her away to the church today. Enya's marriage to Sullivan had happened fast, within hours of Bellamy's conspiring.

If Alannah had another job lined up, someplace else to go, then she wouldn't need to consider a match right now, would she?

"At least think about it," Bellamy continued. "You might even find that you're more than ready."

Kiernan gave a curt shake of his head. "Or maybe she'd just like to work a while longer."

Once again, Bellamy quirked a brow at him.

"I'll help her find another domestic position." Kiernan's mind dashed through the possibilities. There were probably at least half a dozen families he knew that would hire her on. But each had larger staffs. More servants meant more gossip. And more gossip could lead to Shaw discovering her whereabouts.

"No, Mr. Shanahan." Alannah backed up another step. "You've already done enough for me."

"Think nothing of it."

What about Shelia? The Douglases? Would they be willing to take on another servant?

For that matter, why not have Alannah work for his family? Now that the brickyard purchase was finalized, he would likely be staying at Oakland for a while since it was near the site of the new business venture. With his presence at the estate, perhaps Mam would agree to the additional hand.

Bellamy was watching him like an employee awaiting permission. But permission for what? Kiernan didn't have the right to determine Alannah's future. However, he could provide her more time to figure it out for herself. Then she wouldn't feel the pressure to rush into marriage with the first man Bellamy presented to her.

Besides, his family home was the perfect place to keep her safe. It was out of the city, away from prying eyes, and had a smaller staff. Shaw wouldn't learn she was there. She would be away from the cholera epidemic as well.

"You'll work for my family." Kiernan spoke with finality. If Mam wasn't agreeable, he would pay for Alannah's wages out of his own earnings. "In our country home."

Although Alannah's eyes widened again, she didn't offer

an immediate protest. She'd been to Oakland for a couple of days during the terrible fire last month. She had to realize, just as he had, that the country home would be another excellent hideaway.

"You can work there until Enya returns." Kiernan knew he had a bad habit of telling people what to do instead of asking them. But in this case, he didn't want to give her the chance to decline the offer.

Alannah seemed to hesitate.

Bellamy was again bouncing his gaze back and forth between them.

It was definitely time to go . . . before Bellamy started to make more out of his helping Alannah.

Kiernan spun and started down the hallway toward the back door. "I'll come for you tomorrow morning, Alannah. See that you're ready."

3

She was riding in a carriage with Kiernan Shanahan. Alannah was tempted to pinch herself to see if she was dreaming, but she'd refrained so far. Over the past weeks of knowing him, she'd only spent time with him in passing, just a few minutes here and there.

Oh aye, she'd thought about what it would be like to have longer, but she'd never pictured taking a carriage ride with him—the most eligible bachelor in St. Louis.

He sat on the seat across from her, more handsome than ever in a blue suit with a matching blue cravat tied about his collar. He'd removed his hat, and his reddish brown hair was combed into rakish waves, lending an air of wildness to his otherwise immaculate and put-together appearance.

With his smoothly shaven face, the dimple in his chin was visible, and the muscles in his hard jaw ticked from time to time. His dark blue eyes were fringed with lashes the same color as his hair.

"I told Torin the plans," he said, his gaze riveted on the

scenery outside the carriage window. He braced both of his large hands on his knees, fingers splayed. He had nice fingernails, clean like most gentlemen, and bluntly cut.

Alannah had plastered herself to the leather seat in the shadows as far from the windows as she could fit, and she hadn't moved since the start of the journey a short while ago. They'd reached the edges of the city, and at the sight of the trees and meadows, she was eager to sit forward and take it all in.

The flat grasslands and forests were different than the rugged hills of County Kerry. But as with the last time she'd been in the countryside during the fire, she relished every single moment of the beauty. It took away the homesickness a wee bit.

"Your brother was agreeable to the new employment," Kiernan continued. "But he still has a mind to have Bellamy find you a match."

She expelled a frustrated breath. It wasn't that she was opposed to getting married. But she didn't want to rush into something, especially not when life was still so hard and uncertain. She'd watched too many young women her age back home get married and have families only to struggle to feed their wee ones. She'd told herself she'd never put herself in that situation, that she'd wait to be secure, maybe have an editing job and be able to provide.

"Torin's a good brother, so he is." He was all she had left of her family, and she couldn't lose him. He was doing what he thought was best for her because he loved her too. "But sometimes he likes to think he's my da."

Kiernan was quiet for a beat. "And your da? Where is he?"

"Watching down on us from heaven."

"I'm sorry." Kiernan's voice was laced with regret.

She tried to offer him a smile, but it hardly reached her lips. "He's happy now. He's holding Mam's hand again."

"Your mam died of hunger too?"

"No, neither died of hunger, thanks be. Mam passed on when I was but a girl. And Da died of a heart attack two years ago." Was she sharing too much? It felt natural to be telling Kiernan more about her family, especially since he already knew how much she loved Torin. Even so, she couldn't forget their boundaries, and that she was just an employee.

"So Torin's taken care of you ever since?"

"We went to live with my aunt and cousins. But aye, Torin took on the responsibility for me and Cagney, my younger brother." Losing him was still raw and painful.

Kiernan didn't say anything, was instead watching her intently, as though sensing there was more heartache to her story.

As a growing young man of fourteen, Cagney had never had enough to eat during those last weeks and months in Ireland. Although Aunt Joan had done her best to provide for their family as well as her brood of children, there hadn't been sufficient food to satisfy everyone. Even with Alannah's favorite of her cousins, Hugh, working at the newspaper as a reporter, his pay had been sporadic, and the shortages of food all over the county had affected everyone.

When Torin's letter with the notes for passage had finally come, she'd been tempted to spend the money on food. She hadn't wanted to leave the place of her birth, the land she loved, or the people she cared about. She'd never gone far beyond the boundaries of Tralee, much less halfway around the world.

But she'd known Cagney's and her leaving would ease the

suffering of her aunt and cousins. So she and her younger brother had boarded the ship and headed for St. Louis where Torin had found work and Irish Catholics were welcome—or mostly so.

If only the days in steerage on the long voyage across the Atlantic hadn't been so terrible. At the start, Cagney had already been too thin and weak. He'd lasted two weeks in the dark and damp bowels of the ship before he'd caught dysentery—or so the ship's physician believed. Her brother had made it another week before being tossed into the sea with many others who'd died on the voyage.

"Cagney, well he . . ." She pushed the words past her constricting throat. "He didn't survive the journey here."

She almost jumped at the sudden pressure of Kiernan's hand upon hers that she'd folded in her lap. But somehow she managed to remain absolutely motionless, even as her mind began to race.

Kiernan Shanahan was holding her hand.

Well, maybe not exactly holding it. But he was touching her—his long, strong fingers offering what he probably thought was a comforting pat.

Her body didn't get the message that the contact was merely polite—a kind gesture. Instead, her blood rushed forward with a strange heat that went directly to her chest, warming her insides, making the already stuffy interior of the carriage suddenly sweltering.

She didn't want to stare at his hand and make it obvious how fascinated she was by him. So she closed her eyes. Even with her eyes shut, she could still picture his fingers covering hers, his skin slightly darker, a dusting of freckles on the back of his hands, the veins pulsing there.

He squeezed her hand, then released her. "I can't imagine how hard this has all been." His voice was surprisingly soft and tender.

Ach, maybe he thought she'd closed her eyes to hold back tears of grief. He'd be appalled if he knew she'd done it so she didn't get carried away by making more of his comfort than he'd intended.

"Now I understand better why Torin's so set on protecting you."

She let her lashes rise and caught Kiernan's gaze again. He'd bent forward, and his face was but a foot away from hers, his eyes dark and crinkled at the corners with sympathy.

She wanted to simply admire his features. But she knew enough about the dynamics between men and women to understand that giving way to admiring glances, a teasing smile, or even a coy batting of her eyelashes would only encourage what could never be.

She'd used such tactics in her youth to gain what she wanted from the young men who'd showered her with attention, especially during that period of her life after her da's death when she'd abandoned God and her faith, when she'd joined Hugh in his revelries with friends.

But here, now? Such flirtatious ploys were too bold and presumptuous between a woman of her low birth and a wealthy gentleman like Kiernan.

"He's probably afraid of losing you," Kiernan continued. "Especially after you've both lost so many people you care about already."

She had. And she didn't like to be reminded of the losses. It stirred the helplessness and the feelings of abandonment. She hated thinking about how alone she'd felt on the ship and after arriving in St. Louis when she hadn't known anyone. With Torin already staying in a men's-only boardinghouse, she hadn't been able to live with him, had hardly been able to spend time with him because of his working such long hours every day.

Aye, she'd even felt abandoned by God, as if her prayers had lifted a part of the way toward heaven and then crashed back to the ground.

Kiernan was still watching her with warm eyes, likely waiting for her to say something more.

But what could she say that didn't sound bitter? She scrambled to find something—anything—and settled on a gentler version of the truth. "I am grateful I'm alive when many others have died. But I cannot deny that I wish I'd never come here. I've only caused problems for Torin."

He'd scooted to the edge of his seat, and his knees nearly brushed hers. "I know nothing I say will bring back those you've lost. But I'm glad you came and glad you're here."

She couldn't keep from locking gazes with him again. She was being too bold as his employee, needed to remember her place in the social order. But at the moment, she craved the comfort, had been without it for so long that she couldn't turn away from it, wanted to drink it all in while he was offering it.

Hugh had been the friend she'd turned to when she needed to talk. He'd listened well, had been there after Da's death, and had always consoled her. She supposed in some ways she was used to a man being her closest friend, and it was all too easy to imagine—even hope—that maybe she could find a friend in Kiernan in spite of their differences.

Up so close, she could see that the blue of his eyes contained flecks of green, a fascinating combination. His gaze held hers a heartbeat longer before circling around her face, drifting to her cheek, her chin, then her mouth.

What was he doing?

His pupils darkened with something she recognized. Desire.

Kiernan Shanahan wasn't thinking about kissing her, was he? No, he was too polite, too much a man of honor to initiate a kiss.

Even so, he clearly found her attractive.

She held her breath and didn't move. She hadn't welcomed Shaw's kiss, hadn't wanted him putting even a finger upon her.

But she couldn't deny that she'd liked Kiernan's brief touch and the closeness. There was also no denying that she was attracted to him. He was a magnetic man and had been from the moment she'd met him.

Yet, where could such kissing lead?

Of course, she wasn't naive. Wealthy gentlemen sometimes had dalliances with their maids. Everyone in service knew it happened. Yet Kiernan wasn't like that. She hadn't known him long, but it had been long enough to recognize he was a good man. He'd never expected favors in exchange for getting her the job at his sister's. He wouldn't expect anything now either.

Besides, a gentleman of Kiernan's wealth and status would never truly be interested in her. Although she hadn't seen him with any women during his visits to the O'Briens, she'd heard his sister tease him about various women, likely the best and wealthiest of St. Louis.

Aye, sharing a kiss with him would be foolish and rash.

She couldn't let it happen now or anytime. Even though she'd exchanged a few short kisses in her life with different admirers, she wasn't in the habit of kissing men whenever she was alone with one. She'd always wanted to save kissing for the person she intended to marry.

She sat back. From the corner of her eye, she could see Kiernan recline against his seat, too, putting a safe distance between them.

He was quiet for several moments, then spoke again. "Maybe you will be able to see Torin more often now that I've made him a supervisor in my new brickyard."

Was he remembering the time when she'd cried over Torin? It had been shortly after she first started working at the O'Briens'. She and Kiernan had been talking, and she admitted how she missed spending time with her brother and how she'd never imagined that once she moved to America she wouldn't be with him.

Hopefully, Kiernan didn't remember that incident. She normally didn't get so emotional around strangers.

"He's no longer working at the glass factory?" She hoped she didn't sound too desperate.

"No, he officially starts working tomorrow at the brickyard. It's south of Oakland by a couple of miles."

Relief swelled inside her. "I'll be happy he's out in the fresh air of the countryside away from the cholera. But 'tis a long way to be walking back and forth to work, to be sure."

"Not to worry. We've started construction for housing. Until then, many are staying in tents."

"'Tis kind of you."

He shrugged. "Torin's a very bright worker, always fiddling around with the machines and trying to make improvements."

"Our da was a mechanic at one of the mills in Tralee, tasked with ensuring that the machines were in working order. Torin takes after him, so."

She wanted to ask Kiernan more about brickmaking and what that was like and why he'd chosen to start such a business, but the carriage turned off the gravel road onto a narrower dirt lane.

She recognized the tall oaks lining either side and the long grass filled with wildflowers. They'd arrived at Oakland.

She leaned against the window to view the sprawling home. She'd never seen an Italian palace, but she imagined that's what Oakland resembled with its square tower, cornices rising from the roof, and balconies on the second floor.

The carriage rolled down the driveway, circled a small pond with a fountain in the center, then rounded toward the front of the home.

Large potted plants graced either side of the entrance at the top of a wide stairway. Long covered verandas spread out on either side, filled with elegant patio furniture and more greenery and flowers.

Towering oaks not only bordered the lane but also surrounded the home, providing plenty of shade. Beautiful flower gardens had been planted behind the house, and the woodland and meadows all around glistened in the morning sunshine.

'Twas a home unlike any Alannah had visited anywhere else, and her breath snagged just looking at it. It might not be County Kerry, but it filled her heart to see so much beauty, and she was more than a wee bit happy to be back.

"Is something amiss?" Kiernan paused in straightening his cravat.

"No. Everything is grand."

"You sighed."

Had she? If so, she hadn't noticed. "I beg your pardon."

He resumed his task of fixing his cravat. "Just making sure you're all right."

Was he now? "I thank you, Mr. Shanahan."

He blew out a taut breath.

"Is something amiss?" She lobbed the question back at him, smiling at the same time so he would know she was teasing.

He was swinging the carriage door open. As he stretched one foot out onto the carriage step, he glanced at her again, and his brows rose.

She supposed for a servant, the bantering was out of line. But after talking casually with him about her family and past, it was all too easy to let down her guard.

Mrs. Christy had warned her against being overly friendly with the family, encouraging her never to forget that even when the boundaries of class seemed to come down, they were still there. The housekeeper had indicated that the crossing of boundaries was the primary cause of being let go from a domestic position.

Alannah couldn't lose her job today, not now that she was here in the countryside. She wanted—no, needed—to stay. She had no other prospects. This was her best option.

Her smile vanished. "I'm sorry, so I am, Mr. Shanahan. I shouldn't have been teasing you."

He gave a slight shrug. "You took me by surprise, and not many people do."

He finished descending, then held a hand toward her to assist her down as if she were a grand lady wearing a fancy gown. She needed to politely decline and climb out for herself without pretending to be someone special.

But he grasped her hand before she could tuck it away. As his fingers encircled hers, the same tingles she'd felt earlier raced along her nerve endings. This time she kept her gaze averted, not wanting to encourage whatever attraction was between them.

She climbed out of the carriage, and as her feet touched the ground, the front door opened and Mrs. Shanahan stepped onto the veranda. A petite woman with brown hair, she had delicate, pretty features that had aged well, making her appear younger than her middle age.

For as delicate as Mrs. Shanahan might look, she was the complete opposite in temperament. During Alannah's last visit to Oakland, she'd learned the matron ran a strict home. While she was stern and exacting, it had also become clear that she loved her family fiercely and had an inner strength that was the backbone of the family.

"Kiernan." Mrs. Shanahan crossed to the top step into the sunshine. "Is something wrong? Whyever are you home in the middle of the morn?"

"Everything's fine." Kiernan turned to face his mam, still holding Alannah's hand. "I've brought you a new maid to work at Oakland."

Mrs. Shanahan shielded her eyes with a hand as her attention went directly to Alannah's hand within Kiernan's. In the next instant, a frown puckered her forehead.

Not wanting to earn the matron's disapproval, Alannah tugged her hand free.

"You remember Alannah, don't you, Mam?" He stuffed his hands into his pockets. "She was here with Enya last month."

Mrs. Shanahan descended two more steps. "Who is saying I need another maid?"

"I'm saying so. I'll be staying at Oakland the rest of the summer to oversee the brickyard. As a result, I'm hiring an extra hand."

"We've plenty of help and need no more."

A flush worked its way up Alannah's face. Mercy. 'Twas obvious Kiernan hadn't consulted his mam before bringing her out. 'Twas also obvious the woman didn't want another maid.

"Last time I was here you said that you had to leave a couple of servants in the city for Riley and Finola, and now you're short of staff."

"Aye, a butler, not a maid."

"Help is help." Kiernan turned and took Alannah's bag from the coachman. Kiernan's shoulder slumped momentarily under the weight, as he was clearly unprepared for the heaviness of her bag containing her collection of books.

She grasped one of the handles. "I'll carry it."

He straightened himself. "Did you pack bricks?"

"No, 'tis my books, so it is." Her collection wasn't large—only a dozen or so. But she loved each precious volume she owned and had carried them with her across the ocean, no matter how heavy they'd made her luggage.

Breaking free of her grasp on the bag, he trotted up the steps. As he reached his mother, he paused. "Alannah will be staying here, Mam."

Mrs. Shanahan shook her head. "That's not a good idea—"

"I've already made up my mind." Though his tone was respectful, it was firm. "She is in danger and needs a safe place to hide and work."

"What kind of danger?"

"Nothing for you to worry about. But I'd like you to make sure the other servants know they're not to mention her being here."

Mrs. Shanahan pursed her lips, looking none too pleased with the information.

"Thank you, Mam." He placed a gentle kiss on her cheek before moving past her toward the front door.

Alannah stood frozen to her spot near the carriage. Should she climb back inside and ask the coachman to return her to the O'Briens'?

As Kiernan entered the house and the door closed behind him, Mrs. Shanahan released a terse breath. Then she settled her critical gaze upon Alannah, taking her in from her white cap down to her black lace-up boots.

What did the woman think of her? That she would now be saddled with an inexperienced servant she didn't need? After all, everyone knew Alannah hadn't been a domestic long and that her position with the O'Briens had been her first.

Alannah didn't want to cower under the woman's scrutiny, so she took a deep breath. The least she could do was offer to leave. "I'm sorry—"

"You'll confine your duties to the kitchen." Mrs. Shanahan's tone was clipped and unfriendly, and her expression was decidedly displeased. "As a scullery maid."

A scullery maid was the most demanding of the domestic positions and the lowest ranking, requiring long hours of scrubbing and cleaning and hauling water. Alannah had heard other young women complain about how the scullery maid was given the worst tasks that none of the other servants wanted to do.

Mrs. Shanahan lifted a brow, as though waiting for Alannah to protest.

But how could she? It was a job, and she'd have a place to live. Besides, with Oakland having a detached summer kitchen near the gardens behind the house, perhaps the work would be a wee bit more bearable.

Rather than turning down the offer, Alannah curtsied. "I thank you, Mrs. Shanahan."

The matron stood stiffly a moment longer, staring at Alannah. Finally, she cast a glance toward the door and then lowered her voice. "You'll be staying away from Kiernan, do y'hear?"

"Oh aye—"

"No talking, interacting, or visiting with him. Do I make myself clear?" Her voice was nigh a whisper but sharp nonetheless. "If I see you so much as make eyes at him, I'll be sending you away with nary a penny."

Without waiting for Alannah's response, Mrs. Shanahan spun on her heels and marched across the veranda into the house.

Alannah had no intention of making eyes at Kiernan Shanahan or any of the other things the woman had mentioned. But now she would have to be extra careful to stay as far from Kiernan as possible.

She'd do her best to prove she was a good maid and live by the old Irish proverb: A good beginning is half the work.

4

"Everyone should rebuild with bricks," Liam said from where he reclined in the wicker chair on the veranda at Oakland next to Kiernan. "And the city council knows it."

The evening breeze was warm and did little to cool Kiernan after the hot June day. But being outside was much more preferable than sitting inside to discuss business with Liam.

Kiernan took a sip of cold lemonade. As he set his glass down, he tugged at his cravat and loosened the top button of his shirt to allow the breeze to cool his neck. He'd already discarded his coat and was tempted to shed his vest too.

Liam took a puff on his cigar, as suave and collected as always, not a drop of sweat on his forehead or his pale face. His dark hair was neatly combed back to one side, every hair in place, his cravat still perfectly tied, and his buttons lined up. He didn't look like he'd spent the day inside city hall laying out the benefit of bricks to the city council.

"So, you convinced them?" Kiernan rubbed at the condensation on the glass.

"I think so." Liam's lips curved into a satisfied smile. "It won't be long now."

"Good." Kiernan hoped his friend was right and the city's leaders would see the need to pass an ordinance requiring all new buildings to be made from brick. After losing over four hundred buildings last month to the fire that had started among the steamboats lined up on the wharf, St. Louis was still reeling from the destruction.

It was obvious—at least to Kiernan—that such large-scale destruction should never happen again. If the council leaders mandated the rebuilding of the city be done with bricks, that would reduce the risk of fire and make everyone safe.

It would also increase the demand for bricks, hopefully massively.

That's what he and Liam were betting on.

With his glass factory turning a tidy profit, Kiernan had been looking for his next investment well before the fire. He'd been considering a sugar refinery or getting into the steamboat-building business. He'd even discussed with Sullivan, his new brother-in-law, the possibility of investing in a train that would connect St. Louis with eastern rails.

But the day after the fire, Kiernan had realized right away that the city would need to rebuild, and he'd decided to meet the demands that would arise.

As he'd considered the materials necessary for rebuilding, he landed upon bricks. Cheltenham to the south of St. Louis already had a handful of clay mines and brickyards. The area was rich in sediment—primarily clay—deposited over the centuries by the Mississippi River. The clay was ripe for mining and firing into bricks.

In fact, after spending the past couple of weeks researching everything he could find about clay mining and brickmaking, he'd become more convinced than ever that brickmaking was the direction he wanted to go. To capitalize on the immediate need for bricks, however, he'd realized he didn't have time to buy land and do everything required to excavate a mine and create a brickyard from nothing.

After scouring the existing brickyards, he'd located one fellow who was interested in selling and had his sights set on the California goldfields. Kiernan had examined the operations and decided it had potential for growth.

The trouble was he'd lacked the capital to make the purchase on his own, having already used his inheritance from his da to buy the glass factory. Of course, he could have sold his factory, but that would have delayed his ability to help with the rebuilding of St. Louis.

For the span of five minutes, he'd considered asking Da to invest with him. But then all he had to do was think of Da's litany of successes.

Aye, Da loved to talk about how he'd immigrated by himself with a small inheritance from his father, a silk manufacturer. Kiernan had heard Da's stories so often, he could almost recite them word for word—how he'd arrived in St. Louis with practically nothing, and how he'd worked with his own *brawn and brain* over the years to become one of St. Louis's most prosperous and prominent citizens. He'd done it all by himself, without any help.

That's what his da expected now of Kiernan with his inheritance. While the glass factory had been a good start and had helped him learn what it took to run his own business and be successful, he'd also concluded that it would never help him rise to the top and surpass his da's accomplishments.

Kiernan needed something else that would prove he had the same ingenuity, resourcefulness, and drive that his dad did, if not more. That something was bricks.

Whether the people of St. Louis knew it yet or not, they would need bricks. And Kiernan planned to be the biggest and best brick producer . . . with Liam as his partner.

Liam had already come into his full inheritance after his father had passed away several years ago and was a wealthy man, certainly more so than any other twenty-two-year-old. Although Kiernan would have preferred to do it all on his own, he'd had no choice but to involve his friend. Fortunately, Liam had been eager to join Kiernan in his new business venture.

Kiernan took another sip of his lemonade. "Even without the city council mandating the rebuilding with bricks, I think most people will do it."

Liam gave a nonchalant shrug. "A little pressure and a few favors to council members will hopefully nudge them in our direction."

Kiernan set his glass down on the side table too forcefully. "No favors." He'd already had this discussion with Liam. Kiernan wanted to do everything with integrity, the same way his da had. No cheating, no swindling, no cutting corners, no breaking of laws, and no twisting of politicians' arms to get their way.

He'd either succeed by his own brawn and brain or not at all.

Liam's easy smile made an appearance. "I'm just jesting. Of course I'm not offering favors."

Kiernan wasn't an idiot. He knew Liam didn't always tell the truth, sometimes said what he thought people wanted to hear in order to keep the peace. This was probably one of those cases, but Kiernan didn't want to argue with his friend tonight and put a damper on their excitement.

He cast his gaze off to the west to the hazy, humid sky hovering over the horizon. The blue was light, the same color as Alannah's eyes. Those beautiful wide blue eyes filled with such life and curiosity and wonder.

He'd briefly searched for her upon his return home a short while ago, hoping to see her and ask her how her first day of work had gone. But he hadn't spotted her anywhere, and with Liam here, he'd decided it was probably best not to draw attention her way.

The slow singing of the cicadas filled the air, and the short buzz of a nighthawk sounded overhead as it began hunting for its feast of insects around sunset. A low, mournful groan of a bullfrog echoed from the direction of Dover's Pond across the road and down just a little way.

Although Kiernan rarely stopped his work long enough to appreciate the sights and sounds and smells of the countryside, he drew in a breath laden with the scent of damp grass and the lavender his mam grew in the side garden.

"And there she is." Liam stood, his sights fixed upon a horse and rider coming around a bend in the road.

Kiernan didn't need to look to know who *she* was.

"Holy mother." Liam spoke reverently. "She's beautiful."

With her thick brown hair, seductive brown eyes, and perfect womanly form, Shelia was beautiful. She always had been, even when they'd been young children playing together when both of their families had escaped the heat and stench of the city for the countryside, even if only for a few days at a time. Together with their siblings, he and Shelia had run through the meadows and woodlands during the endless summer days.

Kiernan had fallen in love with her almost from the start and always believed he'd marry her. He'd assumed she'd felt the same way about him.

Then eighteen months ago, she'd left for a trip to Europe. He'd been busy with his new glass factory at the time and had hoped that when she came back, he'd have enough saved to build her a house. When she'd returned, instead of rushing into his arms the way she always had, she'd been tucked against Liam's side. While gallivanting around Paris, she'd connected with Liam, who'd been there for a short trip.

Liam's short trip had turned into a long one accompanying Shelia and the Douglas family for the rest of the six months they'd remained in Europe. By the time everyone arrived home in St. Louis, Liam and Shelia had been courting. Over the past year they'd been home, Liam hadn't yet proposed since Shelia's parents wanted her to wait until she was eighteen to get married.

With her eighteenth birthday in one month, Liam had already been planning how he intended to propose to her and talked about it all the time. Kiernan was tired of hearing the details about the proposal to the woman he'd thought would be his wife. But he didn't have the heart to tell Liam to stop.

Liam took a last drag on his cigar, then stubbed it out in the ashtray on the table. "It's getting harder to wait." Liam was watching Shelia approach, his eyes dark with desire.

"You need to. It's the right thing." Kiernan couldn't keep his tone from turning hard, maybe because it was difficult to think about Liam and Shelia together in that way.

Liam's grin kicked up. "That's swell coming from the

fellow who's slept with half of St. Louis's most beautiful women."

Kiernan resented the reputation he'd earned because the truth was, he hadn't slept with any women. Maybe he'd kissed a few . . . or maybe more than a few in his attempt to forget about Shelia. Kissing was as far as his interest in another woman ever went.

Earlier in the year, he'd been eager for the matchmaker to find him a good and decent match to end the rumors and help him shut Shelia out of his thoughts once and for all.

Naturally, Da had wanted to secure his older sister Finola's match first. Then Enya had gotten herself into a predicament and needed the matchmaker next. Shrove Tuesday had come and gone, and for the Lenten season, everyone had put on hold engagements and weddings. Once Easter had passed, Kiernan had debated contacting Oscar or Bellamy. Before he could do so, the city had experienced the fire in May, along with the aftermath, so he'd let the thought of a match go.

Now that June was well underway, was it finally his turn?

He'd most certainly benefit from a sizable dowry he could put toward the brickyard, especially so Liam didn't end up having the greater investment. The truth was, at some point when the clay mine was profitable enough, Kiernan intended to buy his partner's portion and then own the mine completely. After all, making bricks had been his idea, and Liam wouldn't have done it if not for him.

Liam was making his way off the veranda as Shelia reined in. "Hello, darling," she called.

Kiernan tried to force himself not to look at her, not to even glance her way. But his gaze slid to her for the briefest of seconds. It was enough to see her pretty face and luxurious brown hair. It was also long enough to see that she was watching him and wasn't paying attention to Liam.

Kiernan sat forward, braced his elbows on his knees, and bent his head. He was over her . . . or at least he'd hoped he was getting to that point. Besides, it didn't matter how he felt. As long as Liam loved Shelia, then Kiernan was determined to let go of her.

He shoved up, then without another word to either Liam or Shelia, he walked into the house and closed the door behind him. He had to shut Shelia out of his life. And he had to do it soon.

The best way was to get engaged himself. Then he'd have no choice but to move on and hopefully learn to love someone else.

5

Alannah turned the page of her book as quietly as she could, hoping no one would notice her in a shadowed corner of the back veranda behind one of the tall potted plants.

After the past four days of working from well before dawn until well after dark, she'd stopped feeling guilty for stealing a few spare moments to read during the daylight hours.

She'd finished soaking the chamber pots with vinegar because Mrs. Shanahan had complained that they smelled. Now, with Cook taking a nap, Alannah wouldn't be needed back in the kitchen to help with the evening meal preparations for a wee bit longer.

The humidity hung heavily in the air, and the temperature had soared with every passing hour so now it was unbearable to do anything but sit in the shade. How could anyone enjoy living in such a climate?

Ever since she'd arrived in St. Louis, she'd decided she didn't want to stay in America forever, that when life returned to normal in Tralee, she'd sail home. That was all the more reason to avoid the matchmaker since there was no sense in getting attached to someone only to turn around and leave him behind.

"I wish you'd wait for your father," came Mrs. Shanahan's voice from the nearby open window of the library. "He'll be wanting to have some say in the matter, to be sure."

Alannah shoved her book into her pocket, then started to creep out of her spot. Even though she had every right to be taking a break, she couldn't risk Mrs. Shanahan glancing out the window and spotting her sitting idly. Although the matron hadn't spoken much to Alannah since that first day she'd arrived at Oakland, she had felt the woman's sharp gaze upon her from time to time.

Mrs. Shanahan needn't have worried about anything developing with Kiernan. He was gone all day, leaving at dawn and not returning until close to sunset. By that time, Alannah was elbow deep in water in the kitchen, scrubbing dishes from the evening meal. Then after tidying the kitchen and polishing silverware and crystal, darkness had fallen and most of the household had retired for the night.

Although Alannah was exhausted after her long days, she always made time for reading every night. With the heat of the dormer room unbearable even with the small window open, she crept outside with a blanket and lantern to the field behind the summer kitchen where she could read and pretend she was back home in Ireland.

"I can take care of things, Mam," came a second voice from inside the library.

Kiernan.

Alannah halted. What was he doing home before the supper hour?

"I'll not be signing any official papers," he said, his voice placating.

"Even so, your da will not be happy you're meeting with the matchmaker without him."

Kiernan was meeting with the matchmaker?

The very idea struck Alannah squarely in the chest with an odd pang. She wasn't necessarily surprised. But she was taken aback, although she didn't know why, since Kiernan was of an age to get married.

"Bellamy's coming. And I won't be swayed from meeting with him."

Alannah pictured the room beyond the window, which the family called the library. She'd been eager to explore it only to be utterly disappointed the first time she'd stepped foot into the corner room. Instead of floor-to-ceiling bookshelves covering the walls, there was one half bookshelf that held knickknacks of various sorts—a globe, a small crystal clock, and several unique pieces of driftwood. But no books. None.

The desk was equally bare of books, containing an elegant lantern, decorative paperweights, and a pretty set of inkpots. Large framed maps hung on the walls, and the rest of the room was cluttered with odds and ends—a basket of blankets, rolls of large paper, a folded easel, and more.

If she ever had a room labeled the library, she'd fill it with books and nothing else.

At a soft tap on her shoulder, she hopped and would have given her position away if the hand on her shoulder hadn't steadied her. She glanced up to find Bellamy McKenna standing beside the window, as tall, dark, and handsome as always.

He pressed a finger against his lips, cautioning her to silence, then he nodded curtly toward the summer kitchen, a small building built in the same style as the house and painted a bright white. It was a dozen paces from the main house, not too far so as to be an inconvenience but far enough that the cast-iron stove wouldn't overheat the already stifling house.

Did Bellamy want to speak with her there alone?

He started across the porch toward the back steps, his tread so light he could have been a wraith. She crawled after him, and when she was well away from the window, she stood and hurried down the steps, her boots tapping even though she tried to imitate Bellamy's stealth.

A raised bed of herbs grew beside the summer kitchen, and the fragrances of basil, thyme, and sage greeted her as they did every time she passed by. The waft of the cooking chicken from the kitchen hung heavily in the air, too, making her stomach growl with sudden hunger pangs.

At times like this, she was more than a little grateful her stomach would soon be full, that the days of constant gnawing were over along with the worries of when and if she'd eat again. But it was also times like this that she felt the greatest sorrow that Cagney wasn't alive to experience a full stomach.

Bellamy stopped just inside the kitchen door, and she moved past him into the now familiar room. A worktable took up the center, and an enormous range filled the south wall. An iron sink stood under a window that faced the gardens and the meadows so that when she was washing dishes for endless hours each day, at least she had a beautiful view.

A white wicker basket of strawberries—small but perfectly red and ripe—sat on the worktable, which meant Zaira had recently been here and had been out picking strawberries again from among the wild plants that grew in the yonder meadow.

At nineteen, Zaira was the youngest of the Shanahan daughters. Alannah had gotten to know her a wee bit during the last stay at Oakland, and this time Zaira had befriended her again.

The class differences hadn't seemed to matter to Zaira. With each encounter, the young woman talked to Alannah as though she were a friend or relative who'd come to visit rather than a servant.

Just that morning when Alannah had been carrying a heavy pail of water from the well back to the kitchen, Zaira had been passing by and taken one side of the handle and helped her haul it the rest of the way. All the while, she'd chattered about the beautiful morning and how she adored summer.

In addition to Kiernan and Zaira, two other Shanahan children were living at Oakland—Madigan who was sixteen and Quinlan fourteen. Both boys spent hours outside every day, hunting and fishing and riding and exploring the woodland.

They both reminded her of Cagney. Even though she tried not to compare situations, it was hard not to think about her younger brother's experiences in the countryside. His had been so different, not carefree in the least as he'd dug in the fallow fields outside of Tralee desperate for something to eat. Even old, withered root vegetables had been better than nothing.

Bellamy glanced out the summer kitchen door before focusing on Alannah. "Torin came to visit me again last night."

"He visited you and not me?" She couldn't stifle her irritation, even though she knew her brother was staying away for her own safety.

"He wanted to see me before moving to Cheltenham to Kiernan's new brickyard."

"And why was he needing to see you, so?" Alannah plucked a berry from the basket, pried off the green top, then popped the ripe fruit into her mouth.

Bellamy crossed toward the worktable. "Even though I assured him you have a new position, he's still insisting that I find you a match."

"I'll visit with him soon enough and set him straight—that I'll not be marrying anytime soon."

Bellamy stopped in front of the basket of strawberries and picked one up. "He'll not be taking no for an answer, I'm afraid."

She hadn't told Torin she wanted to go to Ireland and that she planned to drag him back with her so that he would be far from the gang trouble. But she would eventually inform him. "I said it before, Bellamy. I'm not interested in marriage, and neither of you will be changing my mind."

"Is that a fact?" Bellamy lifted his gaze, his brown eyes probing hers.

"Aye, 'tis so." She reached for another strawberry and wedged off the leafy part.

"I told your brother I have someone in mind."

In the process of lifting the strawberry to her mouth, she halted. "No—"

"I suspect you'll like my choice."

She shook her head. "I suspect I won't be liking anyone."

Bellamy returned the strawberry he was holding to the basket. "Let's have a wager."

A wager? As in a bet?

His expression was serious, but something lit his eyes, as if he was enjoying their conversation more than he was letting on. "I'll bet that you fall in love with my choice by summer's end. If I win, you agree to marry him."

"And if you lose?"

"I'll convince Torin you're not ready."

She wouldn't fall in love with Bellamy's choice, not in just a few months. Especially because she wouldn't have time to court anyone, except for perhaps on Sunday afternoons when she wasn't required to work.

"Agreed?" He shifted the basket of strawberries, took a step back, then cocked his head as he studied the scene like he was considering the aesthetics of the whole kitchen.

The white basket of berries did make a pretty picture on the light oak tabletop with the window and flower-filled meadow in the background.

Could she agree to Bellamy's terms? If Bellamy had someone in mind, couldn't she at least spend a little time with the fellow?

Besides, Torin was stubborn and probably wouldn't let the matter go until she proved to him that she didn't need a matchmaker, that when she was ready to get married, she'd find her own man.

"Alright, Bellamy. I'll agree to your wager, so I will. But I'll give you two months, just until the beginning of August. I won't be needing more time than that."

"True enough." A smile spread across Bellamy's face, one that seemed to say he'd already won.

"Don't be getting your hopes too high."

"All I ask is that you give the fellow a fair chance. Can you do that?"

Could she? Aye, she wouldn't make a wager with Bellamy and not follow through on her half. "I'll do my best, Bellamy. You have my word."

"Good."

"Will you be telling me who the fellow is, or am I to be surprised when he comes courting on Sunday?"

"He won't be coming to court you."

"No?" That was strange but perfectly fine with her.

"No." Bellamy started to cross to the door. "He won't need to come because he already lives here."

Her mind raced with the possibilities among the staff. The positions of cook, housekeeper, housemaid, and now her position as scullery maid all belonged to women. There were only two men—the coachman who was middle-aged and a gardener who was grandfatherly. Surely Bellamy could find someone younger than either of those men.

Bellamy halted near the door, his expressive eyes still alight. "Figure it out yet?"

"Go on with you now. Just spit it out."

"'Tis easy enough." Bellamy paused. "Kiernan Shanahan—"

"What about Kiernan?" A young woman spoke from behind Bellamy.

His eyes widened with surprise—and something else Alannah couldn't name.

Zaira sidled past Bellamy and into the kitchen. The young woman reminded Alannah of Mrs. O'Brien—Enya. Both had vibrant red hair and lovely green eyes. Both also had stunning features that put them in a class of beauty all their own.

While Enya had a polished style with elegant gowns and coifed hair, Zaira was less formal, less concerned with her appearance, less put together. She often wore her hair free of a chignon, tied back with a simple ribbon, like at the moment, so the long waves dangled down her back with loose strands floating about her face. Although Zaira donned the fine gowns expected of someone in her position, Alannah had heard the housemaid and cook gossiping about how Zaira refused to wear a corset and crinoline.

Regardless, she was like a beautiful bird flitting about, full of energy and life. Now as she crossed into the kitchen, she smiled warmly at Alannah before she spun around and faced Bellamy.

"Bellamy McKenna, so nice to see you again." The young woman's smile curled up a little higher.

Bellamy didn't respond, not even with a smile. Instead, he backed up a step into the doorway as though in a hurry to be on his way.

If Zaira noticed, she didn't let on. "And how is the gentleman you've been helping?" She paused, tapped her lip as if in thought, then nodded. "Oh aye, W. B. Moore. How is he getting on these days?"

Bellamy narrowed his dark eyes on Zaira. "He's doing just fine."

"That's fabulous. Just fabulous."

Alannah could hardly focus on the awkward exchange since her mind was still reeling with Bellamy's declaration from a moment ago that Kiernan was the man he'd chosen for her.

Kiernan Shanahan.

Was Bellamy daft? She wanted to ask him what he was

thinking by trying to match her with Kiernan. But with Zaira in the kitchen, she'd never be able to bring it up. She couldn't chance Zaira finding out about Bellamy's suggestion and telling her mother. If just one peep reached the matron, she'd boot Alannah out of the house and slam the door behind her.

"I best be nipping along." Bellamy turned to go.

Zaira took a quick step after him, then stopped, her cheeks suddenly flushed. "Is Mr. Moore still managing to paint?"

Bellamy's back faced them, and he stiffened. Usually, Bellamy was so calm and casual, never letting anything or anyone perturb him. But for some reason, Zaira seemed to be aggravating him.

He glanced at the young woman over his shoulder, his eyes filled with warning. "Mr. Moore's business is private." Then without another word, he exited the kitchen and stalked toward the house.

Zaira retreated to the doorway and didn't bother to hide the fact that she was watching Bellamy. After a moment—likely after Bellamy disappeared into the house—she released a sigh. "That man." She gave a small laugh and fanned her face. "He's simply divine, isn't he?"

Divine? Alannah wouldn't exactly describe Bellamy that way. To be sure, he was fine looking. But she wasn't attracted to him.

Unlike Kiernan, who she was very attracted to but shouldn't be.

Without waiting for an answer, Zaira motioned at the basket of strawberries and beamed. "Aren't the strawberries delicious?"

Alannah could only nod, still too stunned by her interaction with Bellamy to know what to say or do. She'd made a wager with the matchmaker. She'd given him her word that she would consider his match for her.

But she absolutely couldn't consider Kiernan. That was asking too much.

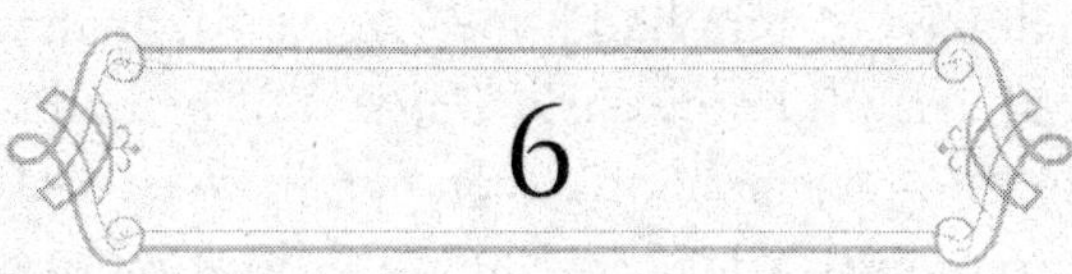

Thank you for coming out here to Oakland to meet with me." Kiernan perched on the wing chair across from Bellamy in the parlor. The room was formal with elegant furniture and elaborate artwork, a fashionable place to entertain and have parties.

"Think nothing of it." The matchmaker was reclining, legs crossed at the ankles and arms folded on his chest. "I was needing to see Alannah about her match too."

Alannah's match? Kiernan's brows rose with surprise. "I assumed you'd halted the matchmaking for Alannah now that she has employment."

Bellamy was once again watching him carefully, analyzing every move he made. "Torin insists that she get married."

"I'll talk to Torin, assure him Alannah is safe here."

"I already found someone for her."

Kiernan, in the process of leaning back, halted. "So soon?"

Bellamy shrugged one shoulder. "It was easy to figure out the right man."

Kiernan pushed up from the chair and paced to the open

window, hoping for a breeze but only feeling more of the sticky air that had plagued them for the past week. He'd been tempted to meet with Bellamy outside. But he didn't want to worry that his mam would walk past and join in the conversation.

A small part of him had hoped to see Alannah tonight, since he'd arrived home early. But so far, he hadn't come across her. In fact he hadn't seen her all week and merely wanted to inquire after how she was adjusting to her new position. It was beginning to feel as though she was purposefully avoiding him.

"Who is the lucky man?" He tried to make his tone casual. "If you don't mind my asking."

"Ach, I wish I could tell you, Kiernan." Bellamy's voice lacked sincerity. "But I cannot be saying so, not until I work on getting the groom ready a wee bit more."

"So he's not in agreement?"

"He will be soon enough."

"If you have to push him, maybe he's not the right man."

"As Oscar always says, it's the job of the matchmaker to help people see the road less traveled because too often they have their sights stuck on the predictable route."

Kiernan frowned. "I don't understand."

"Sometimes a person needs a nudge toward a choice they might not normally consider."

"So you're nudging Alannah?"

"Oh aye. And her groom."

Kiernan wasn't sure he liked the sound of Bellamy's plan for Alannah. But there was no sense getting riled up about it. He would talk with Torin tomorrow and tell him to call off the matchmaking. Then no one would be pushing Alannah for good, bad, or otherwise.

Kiernan returned to his chair and lowered himself. "Listen, Bellamy. Instead of focusing on Alannah, focus on me instead. I've been waiting for my turn to have a match even before you found matches for Finola and Enya."

"Aye, so you have." Bellamy spoke with such certainty Kiernan could almost believe the fellow knew how hurt he'd been when Shelia had chosen Liam. Maybe everyone did. Not that Kiernan had made any claims on Shelia before that Europe trip. Not that they'd even promised each other a future together. After all, she'd been too young at the time. But he had assumed they both wanted to be together and that they would wait for each other. He'd waited.

He slipped a hand into his pocket and pulled out a sheet. "Here are twelve qualities I'm looking for in a wife." He'd come up with the list earlier in the day and had added a couple more qualifications to it when he'd arrived home. He'd been doing so when Mam had cornered him in the library and chastised him for meeting with the matchmaker without Da.

Da was back and forth between Oakland and their home in the city, and Kiernan had been spending every spare moment at the brickyard. With as busy as they both were, they hadn't seen each other much lately. Surely Da would understand the need to move forward with the matchmaking without his involvement.

Bellamy didn't even glance at the outstretched sheet. Instead, he stood, picked up his flatcap, and placed it on his head. "If you have that kind of list, then you won't be needing my help."

"I'd like you to set up appointments over the next couple of weeks, arrange meetings with each of the eligible women."

"Would you now? I suppose you'd also like me to parade them in front of you?"

Kiernan ignored the sarcasm and extended the sheet farther. The list would narrow down the candidates, allowing Bellamy to find the most advantageous match. "Use it."

"You use it." Bellamy started toward the door. "I'm sure you already know a dozen women who meet the standards on your list."

"A few. Not a dozen."

Bellamy just shook his head.

As the matchmaker reached the door, Kiernan stood. "Wait, Bellamy."

Hand on the knob, Bellamy halted.

"I'd like to have some input in the matter. That's all."

Bellamy expelled an exasperated breath. Then he turned and nodded at the list. "Input, aye. But that list is your attempt to do my job."

"Your job is to find the kind of woman I'm looking for. The list will help."

"My job is to decide on the kind of woman you need. Your list won't do that."

Kiernan swallowed his rising irritation. This meeting with the matchmaker wasn't going the way he'd anticipated. Maybe he ought to talk to Oscar instead. No, Oscar would probably grab the list, rip it to shreds, then laugh in his face.

"All right." Kiernan kept his voice level. "I see your point."

Bellamy crossed his arms and leaned back against the door.

"But at least look at the list. Then you'll know my standards." The Shanahan standards—everything his da and mam would expect of him as the firstborn son who would carry on the Shanahan name.

He needed a woman from high society, well-bred, and well-educated. He preferred a woman who could manage a large household and host parties to entertain his business associates. A St. Louis native would also be helpful, someone with knowledge of the important people in the city and how to interact with them. He needed her to be polished, poised, and pretty.

He also wanted a woman from an affluent family who could bring that wealth into their marriage and into his business ventures. He'd been telling himself that there was nothing wrong with striving for a beneficial marriage and that most men in his social circles were endeavoring after the same thing. But he couldn't deny that having to rely upon a dowry rankled him, made him feel weak, as though he couldn't quite measure up to all that his da had accomplished on his own.

Bellamy was staring at him, his brows drawn. "I can already tell you that the woman I have in mind won't meet your qualifications."

"How do you know? Look at the list first."

"I can't help you, Kiernan. Not if you're already so set on what you want."

"I'm not set."

"Then prove it."

Kiernan bit back more annoyance. Maybe he should consider finding his own spouse. He could set up the invitations with the various women himself.

But what about having Bellamy's objective advice guiding him? The matchmaker had proven himself to be wise and enterprising and even strategic while working on the matches for his sisters.

Besides, if the appointments with the women didn't end well, Bellamy could be the one to tell each of the ladies the news. It would all be so much more professional that way.

"I'd prefer to have your help, Bellamy. But I can't throw away my list."

Bellamy was silent for several long heartbeats before speaking. "Let's have a wager."

"No, Bellamy—"

"I'll look at your list and arrange visits with women over the next month." Bellamy pushed away from the door and straightened. "But if you don't fall in love with one of them during the month, then we'll burn the list, so we will, and you'll agree to marry the woman I pick out for you by the end of the next month."

Kiernan hesitated. "I never said anything about falling in love with a woman."

"Ach, love needs to go at the top of your list, Kiernan. 'Tis not meant just for fairy tales, doncha know?"

All the while he'd been writing his list, he'd never once thought of adding love to it. Was *love* really important? Or would *liking* his bride be enough?

"As long as you choose women this next month that meet the qualifications on my list." Surely one among the batch would catch Kiernan's attention and he'd be attracted to her. He might not fall in love, but he'd at the very least develop some feelings.

Bellamy crossed to him and took the list. Without looking at it, he folded it. "I'll be fair. I give you my word."

"I give you my word too."

Bellamy stuffed the paper into his trouser pocket, then stuck out his hand. "Good. Then we have a deal."

Kiernan shook the matchmaker's hand and quelled the unease inside. What was he doing? He'd all but agreed to get married this summer one way or another. He hoped when the time came, he would choose the right woman.

◆ ◆ ◆ ◆ ◆ ◆ ◆

Kiernan pressed his glass of lemonade to his cheek as he walked out of the summer kitchen. The liquid wasn't cold, but it was refreshing nonetheless.

With the fall of night, he had hoped for relief from the heat. But in the humidity and staleness of his room, he'd tossed restlessly on his bed, even with the windows and balcony door open.

Finally, he'd tiptoed downstairs and outside, needing something to quench his thirst. His feet had taken him to the summer kitchen, just as they had many times when he'd been a boy.

He stopped in the grass and took a long drink. The land behind the house was bathed by the moon, the light of the fireflies twinkling in the darkness. He liked being away from the hustle of the city once in a while and relished the prospect of living at Oakland for the next couple of months. The place held many nostalgic memories and was still invigorating.

The only trouble was that staying in the country might make the matchmaking more complicated. He'd have to ride back to the city to meet with some of the women, but he guessed there were also plenty who were residing in the countryside for the summer or at least until the cholera was gone—if it ever went away.

His gaze snagged on a flicker of light in the flower garden. What was that? He narrowed his eyes to find what appeared to be a flame.

Quietly, he started in the direction of the light. He rounded several raised beds containing flowers, passed the gated vegetable garden, until at last he reached the edge of the meadow with its wild, untamed grass and flowers.

The light took more form, a lantern with a low-burning wick. A blanket was spread out on top of the long grass, flattening it. And the lantern was at the center of the blanket with a person—a woman—stretched out beside it. She was lying on her stomach, her long white nightgown tangled in her legs. Propped up on her elbows, she held a book close to the lantern and was reading.

Was this Zaira? His youngest sister was an avid reader and free-spirited enough to escape the heat of the house to do something like this.

As he drew closer, his foot landed in a patch of dried leaves, and a crackling broke through the soft trilling of the crickets.

The woman on the blanket glanced his way. With a startled intake, she scrambled to sit up.

The lantern light glistened now upon her hair, revealing blond waves falling all around her, nearly reaching her waist. Her face was also fully visible, her beautiful features creased with apprehension.

"Alannah?" He halted. "What are you doing?"

"Mr. Shanahan." She didn't move, except to close her book. "I'm getting a breath of air."

He frowned and surveyed the property. "It's not wise to be out here by yourself."

She followed his gaze. "I'm alone, or I was until you scared me."

"What if I'd been someone else? Someone less honorable?" His sights dropped to her nightgown. Even though a part of him knew he shouldn't look at her state of undress, he took her in anyway. By the glow of the lantern, it was all too easy to see the way the light cotton material clung to her curves and the bare patch of her ankles and calves where the gown had crept up.

As though realizing her indecency, she hurriedly tugged at the hem of her nightgown, trying to cover her feet. In her haste, she yanked too hard, and the garment slid off her shoulder on one side, drawing his attention to the bare stretch of her collarbone and the elegant curve of her shoulder visible beneath her hair.

Her fingers flew to the neckline, and she slid it back up. At the same time, she was taking him in, her gaze widening with obvious embarrassment.

He peered down at himself and then remembered that he'd hastily donned his trousers and suspenders before leaving his room, but otherwise he was bare chested and had bare feet. He wasn't decently attired either—not for an encounter with a woman.

He took a step back. "You should go inside." His voice came out rougher than he intended.

She dropped her gaze to the blanket in front of her and held herself stiffly. "'Tis a pleasant night, and no one knows I'm here. If you don't mind, I'd like to stay a wee bit longer."

"Not out here by yourself." He released a low scoff. "No."

"I've been fine every single time I've come out here—"

"You've done this before?"

She hesitated.

That was all the answer he needed. "No more coming out at night."

Even in the dark, he could see a flash of stubbornness in her expression. "While I'm not on duty, I'd like to be deciding for myself—"

"I'm deciding it for you." He cocked his head in the direction of the house. "Now come on with you."

Lifting her chin, she sat up straighter. "You might own me during the day, but my time belongs to me at night."

"Own you?" He couldn't keep his tone from rising at the absurdity of her declaration.

"Aye. I'm not a slave."

"Nobody said you are." He blew out a tense breath. The conversation wasn't going well, not at all how he'd envisioned it. Not that he'd envisioned talking with her. . . . Well, maybe he had imagined it a time or two, primarily finding her at work someplace in the house and then conversing for a few minutes.

"It wasn't my intention to make you feel like you have no freedom." He gentled his voice. "But I would have said the same thing to Zaira if she'd been the one out here. It's simply not decent—or safe—for you to be out here alone."

Alannah held his gaze for a moment before looking away. "I thank you for your concern, Mr. Shanahan. But I've sensed no danger here."

"Even though you might feel safe, we can never forget that Shaw could still be searching for you and might trace you here."

She examined the landscape shrouded in moonlight, and her features gentled. "I understand the concern, so I do. And

I promise from now on I won't stay long, and I'll be more watchful."

He opened his mouth to protest again.

But she continued before he could say more. "Being out here reminds me of home, and I need just a little time for it."

How could he argue with that reasoning?

"Please?" Her plea was soft.

He absolutely couldn't argue. That was the truth of the matter.

Silence settled between them with a distant squeak of bats out hunting. He drew in a breath of night air, relishing the scent of the grass and the soil and the freshness of it all.

If coming out to the field to read at night was so important to her, then he'd have to find a way to allow it so she remained safe. Should he accompany her? Or would that be inappropriate?

He didn't want to bring harm to her reputation in any way by being with her at night in the dark alone. But if they both remained fully clothed and a proper distance apart, that would be sufficient, wouldn't it?

A part of him knew it wouldn't be enough, that he'd still put her in a compromising situation. Yet another part of him wasn't willing to force her to stop her nightly rendezvous. Besides, even if he forbade her from coming again, perhaps she'd find a different spot that was less secluded and less safe.

What would it be like, instead, to sit on the blanket near her, talk to her for a while, and then maybe lie on his back as she read?

The very prospect of watching her in her nightgown with her hair flowing around her sent a spurt of heat through his blood, a heat he hadn't felt in a long time, a heat that made him want to cross over to her and pull her into his arms.

No, he couldn't think about her that way. He had to douse any and all heat. At the very least, he couldn't act upon it. Not now and not ever. Instead, he had to keep his thoughts—and his eyes—from straying where they shouldn't.

He was a strong man, and he could do it.

Regardless, his reaction to Alannah was all the more reason to start the process of finding a bride. He was clearly ready.

7

Alannah chanced another look at Kiernan standing near the edge of the blanket.

Oh, saints above. His chest gleamed in the moonlight, showing every hard and rounded muscle in his upper body—a body that was honed and tough, so much so that his suspenders pulled taut against his bare flesh.

Aye, she'd witnessed men without their shirts on before, especially in the crowded living conditions at her aunt's house and then on the ship to America. But she'd never seen a man who looked like Kiernan, either with or without his shirt.

She had the unholy urge to press her palms to his chest and feel the strength of his body rippling against her.

As though sensing her perusal, his gaze connected with hers, direct and intense and filled with interest.

Something sparked to life in the air between them, making her stomach flutter with a rush of warm pleasure.

Had Bellamy told Kiernan about their match? Was that why he'd sought her out? And was that why he was looking at her with undisguised desire?

If Bellamy intended to see them matched, why not get it out in the open? At the very least, she could hint at the subject. "So you met with Bellamy earlier tonight too?"

He seemed to wrench his attention from her and focus instead on the night sky. "Don't worry. I told him I would discuss it with Torin tomorrow."

A shiver shimmied up her spine. Did Kiernan really want her? It seemed unfathomable. But if he was talking to Torin about it, then maybe he was asking her brother for permission to have her hand in marriage.

"I'm not sure how Torin will react." She plucked the long-stemmed daisy beside the edge of the blanket. What would her brother think about her being matched with his boss? For that matter, how did she really feel about it?

Since Bellamy had brought it up, she'd mostly put the possibility out of her mind, hadn't believed Kiernan would agree. After all, he could have any woman he wanted in St. Louis—or in all of America. Why would he settle for a poor nobody like her? And should she let him? Maybe she ought to tell Bellamy that Kiernan deserved someone better.

Besides, even if Kiernan agreed to the match, she couldn't imagine his parents allowing it, not after Mrs. Shanahan's warning that first day of employment. But maybe Bellamy would know how to convince Kiernan's parents and smooth over any problems.

"Torin wants you to be happy." Kiernan's voice held his usual note of confidence. "Once I assure him you're happy here, he'll be fine."

How could Torin find fault with a man like Kiernan? How could she?

But could she push aside her concerns and fears about getting married and starting a family? The fears that had taken root after all she'd witnessed those last months in Tralee?

She pressed a hand against the lump in her skirt pocket, feeling the outline of the hard roll she'd stuffed there after supper. She wasn't sure why she'd felt the urgency to save it for Cagney. But she had. How long before everything became only a memory instead of a pulsing worry that still lingered at the back of her mind?

"You are happy here, aren't you?" Kiernan slid a sideways look her way.

Was she? Her work for the O'Briens had been easier, and Mrs. Christy had been a wonderful and kind housekeeper. But Alannah certainly couldn't complain about Oakland.

"You're not happy." Kiernan's brow creased.

"No, I am."

"You hesitated. That means something."

"It means I'm still adjusting, so it does."

The creases in his forehead didn't go away.

"What's not to like about all this?" She waved a hand at the countryside. If she went through with the match with Kiernan—and she hadn't decided yet if she would—then she would get to live at Oakland all the time. And she wouldn't be working as a servant anymore, would she?

'Twas too odd to think about living in the house as a part of the family and not the hired help.

He was silent for a beat. "The work is too much."

"No, I'm a lucky lass to have it, and I won't be complaining."

"I'll talk to my mam about it."

"You can't." Her response came out emphatic.

He quirked a brow at her.

She climbed to her feet, as though doing so could block him from going to his mam. "She'll think I put you up to it and dislike me even more."

"She doesn't dislike you."

Mrs. Shanahan might tolerate her but would never like her, which was one more reason not to push forward with Bellamy's crazy idea.

"Hey now." Kiernan reached out a hand toward her arm but stopped before touching her and instead swatted away a firefly. "My mam can be an opinionated woman, but she'll eventually grow to like you."

"Do you really think so?"

"Who wouldn't like you?"

She could feel a smile working its way free. "Don't be flattering me now. You know what they say about blarney, don't you?"

"Remind me."

"Soft words butter no turnips."

"They also say: A kind word never broke anyone's mouth."

"Aye, so they do. But I've heard it said: 'Tis often that a person's mouth broke his nose."

His grin inched up on one side, a lopsided one that made him all the more attractive, sending her stomach tumbling end over end.

She liked Kiernan. She had no reason to deny it any longer—not now that Bellamy was working on their match.

"What are you reading?" He nodded toward the book she still held, now tucked into a fold of her nightgown.

"'Tis *Oliver Twist*."

"Is Dickens your favorite?"

"I like him well enough."

"I would have guessed you are a Jane Austen enthusiast."

"I've actually never had the opportunity to read any of her novels." Most of Alannah's books had belonged to her mam—books her da had purchased for Mam long before the hard times had fallen on their family, during the days when they could afford the luxury of buying a book.

Mam had loved reading more than just about anything else. In the years before her passing, she'd met one of her favorite authors and had started editing for him. She'd had a keen eye for mistakes and also a way with words so that eventually other authors had sought out her editing skills.

Alannah had been told she had a keen eye, too, and she hoped to follow in her mam's footsteps. She'd been making some progress before leaving Ireland, editing for her cousin Hugh and a few other journalists who worked with him at the *Kerry Evening Post*. But she hadn't done any editing in the many months since she'd sailed away from Ireland.

Standing but a foot away, Kiernan stuffed his hands into his pockets. The motion only drew her attention back to his bare chest and the well-rounded contours.

His gaze swept over her again too.

What was she doing alone with Kiernan in nothing but her nightgown? It was indecent, that's what.

He tore his gaze from her and shifted around to face the house instead. Obviously, he knew their predicament was indecent too.

He cleared his throat. "I should go."

"Aye, 'tis late, to be sure."

With his hands still shoved into his pockets and his arms stiff, he started through the flower gardens. She wanted to gather up the blanket and lamp and walk back with him.

But 'twas likely for the best if they made their way inside the house separately just in case any of the other servants or family were awake and happened to see them.

When he disappeared from sight, she released a tight breath and the tension she hadn't known was building inside her.

Marry Kiernan Shanahan? Bellamy's suggestion was too farfetched to be true. She never would have had the courage to propose a match like that on her own, not ever. But Kiernan hadn't seemed opposed to it. In fact, he hadn't uttered one negative word about it.

Was it possible Kiernan could want her? That he looked beyond all the reasons they weren't right for each other and saw only the reasons they were?

And what exactly were those reasons? Bellamy must have seen something about them he thought made them fit well together.

She released a shaky laugh, then bent to retrieve the lantern and the blanket. "No, Bellamy. I'm no fool. This cannot work."

But even as she stood and watched the house, studying the window that belonged to Kiernan's room on the second floor, her heart pounded a traitorous extra beat. Kiernan had been good to her and Torin, had already done so much for both of them, even though he hadn't needed to. He was hardworking, knew what he wanted, and wasn't afraid to go after it. He loved his family and was loyal to them. Those were just a few of the things she liked about him, and there were more.

Maybe it wouldn't hurt to get to know Kiernan better. After all, she'd told Bellamy she would give the matchmaking a fair chance, and she couldn't go back on her word.

The trouble was, she and Kiernan were both so busy. How would she find any time to spend with him? Alone?

It would have to be alone. As inappropriate as that might be, she couldn't risk Mrs. Shanahan discovering her with Kiernan. Not yet—not until she was more certain of what the future held.

◆ ◆ ◆ ◆ ◆ ◆ ◆

The next morning Alannah was up at dawn, as usual, before the family awoke. It was only in those few moments of forcing herself from bed that she regretted her late-night reading habit and determined not to read so late. However, once she was in the kitchen and had a mug of coffee in hand, her resolve faded.

As she washed the remaining dishes from the previous evening's meal, she scrambled to find excuses to go inside the house so she might orchestrate an "accidental" meeting with Kiernan as he rushed to leave for the brickyard.

But as soon as she finished with the scrubbing, Cook set her to kneading dough for rolls and bread at the center worktable. They needed to do as much of the baking as they could in the early hours of the day before the heat became more unbearable than it already was.

After Cook left carrying a fresh pot of coffee to the dining room, Alannah paused and watched out the window. The scene was too beautiful to miss with the rising sun casting a haze over the meadow where she and Kiernan had met last night. A doe and her twin babes were grazing, their ears flickering back and forth at every noise they heard, their large eyes wide and alert.

Alannah wiped her hands on her apron and approached

the window to get a better view. She'd already seen the trio several other times during the week, and she never tired of their visits.

At a soft rap against the doorframe behind her, she startled and spun.

Kiernan stood in the open doorway, attired in one of his sharp suits, this one a light charcoal with a cravat that matched his black hat.

"Good morning," he said softly. By the light of day, his blue eyes, though still dark and intense, were less intimidating. And his expression was less imposing.

Even so, she couldn't seem to find her voice to respond to him. It had been so much easier to talk to him in the darkness.

He ducked inside and then stood with his arms behind his back, taking in the center table with the abandoned lumps of dough amidst the flour. Then his gaze shifted to her, pausing on her cheek and nose.

"Do I have flour on my face?" She lifted a hand and swiped at the spots, hoping to make herself more presentable. Her hair was coiled into the required knot and stowed under her maid's cap, and her apron was mostly clean over her black uniform.

"You're making it worse." With a grin making its way up his lips, he started around the table toward her.

She took a step back until she bumped against the wall and window. Several glass bottles on the sill rattled together, and she spun to keep them from toppling. As she started to straighten them, Kiernan's arm swept past her.

Standing directly behind her, almost boxing her in, he steadied one too.

She was suddenly conscious of his clean, masculine aftershave—a woodsy scent she'd noticed on other occasions but that was pungent this time of day and at his proximity.

His fingers lingered on the bottle, even though it was safe, and he seemed to be looking past her out the window. "Ah, the doe and her fawns are out this morning." His voice rumbled low beside her ear, and his chest was near her back and radiated warmth.

She was almost tempted to lean into him, but she held herself still and pretended she didn't notice how close he was, focusing instead on the deer. "They're beautiful, aren't they?"

He didn't respond.

As with that morning in the carriage ride to Oakland, she felt an invisible tug toward him, something magnetic and powerful. Kiernan Shanahan was a difficult man to resist. And she wasn't sure if she wanted or needed to resist him anymore.

Her thoughts were tangled, the threads of her reasoning crisscrossing first one way and then back the other. There were so many reasons why she needed to keep herself from falling for him. There were also reasons why she wanted to throw aside caution and embrace the possibilities.

Whatever she decided, she couldn't stand in the kitchen practically in his arms. Cook would be back soon. For that matter, anyone could come by, including Kiernan's mother.

She sidled away from him. "You're usually gone from the house by this hour."

He didn't move from where he stood, except that his gaze followed her. "I didn't realize you paid attention to my schedule."

"I don't." A flush climbed into her cheeks as she rounded the worktable and returned to her spot in front of the dough. "It's just that you've been gone such long hours each day this week."

"So you've noticed I'm gone."

She reached for the dough, her flush working its way higher. "Mr. Shanahan, I assure you—"

"Call me Kiernan."

She paused, her knuckles fisted and ready to begin kneading again. She didn't have the right to call him Kiernan. Not yet. Maybe not ever.

Blowing out a terse, almost exasperated breath, he shifted around to face the window, his shoulders turning rigid. He held himself motionless for several heartbeats.

She didn't dare move either. Was he upset at her or himself?

Finally, he pivoted with a scowl. "I just came to say that I've thought about it more. You're not to go out again at night. Stay in the house."

It was her turn to stiffen. She'd been bold to speak her mind with him last night, but she couldn't do so again today. After all, as the old saying went, a little dog can frighten a hare, but it took a big one to catch it.

She was nothing more than a little dog. What could she really do other than bark? Her bite had no strength.

He didn't wait for her response, was already striding toward the door, his heels clicking with finality. Without another word, he exited, leaving her staring after his retreating back.

Ach, Kiernan Shanahan was a vexing man, warm toward her one moment and in the next as cold as the ocean in winter. 'Twas clear that he didn't know what he wanted either.

Even though she'd told Bellamy she would give the match a chance, she'd said so before she'd known he had Kiernan in mind. Surely she wasn't obligated to follow through now that she knew Bellamy had planned something so impossible.

Because the truth was . . . a match with Kiernan would never work.

8

Kiernan's gut roiled with frustration. At himself.

With a curt nod, he handed off his mount to one of the lads who worked at the brickyard. He couldn't remember the kid's name, since there were several who had already been employed when he'd taken over the ownership.

With his usual long stride, Kiernan made his way toward the kiln, the tall rectangular brick building that rose above the others in the brickyard.

Even at the early hour, the morning sunshine was hot and the humidity heavy, and he was already perspiring beneath his coat and vest. Actually, he'd been hot since the moment he'd stepped into the summer kitchen, and he couldn't blame the heat emanating from the stove, although he'd tried.

No, he was an honest and direct man, and he had to be honest and direct with himself. The truth was, his body temperature had climbed the second he'd laid eyes upon Alannah, maybe even as he'd been crossing the yard and envisioned the way she'd looked in the moonlight with her nightgown clinging to her body.

He didn't want to think about her, didn't want to imagine her, didn't want to desire her. But every time he was around her, he couldn't seem to control his reactions. He liked her too much, especially her independent spirit that somehow seemed to challenge him.

He should have walked directly past the kitchen. But he'd had to insist that she not go out at night. As homesick as she might be and as much as he wanted to allow her the freedom to sit and read, she wasn't safe alone and her reputation could suffer if he was there with her. Besides, he didn't want to lead her on and certainly didn't want to take advantage of her in any way.

The pounding of hammers and the slicing of saws filled the air on a patch of land a short distance away, just beyond the enclosed yard where stacks of bricks awaited transportation to the city. The shell of the boardinghouse was already well underway, the newly cut beams gleaming in the sunlight.

Beyond the construction site lay a small town of tents, simple canvas held up by ropes. The campfires scattered among the tents had been doused, but a haze lingered in the air along with the scent of smoke.

The entrance to the clay mine was on the opposite side of the brickyard in the hillside where thick four-by-four slabs framed the dark chasm. The main shaft wasn't long, and it sloped gradually down into the shale deposits. A miner was exiting with a team of oxen pulling a wagon filled with buckets of the excavated reddish clay.

The shale deposits, which were fire-resistant and made the sturdiest of bricks, weren't as close to the surface as some of the other types of clay. Even so, that shale layer was still easy to access with a depth of not much more than a hundred feet down.

The *winning*, as the process of extraction was called, was done by free Black laborers who were willing to do the dirtiest of the jobs. Not only was it the dirtiest, but it was also the hardest and most intensive of the work. The clay had to be shoveled by hand, then loaded into buckets and hauled to the surface.

From there, a different group of laborers—primarily Irish immigrants—took over the process of hand-packing the clay into wooden molds. After the bricks were formed, they were stacked in one of several drying sheds, which were roofed but had open sides to ensure the necessary circulation. Finally, after about a week or two of drying, the bricks went to the kiln, where they were heated and cured in another weeklong process.

Kiernan had put Torin in charge of the heating process in the kiln, where the fires had to be maintained at 1600 to 2000 degrees. It was hot work, but Torin had claimed he could maximize the process so they could cut back on the amount of coal they were using as well as the time necessary to cure the bricks.

Since Torin had already proven himself to be resourceful at the glass-cutting factory, Kiernan had given the young man permission to tinker all he wanted with any of the machines and mechanisms. And tinker he did—at all hours of the day and night, creating new devices and always planning for more.

Torin had also brought with him a group of new immigrants eager for employment. Some were helping with the construction of the boardinghouse. Others were working with an architect to build another kiln. Still some were digging a new shaft to reach more of the shale deposits.

Whatever the case, Torin was easily the smartest and best worker Kiernan had. He'd always liked the fellow, even from the first day Torin had shown up at the glass factory asking for a job.

As Kiernan drew nearer the kiln, the dirty scent of coal smoke filled his nostrils. Torin was outside the kiln beside one of the loading doors. He was on his back, head poked into a section, a level in one hand and a hammer in the other.

Kiernan halted beside the fellow and waited for him to finish his task. A short distance away, a group of new workers leveling out the area for the new kiln cast him curious looks.

Maybe they were accustomed to working someplace where the owner never got involved in the operations. But they would learn soon enough that Kiernan wasn't like that. He took a vested interest in every aspect of his businesses.

After a moment more of fiddling, Torin slid out and peered up at him. Even though his spectacles were dusty, there was no hiding the blue that was the same shade as Alannah's. Pale blond hair that also matched Alannah's fell over a scar on Torin's forehead and curled around his ears and at the back of his neck. The scruff covering his jaw and chin was lighter too.

"Mr. Shanahan." Torin sat up, took a rag from his coat pocket, then wiped the grease from his fingers. "What's the issue today, sir?"

"There's no issue, Torin." Kiernan assured the young man. "But I do need to speak with you about a personal matter."

Torin's brows gathered together like storm clouds. "Is she all right?"

Kiernan slid a glance toward their audience, the men now leaning against their tools and watching the two of them openly.

Torin stood, tossed his rag to the ground, and then nodded at the group. "Keep working."

The half a dozen men resumed their raking and shoveling at double the speed. Regardless, Kiernan led the way toward a private area near one of the drying sheds that was half full of drying bricks.

Once they were alone, Torin's eyes took on a wildness that never failed to move Kiernan. He appreciated how the young man cared so deeply for his sister.

"What is it?" Torin's question was low and quiet, his gaze darting around as though he feared Shaw or someone else from the Farrell gang would jump out on him.

Kiernan couldn't imagine having to live in constant fear of someone hurting him or one of his family members, and he respected Torin for doing everything he could to keep Alannah out of trouble.

It was at times like this when Kiernan had to remind himself that his life was easy. Even though he was striving hard to establish himself as a successful businessman in his own right, he couldn't take for granted the privileges he'd gained by birth, the advantages these poor immigrants didn't have.

"Did something happen to Alannah?" Torin asked.

"No, she's still safe." Guilt pricked him. Maybe he was overstepping his role and needed to simply leave Alannah and Torin to work out their differences regarding the matchmaker for themselves.

Torin glanced toward the far end of the mine. "Saw a couple fellas from the Farrell gang loitering out there today."

Kiernan's gut hardened. "We knew it wouldn't take them long to track you here."

"Was hoping to buy more time."

Kiernan had hoped with the move that Shaw would finally stop harassing Torin, but clearly that was wishful thinking. "They wouldn't risk coming in here and starting problems any more than they could come into the factory." Kiernan had already gotten the police involved in the gang activity outside the glass factory. The officers had informed Shaw and his men—at Kiernan's prompting—that if they came into his factory to stir up trouble, they would be arrested.

Torin shrugged. "As long as they don't figure out where Alannah is, then it doesn't matter if they know where I am."

"Just one more reason to tell Bellamy to call off the matchmaking for her. We don't need fellows coming out and courting her and giving away her location."

Torin opened his mouth to respond but then just as quickly closed it. His blue eyes scrutinized Kiernan, confusion creasing his brow.

"I spoke with her again last night about it—"

"Last night?" Torin's tone dropped a notch.

"She likes living at Oakland, and there's no need to uproot her again so soon."

Torin narrowed his eyes upon Kiernan. "Or maybe 'tis you who doesn't want her going."

"What does that mean?"

"It means I thought I could trust you, and now I'm not so sure."

Kiernan wanted to pretend he didn't know what Torin was talking about. Even worse, he wanted to deny the insinuation.

But how could he? Not when he'd blatantly lusted after Alannah last night and then again this morning.

Before Kiernan could come up with an honest response, Torin bumped against him, pressing the tip of a knife to his chin. The look in his eyes was lethal—a crazed hollowness of someone who'd killed before and wasn't afraid to do it again.

Kiernan knew he ought to be frightened, but he wasn't. Torin wouldn't kill him right here and now at the brickyard. If he really wanted to kill him, he'd do it in private later.

Besides, Kiernan had his revolver tucked away under his coat, which he'd started carrying when the gang problem had landed on the doorstep of his glass factory.

Torin pressed the blade harder. "Tell me you haven't touched her."

The prick against Kiernan's chin wasn't drawing blood, at least not yet. "I haven't touched her." Patting her hand to comfort her in the carriage hadn't counted, had it? Thinking about touching her didn't count either. Thank the sweet Mother Mary for that because he'd be a dead man for sure with all the thoughts he'd had since meeting her.

He couldn't deny that he'd been thinking about her since the first time he'd met her, and maybe he had made up excuses to stop by Enya's to see Alannah and talk to her. Maybe he'd even orchestrated the move to Oakland so that in addition to keeping Alannah safe, he could see her more often.

Whatever the case, he hadn't done any of it purposefully, hadn't set out to seduce her. In fact, the very thought of using her made him sick.

Torin was watching him without twitching a muscle, his

gaze still filled with murder. Could the young man somehow read his thoughts?

That was impossible, but still Kiernan needed to be careful with how much he revealed to Torin of his inner struggle.

"I won't deny Alannah is a desirable woman," he stated carefully, the blade still sharp against his chin. "But I don't have any designs for her. I vow it."

Torin's hardened face didn't look convinced.

Kiernan grabbed Torin's arm and wrestled against the hold, unwilling to be intimidated any further.

But Torin was stronger than he appeared. And quicker. In the next instant, he had another knife out and this one pressed against Kiernan's chest, the tip right near his heart.

Should he get out his gun? Even if he did, he'd never use it on Torin. So what was the point in drawing it?

"Calm down." Kiernan latched on to Torin's other arm, so that now he was straining to hold both of the young man's hands. "I have the matchmaker working for me now too. I'll be wed before summer's end."

Torin didn't relent with his knives. "Having a woman, even having a wife, doesn't stop men from taking advantage of innocents like Alannah."

"Once I'm wed, I'll never look at another woman again." He intended to be as faithful as his da had been to his mam. As far as Kiernan was concerned, there was no other way.

Torin's gaze bore into him.

"I vow it." He was not only vowing it to Torin, he was vowing it to himself.

"That's all well and good, Mr. Shanahan. But what's to stop you now from using my sister before you get married?"

"My respect for her."

"I've heard about your reputation with women."

"You don't know anything." Kiernan spat the words.

After another long few seconds, Torin dropped both hands and slipped his knives back into their sheaths, one in his boot and one at his hip. He glanced around, and seeing that they were still alone, he pressed in close again. "If you lay a finger on Alannah, I'll cut it off first, then I'll kill you."

Kiernan shoved Torin, but didn't respond. What could he say? Of course he wasn't planning to touch Alannah. But he wasn't perfect.

Torin took several more steps away. "Don't think I won't do it, because I will."

"I realize that."

"Good." Torin shook his shoulders as if shaking off the incident.

Kiernan shook it off too. He wouldn't hold the knife threat against Torin. How could he, when he was actually relieved to know that Torin wouldn't allow anyone to take advantage of Alannah, at least not without paying for it?

Even so, Kiernan had put up with enough threats for one morning. He spun on his heel and began to walk away.

"She'll be safest married," Torin called after him. "And you know it."

Kiernan didn't respond. Torin was probably right. Alannah would be safe from Shaw . . . and from any other man who tried to use her, including him.

Aye, he'd deserved Torin's warning not to lay a finger on Alannah, and he'd do well to heed it.

9

She wasn't watching for Kiernan's return. She really wasn't.

Even so, at the thudding of a horse's hooves on the lane in front of the house, Alannah halted in the backyard and set down the bucket of water she'd been hefting from the well to the kitchen.

She wiped a sleeve across her forehead, the early evening still warm. Then she tucked several loose strands of hair into her braid before brushing at the stains upon her apron and straightening it as best she could.

After Kiernan's visit with her in the kitchen that morning, she hadn't been able to put him out of her mind. She'd been a wee bit giddy that he'd sought her out, had talked to her, and had even seemed interested in her—if his lingering behind her while straightening the bottles was any indication. He'd even asked her to call him by his given name. He wouldn't have done so if he saw her only as a hired worker.

The more she was around Kiernan Shanahan, the more she wanted to get to know him better. She still wasn't sure she had any right to speak with him, spend time with him, or even think about him. But her wager with Bellamy kept forcing its way into her head.

As the clopping drew nearer, Alannah shielded her eyes against the sun's rays in the west, her stomach fluttering at the prospect of seeing Kiernan again.

When the rider came into view, Alannah expelled a breath of disappointment. Zaira. The young woman had left earlier in the afternoon for a ride through the countryside—at least that's what Alannah had overheard her tell Mrs. Shanahan. But Alannah suspected that the ride had been to someplace specific for something important, especially because the young woman had carried a leather satchel strapped diagonally across her shoulder and body.

Normally, Zaira was full of energy and a zest for life that spilled over onto everyone around her. But now with her shoulders slumped and the tears streaking her face, 'twas easy to see the woman's ride hadn't been a happy one.

As Zaira crossed toward the barn, she caught sight of Alannah and veered in her direction, whisking the moisture from her cheeks.

Alannah wanted to say something to acknowledge Zaira's despondency. On the other hand, she didn't want to inquire into personal matters and overstep boundaries.

"How was your day?" Zaira asked with a forced smile.

"I helped Cook make jam with the strawberries you picked."

"That sounds much more delightful than my afternoon."

The young woman clearly had no idea how hot and sticky jam-making was. In fact, Zaira probably had no idea how hot and tiring most of the kitchen work was. But Alannah couldn't complain. She had employment, even if it was a far cry from working in the newspaper office as an editor as she'd hoped to do.

Zaira reined in beside Alannah, the leather satchel still in place.

Alannah rubbed a hand over the horse's flank. "I can take your horse to the barn, if you'd like."

With a heavy sigh, Zaira dismounted. As she steadied herself, she stared off into the distance. "I thought my skills were better than they are. And today I learned I still have much to learn."

What skills was Zaira referring to? As open and kind as the young woman was, Alannah held the question back. She couldn't push past the roles of servant and mistress quite as easily as Zaira could. Instead, she tried for encouragement. "We all have much to learn, so we can't be too hard on ourselves."

"But at this rate, I'll never accomplish anything."

"You know what they say: However long the day, evening will come."

Zaira patted the leather satchel. "It looks like the day is going to be an exceptionally long one for me."

Alannah waited, unsure if she ought to say more or hold her tongue.

Zaira glanced around. The backyard was deserted except for a few chickens scratching about in the dust and a calico barn cat perched on the garden fence post, giving itself a bath.

"I don't share my aspirations with many people—only my sisters know. And I've told Madigan. But now that I've failed, I guess it doesn't matter who knows since my career is over before it even began."

"Career?"

Zaira lowered her voice to a conspiratorial tone. "I've been writing stories."

With as creative and vibrant as Zaira was, the news didn't surprise Alannah. "I'm sure you're very talented."

"That's just it." Zaira flipped open the latch on the satchel. "I gave the manuscript to McDonald and Sons publisher. When I retrieved it today, they'd only read five pages and left a note on the first page that says, 'Needs more work.'"

As much as Alannah loved to read, she'd never aspired to be a writer, unlike her cousin Hugh who'd dreamed of becoming a journalist since he was old enough to read and write.

"I could do a little editing if you've a mind to let me. I've been told I have sharp eye for catching mistakes." The words slipped out before she could stop them, probably because she'd just been pining for an editing job moments ago.

She cringed, waiting for Zaira to scoff at her or at the very least to look at her as though she were a deranged lunatic for making such an audacious suggestion.

But Zaira cocked her head, studying Alannah as though she was seriously contemplating the offer.

"My cousin is a journalist. I always read his articles and offered feedback." Hugh had even encouraged the newspaper owner to hire her as an editor.

Of course, Mr. Graves had been older and set in his ways, of a mind that young women ought to marry and not be bothered with anything besides being a good mother and wife. Hugh had assured her that he would get Mr. Graves to change his mind eventually. She was hoping he still would.

In the meantime, she could help Zaira.

Zaira opened her satchel and pulled out a bundle of papers tied with twine. She ran a hand over the front page reverently, as though the book were an infant who needed reassurance. "I've never let anyone read any of my writing before."

"'Tis your eventual goal, is it not?"

Zaira nodded, the sunlight glinting off her hair and turning it a brilliant red.

"Then start with me."

"Really?"

"Oh aye. I promise to offer honest feedback, even if I can't promise publication."

She stared at her manuscript, gripping it hard. "Do you have the time?"

"I'll find it."

Zaira hesitated a moment longer, then thrust the bound papers at Alannah. "Thank you for being so kind and helpful."

Alannah took hold of the manuscript with care, suddenly feeling the weight of what she'd agreed to. "I'm sure you're aware that even with all the editing in the world, your manuscript might still face rejection."

"Perhaps."

"Especially as a woman."

"The publishing industry is starting to make room for female authors."

"Let's hope so."

Zaira glanced around hesitantly. "You must keep it a secret. No one can know about it for now."

"I'll be careful, so I will." Alannah hugged the stack of paper to her chest. "You could take a pen name. A man's name." She hated to suggest it, but if it helped Zaira to break into the men's world, she could eventually reveal herself after she was well-liked and respected.

"I'm already writing with a man's name. And I'm still not lucky."

"You'll get there. Besides, you know what they say about luck: The only sure thing about luck is that it will change."

A pretty smile finally curved up Zaira's lips. "I like you, Alannah. I think we're going to be grand friends."

◆ ◆ ◆ ◆ ◆ ◆ ◆

Alannah raced up the narrow servants' stairway at the back of the house, a fresh energy coursing through her. She wasn't sure if Zaira's declaration about friendship would really come true. But after the past months of missing Hugh, she felt a surge of hope that perhaps she could find new friends.

As she reached the dormer level, she hurried down the windowless hallway until she reached the door to her room. Even though dusk was falling, she had several more hours of work before Cook would release her from the kitchen for the night. The editing would have to wait until then.

In the meantime, she had to stow Zaira's manuscript in a safe place where no one would find it. The servants' quarters were deserted during the busy hour of the evening, but she didn't want to chance anyone seeing her with the bundle.

She slipped into her room, ducking under the slanted ceiling. A chest of drawers, bedside table, and bed took up the majority of space, leaving a narrow pathway between the furniture.

A circular window above the bed afforded some natural light, revealing her nightgown and coat on the pegs on the back of the door, a lantern on the bedside table, a basin, pitcher, and towel on the dresser, and her books stacked neatly beside them.

She started toward the dresser. The empty bottom drawer would probably be the best spot to keep the manuscript.

As she reached for the knob, she stopped short at the sight of a book on her pillow. How had it gotten there? Had someone come into her room and sorted through her belongings, leaving it out?

Her chest drummed with unease.

She finished stowing Zaira's story in the bottom drawer, then straightened and read the title of the book on her pillow. *Sense and Sensibility* by Jane Austen.

She drew in a breath. "Kiernan." Her gaze swept over the room as if he would magically appear from a corner. She had no doubt he was the one who'd left it for her. But how? When?

A smile tugged at her lips, and pleasure sifted through her. Kiernan had remembered their conversation of the previous night and brought her a book. No one had ever done anything so kind for her before.

She picked up the book reverently. Where had he found it? She didn't remember seeing the book anywhere around the house since there were very few books, mostly those Zaira kept in her room.

Carefully Alannah opened the cover and flipped through the pages until she reached the first chapter. The words beckoned to her. But she closed the book and fingered the spine, relishing the hard length. She smoothed her hands over the front and back, then forced herself to put the book back on her pillow in the exact spot she'd found it.

As she exited the room, she prayed she wasn't dreaming and that she would find the book there later when she returned.

She'd never met a man like Kiernan. He was imposing, intense, sometimes even short-tempered. But underneath all of that, he was genuinely caring and considerate. And sweet. There was no other way to describe what he'd done.

Unable to wipe the smile from her face, she made her way down the servants' stairway. Rather than taking the long way out of the servants' side exit, she slipped into the hallway that led to the back door.

As she stepped up to the door, it swung open.

Kiernan stalked over the threshold, nearly barreling her over but stopping just in time. He pulled himself back. "Blast, I'm sorry."

She found herself almost hungrily taking him in from his bare head and unruly waves of auburn hair to his jaw shadowed by a layer of scruff. He was usually clean shaven, so the day's worth of stubble made her fingers twitch with the urge to scrape her fingers over it. And that dimple in his chin, she would linger there, to be sure.

"Mr. Shanahan," she started, but then stopped at the

quick frown that wrinkled his forehead. Was he serious about her calling him Kiernan?

As if hearing her silent question, he crossed his arms and cocked his head in an almost arrogant manner. If he hadn't been her employer, she might have crossed her arms back in a battle of wills. But she couldn't make her muscles work to do anything but stand and stare at him.

"Alannah." The tenor of his voice sent a tingle up each bone of her spine. "Say it."

"Say what?" She was embarrassed at how breathless she sounded.

"My name."

"I did."

He narrowed his eyes, hiding the darkening blue. Something even in that narrowed gaze pinned her in place and commanded her heart to beat harder for him.

At the closing of a door from a room at the front of the house, he flicked his gaze beyond her. As if assuring himself that they were still alone, he took a step toward her so he was less than a foot away, close enough that she could almost feel the heat of his body.

She couldn't say his name and risk anyone hearing her being so casual. But before she scurried away, she had to bring up the book. Especially because there was no telling when she'd see him again. "I thank you for the book."

"Of course."

"I was surprised to find it in my room just now."

"I had one of the lads at the mine ride into town for it, then bring it here."

He'd had someone do that specifically for her? "I don't know how I can thank you."

"I do."

Mercy. This man was too much.

"Say my name, Al-an-nah." He dragged out her name, and with each syllable, she felt it to her core.

She pursed her lips together to keep from doing as he asked.

A grin tilted up one side of his mouth, sending her off-balance like someone who'd been dared to walk atop a narrow stone wall. She wasn't sure how much longer she could keep her footing without falling for him. Maybe it was already too late for that.

"Fine. Kiernan."

"That wasn't so hard, was it?"

"'Twas fearsome hard, so don't be asking me to do it again now."

At the clatter of footsteps coming from the opposite end of the hallway—the sharp ones that belonged to Mrs. Shanahan—Alannah froze.

"Alannah?" the woman called. "Could you please come here?"

Alannah turned to find the matron standing just outside the parlor. She was attired in a fashionable evening gown and her hair neatly arranged into a chignon. She appeared as lovely as always, and her voice was pleasant enough, but it contained a hint of a warning.

Had the matron overheard the conversation with Kiernan? Had she heard the informality between them? What if she'd heard about the gift of the book?

Alannah's stomach dropped with a sickening thud. This was exactly the kind of interaction with Kiernan Mrs. Shanahan had warned against. Now the woman would follow through on the threat to send her away without a penny.

Alannah pressed a hand to her middle.

Kiernan's grin faded, and he leveled a stern look at his mam. "What business do you have with Alannah? You're not intending to punish her for talking with me, are you?"

Alannah liked how direct Kiernan was. It was a refreshing change from the games most people played. Even so, she didn't dare glance down the hallway again at Mrs. Shanahan. No doubt Kiernan's question would only stir up more trouble.

"Kiernan Shanahan." Her tone was like that of a mother scolding a five-year-old boy. "'Tis not your concern what I am doing or not doing with the hired help, so it isn't. See to your own matters, and let me take care of mine."

"You'll leave her be. She's innocent."

Alannah kept her attention on the floor. Even so, the matron could likely see everything inside her—everything she was feeling toward Kiernan and how much she was thinking about him.

"If you're upset about the interaction," Kiernan continued, "speak with me instead."

"Very well." Mrs. Shanahan's voice took on a haughty note. "Then, Alannah, be on your way to do your evening duties. And, Kiernan, let's go sit on the front veranda, and we'll speak there."

Alannah didn't have to be told twice to leave. She sidled past Kiernan and exited, letting the door slap closed behind her.

All the while, mortification burned her cheeks. What would Kiernan tell his mam? That Bellamy was setting up a match between them? Or maybe Mrs. Shanahan already knew.

Either way, Mrs. Shanahan disapproved of her and was making that clear.

Alannah honestly couldn't blame the woman. Who would want a penniless immigrant maid for a man of Kiernan's potential?

Wager or not, the next time she saw Bellamy, she'd tell him she'd given his idea great consideration, but that there were more chances of leprechauns flying than of having a match with Kiernan.

10

The past few nights of visiting with Bellamy's prospects had gone well. Kiernan had met with three possible brides, and each one had potential. Bellamy had assured him he had four more meetings lined up for next week.

Kiernan tugged off his cravat and tossed it on his bed. If everything was going splendidly, why did he feel so restless?

Unbuttoning his vest, he stepped to his open window and let the cool night breeze soothe him. After the recent rainy days, the heat and humidity had dissipated, replaced by cooler temperatures.

Even though his dinner with tonight's prospect had taken him to the city, he'd decided to return to Oakland. It was more convenient for reaching the brickyard. And it was safer. Every day, they were getting reports of the increasing death toll in the city. While cholera was still more rampant in the immigrant communities than elsewhere, it was no respecter of a person's neighborhood or family and would eventually reach everywhere in St. Louis.

Kiernan finished with his vest and shed it. As he started

unbuttoning his shirt, his gaze snagged on a flicker of light in the field beyond the summer kitchen. He stopped short and peered more closely. The light was too big to belong to an insect. It had to be the flame from a lantern. Alannah's lantern.

"Blast." He scowled, frustration curdling inside his gut.

She hadn't gone back outside at night since that time he'd caught her and warned her against it—at least that he'd been aware, and aye, he'd been looking. He'd assumed she'd heeded him. But maybe the reason she'd refrained was because of the wet weather. Now that it had finally stopped raining, had she decided to resume her nightly ventures?

He should have known she was too independent to rely upon him for advice. And she was too much like a wildflower to be confined inside. She seemed to thrive on the fresh air and the beauty of nature and the openness of the sky. Already in just a week of her living at Oakland, her skin had gained color, her hair was more golden, and her cheeks were rosier.

The move to the country had been good for her. If only he could convince his mam of the same.

He expelled a tight sigh. He could admit another reason he was coming back to Oakland every night was to make sure his mam didn't fire Alannah after she'd witnessed them talking together by the back door earlier in the week.

Mam had expressed her concern about his forming an attachment to a maid, reminding him of their household rule not to dally with the hired staff.

"She's a pretty young thing, so she is," Mam said, as they sat stiffly together on the front veranda. "And naturally you might feel some attraction."

Oh, he felt attraction to Alannah, and it was only getting

stronger. However, he didn't intend to do anything about those feelings . . . except douse them, which he'd been trying to do, especially since his conversation with Torin. Kiernan still had a knife prick under his chin to remind him of Torin's threats.

"You'll be keeping your eyes and hands off that maid," Mam continued in her usual blunt manner. "I won't stand for you using her or any of the staff."

"Don't worry." He'd been slightly embarrassed by the nature of the conversation, but he couldn't fault Mam for bringing up the issue. "She's like a little sister. That's all."

Maybe that wasn't exactly all. But that's what he was aiming for—treating her like a sibling.

His mam shook her head. "You'll also not be putting notions into her head so she starts thinking of herself as more important than she really is."

The comment needled him in all the wrong places. "Just because she's a maid doesn't mean she's not important."

"You know what I mean, Kiernan."

Aye, he did know. If he made it clear to his mam that he would behave honorably, would she leave Alannah alone? "I have no intention of having a dalliance with a maid. Not now. Not ever. And as far as courting her, she's not someone I would ever seriously consider."

"Good, because the cook tells me she knows nothing about all the uses of silverware, doesn't understand mealtime mannerisms, and doesn't know the appropriate way to serve tea."

He wanted to chastise his mam for her emphasis on such trivial things. But how could he when his list of wifely requirements had included things like having a well-bred wife, one from high society who was poised and could manage a large house?

The conversation hadn't gone much differently for the rest of the five minutes or so that they'd talked. He'd finally ended it by telling Mam to treat Alannah fairly and to leave her alone.

Unease had nagged him ever since. He sensed that Mam had made up her mind to dislike Alannah from the day he'd first brought her to Oakland. Lucinda Shanahan was stubborn and determined and wouldn't be swayed. But he was equally as stubborn and determined, and he didn't intend to be swayed either.

Alannah was staying, and that was all there was to it.

And since she seemed bound to read alone in the moonlight, he would have to make sure she stayed safe.

Without bothering to don his vest or coat, he headed outside, going as quietly as he could so no one—especially Mam—would hear him sneaking around. A part of him resented that he had to sneak at all. But he didn't want to get Alannah into trouble. And it would certainly be best for her reputation if no one knew of his presence there with her.

As he passed by the flower beds, he breathed in the brisk air and felt the restlessness begin to fade. Once again, at his approach, she didn't notice or hear him, was too engrossed in her book—the Jane Austen he'd given her. As before, she was lying on her stomach in her nightgown. But this time, she was wearing a cloak.

He paused at the edge of the blanket she'd spread out, folded his arms, and waited for her to glance up and see him.

After a moment of standing, frustration pooled low inside. The entire Farrell gang could have surrounded her, and she wouldn't have heard them.

He exhaled a huff of exasperation.

At the sound, she released a soft squeak of surprise and slapped her book closed. Her gaze flew up to him, her eyes wide and guileless. Her face was soft in the lantern light, a warm tan, with pieces of hair framing her cheeks and the rest contained to a braid.

"You scared me." She pushed herself up so that she was sitting.

"I told you not to come out here."

She lifted her chin, and her eyes flashed with sudden defiance. "I tried to stay away, but I needed just a few minutes."

He didn't wait for an invitation to join her. He stepped onto the blanket and began to lower himself. "Since you refuse to listen to me, you leave me with no choice but to join you and watch over you."

She reached for the lantern and her book, sliding them aside. Was she so easily making room for him and welcoming him to be here with her?

He took the spot beside her. As he stretched out his legs and then leaned back on his elbows, he glanced at her sideways.

She was watching him, her eyes still wide, her long lashes framing them and making them even more beautiful.

The words "You're beautiful" pushed to the tip of his tongue. But he couldn't say anything like that, had to treat her like a sibling, had to prove to Mam that he had no intention of having a dalliance with Alannah or anything else even close to it.

"How do you like Jane Austen?"

Alannah caressed the back cover of the book. "I love her. She's my new favorite author." A long daisy stuck out of the middle of the book where she'd closed it.

He couldn't stop a strange pang of jealousy, that she didn't like him as much as the book and that she was caressing the inanimate object rather than him. He swallowed the desire for her attention and touch and instead focused on the stars overhead. The rain clouds were gone, leaving a few wisps behind.

"Looks like you're about halfway done." He forced his tone to remain casual.

She released a soft laugh. "This is my second time reading it, so it is."

"Really?"

"Really." She lowered her head, an embarrassed smile playing over her lips.

"You're a fast reader."

"Oh aye." She hesitated, then her smile widened. "I admit, I stayed up most of the night after you gave it to me."

"You must have been tired the next day."

"I was, but reading it was worth the loss of sleep." She pulled her cloak around her tighter. "I promise I'll return it to you when I finish this time."

"I don't want it back."

"You don't?"

When she turned her wide eyes upon him, he suddenly felt like he was drowning in their depths and couldn't come up for a breath.

What was it about this woman that made him react this way?

He scrambled to find his breath and his sanity. He had to remain in control of himself and of the situation.

"I can't keep it," she persisted.

"It's a gift, Alannah." Somehow his words came out calmer than he felt.

"And I can't be taking gifts from you either." Her tone held a note of chastisement. "Your mother won't be liking that—"

"Mam's not making life miserable for you, is she?"

"No, she's not said a word to me all week."

"Good."

"You know what they say: A storm is always brewing on the horizon."

"You know what they also say: Sunshine always follows the rain."

She laughed again lightly.

He liked listening to her laugh, liked seeing her smile, liked knowing he could make her happy with something as simple as a book. He'd have to get another for her.

She was quiet for a long moment, the gentle rustle of the breeze in the grass filling the lull.

He felt strangely content lying beside her.

She shot him a sideways glance. "Miss Douglas came by earlier this evening looking for you."

The comment was like a bucket of cold well water dumping over him and waking him up to real life. He didn't want the reminder of Shelia. He didn't want to think about her or Liam or the upcoming engagement party.

Alannah seemed to be holding her breath.

He forced down a brusque retort. He couldn't take out his frustration on her.

"I'm sorry for bringing it up, so I am." She spoke hesitantly. "The gossip is none of my concern—"

"What is the gossip these days?" He couldn't keep the bitterness from his tone.

"We can talk about something else."

"Since you know about Shelia, you may as well know the truth and not hearsay."

She fingered the lettering on the front of the book. "Do you still love her?"

Did he still love Shelia? Maybe there were still times when he cared about her and thought about what he could have had with her, but he had forced himself to let go of her for Liam's sake.

"She was my first love." He stared ahead at the meadow shadowed with darkness and the dense woodland beyond. For a short while, he shared with Alannah about growing up next door to Shelia, becoming friends, and then falling in love with her. He told about her trip to Europe and how she'd shifted her affection to Liam at that point.

"I suspect she was pressured by her family," Kiernan finished. "After all, Liam is one of the wealthiest men in St. Louis, and though I have means, I am still trying to make my own way."

"Ach, if she truly loved you, that wouldn't have mattered." Alannah's voice held a thread of indignation, and he liked it, liked that she was upset on his behalf.

"She and Liam are having an engagement party this summer." Because of the cholera, it would be a smaller gathering than it would have been otherwise. Even so, the Douglases would likely make it as grand as possible.

"You'll be feeling obligated to go?"

"He's my business partner and best friend. I have no choice in the matter."

"He doesn't sound like any best friend I'd care to have." This time Alannah's voice didn't have just a little indignation. It was loaded with it.

Kiernan lowered himself the remainder of the way so his head rested against the blanket. Not so he could see her face better, but it didn't hurt to have a better view. "Liam's a good fellow. I don't think he ever realized that I harbored feelings for Shelia."

Alannah made a scoffing sound. "Seems to me a best friend ought to be the first to know about a love interest. My cousin Hugh was my closest friend, and he always knew who I liked, sometimes even before I was willing to admit it."

"And exactly how many hearts have you broken?"

Her lips curled with a smile, showing off that tiny pucker in her upper lip, a pucker he wanted to trace, even if for just a second.

"Who says I've broken any hearts at all?"

"I do."

She cast her eyes down, her lashes falling against her cheeks. She clearly liked his roundabout compliment. He was tempted to be more direct, but if he had any hope of keeping his relationship with Alannah platonic, then he couldn't get carried away.

"So?" he persisted, not sure why he cared so much about the previous men in her life, but he did.

She hesitated a moment longer before telling him the stories of different boys and men who'd tried to win her hand. Kiernan wasn't surprised that she'd had more interest than she could keep count of.

But she'd only ever had two that she was serious about. One had been a family friend her da had wanted her to marry. But apparently after her da died, the relationship hadn't lasted.

The other had been with a fellow who had joined a rebel group, the Young Irelanders, with Torin in an effort to fight for Ireland's independence from Great Britain. The young man had died of a gunshot wound he sustained during a skirmish during the uprising in '48.

"What about here in St. Louis?" Kiernan couldn't keep himself from probing, a strange need driving him.

She twisted the loose hair at the end of her braid and didn't meet his eyes.

His gut cinched. "You do like someone."

"Maybe." Her response was tentative.

Maybe? What kind of answer was that? "I haven't seen you with anyone." Did this have to do with Bellamy? Had Torin gone through with using Bellamy even though Kiernan had asked him—no, ordered him—to call off the matchmaking?

Kiernan pushed back up to his elbows, frustration mounting within him. He had no right to interfere with Torin and Alannah's decision in the first place.

"So do you think you'll marry him?" The question popped out before Kiernan could censor it. It was meddlesome, but once spoken, he refused to take it back.

Alannah still didn't look up, kept her focus on the tip of her braid. "I'm trying to figure it out."

Kiernan wanted to tell her that he'd figure it out for her by canceling all plans with the fellow. But he'd already been forward enough.

"How about you?" Her cheeks were most definitely turning rosier. "Do you think you'll marry Bellamy's choice for you?"

He had a wager to uphold. And one way or another, he was getting married. "I'm still trying to figure things out too. But I gave him my word I'd cooperate, so that's what I'm doing."

Her smile faded. "Oh. So it's been difficult for you?"

His thoughts returned to the three women he'd met with over the past few nights. Bellamy had done well. Each had all twelve qualifications on his list, and the visits had been pleasant enough. But at the end of each, he hadn't been attracted to any of them, not even a little bit.

"I'm trying to move on," he said. "But it's been difficult."

Alannah nodded, her expression still solemn. "It's alright. There's no rush. As they say: If you don't know the way, walk slowly."

He wished he could take reassurance from her. But he wasn't one to sit around and wait for things to happen. He preferred to make the moves first.

She pushed herself up so she was standing, tucked the book under one arm, and took up the lantern in the other hand. "Friendship is always a good place to start any relationship." She offered the words of advice almost shyly.

"So it is."

"I think you'd make a great friend."

"You don't know me."

"I know you well enough."

He'd lost track of the trajectory of the conversation. How had they gone from talking about his matchmaking to their friendship?

He stood and gathered the blanket.

"Friendship, then?" She ambled toward the flower beds.

He'd gotten a glimpse of her ankles and calves the last

time they were out in the field, and now he caught sight again of that stretch of her legs, the creamy skin, the smooth shape. Just the tiniest look sent a trail of heat blazing through him.

He tore his gaze from her. What was he doing? He had to stay far away from lusting after her. Was the best way to do that to focus on being friends, the way she was requesting?

"Well?" She stopped beside one of the raised beds. The blooms were an array of colors that even in the darkness held a vibrancy and heady scent.

"Friendship it is." What did two people do when they were agreeing on becoming friends? Should he offer a handshake?

She gave him a smile, one that was warm and encouraging. "It'll be good. Kiernan."

At the use of his given name, the last resistance inside him came tumbling down, and he smiled in return. Friendship with Alannah wouldn't hurt anything. In fact, maybe it was just what he needed.

11

Zaira was a talented writer. 'Twas easy to see.

Alannah used an insert sign and wrote a missing word in the margin of the page open before her. Now that she was nearing the end of the manuscript, she was having a harder time giving feedback and not getting lost in the story itself.

Sitting in the grass in the shade behind the summer kitchen, she'd been editing for the past hour while Zaira took her position inside the kitchen, helping Cook clean up the evening meal.

It felt awkward to switch places and hand her apron over to Zaira. But whenever she protested, the young woman smiled brightly and claimed it was the least she could do to allow Alannah the time she needed to edit.

Alannah had tried to work on the manuscript at night in her room. But with how exhausted she was, sitting on her bed invariably led to her falling asleep, which was one more reason why she liked reading outside, so she didn't fall asleep so easily.

She'd considered bringing the manuscript with her during her nightly ventures to the field. But with Kiernan joining her every night for the past week, she'd hadn't wanted to reveal Zaira's secret. She didn't think Kiernan would mind that his sister was writing a novel and trying to get it published, but the decision to involve Kiernan was Zaira's.

Besides, even if Alannah brought the manuscript out to the blanket, she wasn't sure how much work she would have accomplished with Kiernan sitting there beside her. On a couple of occasions, he'd brought a book, too, but he'd only read for a little while before he closed it.

Whenever he did that, she put her book down, too, even though he insisted that she keep reading. The truth was, she was more interested in talking to him than reading anything written on the pages.

And . . . he was too distracting lying on the blanket with his arms crossed behind his head and his muscular body stretched out in all its brawny glory. Without his cravat and vest and coat, he seemed more at ease. Sometimes he even had a button or two of his shirt undone or his cuffs rolled up.

Besides, when she kept reading, he watched her, making her self-conscious. Every time she glanced at him, he pretended to study the stars and told her he was there to make sure she was safe.

But it was more than that. . . . At least, it felt that way to her.

Alannah paused with her pencil above Zaira's manuscript and smiled. She couldn't help it. Kiernan made her happy. Spending time with him was satisfying enough, even when they weren't talking. But she loved their conversations too.

He was interesting, and they could discuss just about anything.

He'd asked her lots of questions about what her life had been like in Ireland, and she'd shared all about her childhood and family. Likewise she'd asked him about his childhood and his family and each of his siblings and his experiences with growing up in St. Louis.

They'd talked about their plans and dreams for the future along with their fears and worries. They'd discussed the problems in Missouri and in St. Louis, particularly among the newly arriving immigrants. And, of course, they'd talked about the gang concerns for Torin.

She was finding that she and Kiernan could converse about everything . . . except for their relationship. It was too awkward to talk about Bellamy and his matchmaking between them, especially because Kiernan had admitted he was still trying to figure out what to do next.

The last thing she wanted to do was push him into something he wasn't ready for. That's why she'd suggested starting out with friendship. Maybe if they learned to be friends, eventually he'd like her as more.

That was working for her. She was liking him more with every passing day.

She stared ahead to the spot where she and Kiernan usually met, the tall grass conspicuously flattened in just one area but growing in profusion everywhere else in the meadow along with the wildflowers.

How could she not like him after he'd given her a second book just two nights ago, another Jane Austen, *Pride and Prejudice*? A man who gave her books was a man who knew the way into her heart.

He was wonderful.

She released a happy sigh. Was God finally smiling down on her?

For so long, God had felt far away, even angry. But she supposed He had every right to be angry. She hadn't exactly been living an upright life over the years before she'd immigrated. She could blame Hugh's influence—his penchant for parties and drinking and dancing. But she could have told him no. Instead, she'd gone along with him all too often and had indulged in the same vices.

Sometimes she wondered if God had punished her by taking away her family. Even if He hadn't directly punished her, at the very least He hadn't been pleased enough to take her side over recent years.

Was that changing now that she'd put the vices out of her life and was living more uprightly? Would God give her something good? Maybe Kiernan?

She dropped her attention back to Zaira's manuscript and poised the pencil above the next line of fine penmanship. Before she could take in a word, hands snaked around her face from behind and covered her eyes.

She startled, and a bubble of panic welled inside her chest. What was happening? Had she grown too comfortable at Oakland, and had Shaw Farrell discovered where she was?

Kiernan had been keeping her apprised of the few times that anyone from the Farrell gang had shown up at the brickyard. They hadn't come inside, but it was clear they were still after Torin.

Did that mean Shaw was still after her too?

With a jab of her elbow, she wrestled against the hold.

Behind her came a familiar laugh. Torin's.

She stopped her struggling. "Torin Darragh. You're a beast for scaring me to death."

He released her and stepped around in front of her. With a wide grin, he peered down, his bright blue eyes behind his spectacles filled with tenderness. His fair hair was overlong and in need of a trim and his scruffy face in need of a shave. But otherwise, he appeared to be healthy, his wiry body filled out and his muscles well rounded.

"It's about time you came to visit," she chided as she set aside Zaira's manuscript and rose to her feet.

Torin was surveying her, taking her in from her head to her toes, likely reassuring himself that she wasn't harmed or in want. She didn't wait for him to finish and instead launched herself against him.

His arms encircled her at the same time she embraced him. For a long moment, she just hugged him, wishing she could see him more often. When she pulled back, she held him at arm's length and examined him more carefully.

Even though Kiernan had kept her well informed on Torin's doings, she couldn't keep from peppering him with questions. "How are you doing? How is work at the brickyard? Are you getting enough to eat? Are you staying safe?"

"Whoa, now." He laughed, his eyes crinkling at the corners in a way that reminded her of their da. "I'm fine. I can hold my own."

Torin had already proven he could survive danger many times over. After all, he'd survived his time as a rebel with the Young Irelanders. He'd survived the hunger and the ship voyage to America. He'd survived the first difficult year of living in St. Louis. And he was still surviving against the gang rivals determined to punish him.

Torin was an intelligent man, and she admired him for his strength of mind and body.

He surveyed the thick trees that bordered Oakland, his eyes narrowing. He probably had a friend or two keeping watch in the woods. He never went anywhere without his companions from the Saints Alley gang. If there was one good thing about gangs, at least they looked out for each other.

It's just that Torin wouldn't have needed looking out for if he'd never joined a gang in the first place.

He shifted his attention back to her. "How have you been?"

She couldn't contain a smile. "I love it here."

"You do?" His eyes held uncertainty and hope, as though he desperately wanted to believe her.

"I do." The workload was still difficult and endless, but as long as she could spend time with Kiernan as well as read her books, she would be satisfied.

"I didn't believe Mr. Shanahan when he told me to call off the matchmaking. But it looks like he was right, that you're happy enough."

Call off the matchmaking? Surely Torin meant that Kiernan had wanted the matchmaking called off with other fellows *except for him*.

"I'm happy," she reassured her brother.

"I've been worried about you living here, that maybe Mr. Shanahan would take liberties with you."

"He's a good man, Torin." She didn't realize how besotted she sounded until his brows dipped into a dangerous glare.

"You like him," he said in a low, ominous voice.

Something in Torin's eyes made her hesitate to admit just how much she liked Kiernan.

What if Torin didn't know that Bellamy had lined up a match with Kiernan? Even if Bellamy hadn't spoken with Torin about the man he'd picked for her, surely Kiernan had mentioned it. He'd said he'd talk with Torin. But maybe he hadn't yet done so.

"I told Mr. Shanahan to leave you alone." Torin hefted his shoulders as though preparing for a fight.

"So you don't approve of the match?"

"What match?"

"With Kiernan."

Torin's brows rose at her use of Kiernan's given name.

"With Mr. Shanahan," she quickly corrected herself.

Torin opened his mouth to respond but then didn't say anything.

It was becoming clearer by the moment that neither Bellamy nor Kiernan had said anything to Torin about the match, and that was strange. Maybe she shouldn't have mentioned it either. But now that she had, she might as well clear up his confusion. "When Bellamy met with me a couple of weeks ago, he told me his choice of match for me was Kiernan—Mr. Shanahan."

"He did?"

"Aye, so he did."

"Whyever for?" Torin's confusion only seemed to be increasing by the moment rather than clearing up.

"I didn't believe Bellamy was serious at first either. But when Kiernan began spending time with me, I realized he's been giving the match a fair try, just as I have."

"Blimey." Torin scrubbed a hand down his mouth and chin. "I never would have expected Mr. Shanahan to agree to something like that. Not with how arrogant he is."

"He's not arrogant. He's actually really wonderful."

Torin halted. "I was right. You've already fallen for him."

A half laugh escaped her lips. "No. Not yet." Even as the denial rushed out, her heart thudded with a strange beat. What if Torin was right? Was she was letting herself get too close to Kiernan too soon?

"You better be careful, Alannah. I like Mr. Shanahan. I do. But I'm having a hard time believing he'd settle for a woman of your status."

She straightened her shoulders and pulled herself up. "Maybe status isn't as important to him as you think it is." She'd gotten to know Kiernan better since living at Oakland, and his friendship was proof that he didn't care about her status, wasn't it?

At a nearby clanking of a pail, Torin's eyes darted around again, taking in every detail of the landscape. As his gaze came to rest upon her, it was grave. "I overheard Mr. Shanahan discussing the business plan for the brickyard with his partner. He's counting on a sizable dowry to help with the expansion. And from what I understand from the rumors going around, he's been meeting with lots of different ladies who are candidates."

A knot formed in Alannah's chest. Was Torin right? "Maybe that was before Bellamy formed the match. Maybe now he's changed his mind."

"The conversation took place yesterday."

"But he's interested in me." She hated the desperation in her tone.

Torin cursed under his breath. "I'll speak with Bellamy. Soon. And I'll get this figured out."

Bellamy wouldn't have misled her. She didn't know the

matchmaker well, but he was too kind to direct her down a path that would lead to nowhere. Of course, he wasn't God and couldn't work miracles. But surely he wouldn't have suggested something impossible.

Even as she tried to defend Bellamy, all her doubts rushed back in. She'd questioned the match with Kiernan all along. Had she been foolish to allow herself any hope?

At a distant whistle, Torin nodded curtly, probably at one of his friends. "I have to nip along."

"So soon?" She started to reach for him, wanted him to stay, but he was putting himself in danger by leaving the brickyard. What if the Farrell gang had followed him to the Shanahans'?

He gave her another hug. "Be careful, Alannah. Stay away from Mr. Shanahan until I talk to Bellamy."

She pulled back. "I can take care of myself. I don't need you to be telling me what to do."

"Don't be a fool." His tone turned harsh.

"I'm not."

"Then listen to me for once, lass."

"I do listen—"

"If you'd listened to me and stayed at the tenement where I told you to, maybe Shaw wouldn't be hunting for you."

The hard accusation was like a slap against her cheek, and she drew back with a sharp inhale.

Torin kneaded the back of his neck. "Ach, I'm not meaning that, Alannah. I'm to blame for everything and not you."

"That's not true. I'm to blame too."

At another whistle, he cursed again. "Before I go, I wanted to warn you that we got word the Farrell gang is planning to do something soon. No matter what happens to me, you need to promise to stay here and not show yourself."

She pressed a hand to her throat. She didn't want anything more to happen to him, but she was so helpless to protect him.

His expression softened. "I love you, Alannah. Take you care now." Without waiting for her reply, he jogged toward the nearest area of woodland. He didn't look back, and within the span of thirty seconds, he disappeared into the dark depths of the brush and trees.

She could only stand watching the spot, her mind reeling with everything she'd learned. One thought crowded to the front more than the others. Kiernan needed a sizable dowry that would help him make his new brickyard successful.

Just last night he'd shared with her how another shaft was nearing completion. In addition to that second mine shaft, he was also building a second kiln, erecting more open storage sheds, purchasing more equipment, and was hoping to at least double the production of bricks by the end of the year. She'd heard the determination in his voice along with the excitement over all he was accomplishing.

She wouldn't have a dowry and couldn't possibly help him achieve what he wanted. Torin was right that Kiernan would never settle for a woman of her status. He likely had his sights set on someone else. Maybe he'd even been courting another woman.

A burn began to work its way up her chest and into her cheeks.

There was one way to find out if she'd been making a fool of herself with Kiernan.

Swiping up the manuscript from the grass where she'd left it, she marched around the kitchen to the side door. As she stepped inside, Zaira was standing in front of the sink, scrubbing a pan and telling Cook a story as she did each time she took Alannah's place in the kitchen.

Cook stood at the center worktable, her preparations for the next day's meals forgotten, her attention riveted to Zaira. Storytelling was a skill Zaira excelled at whether written or vocal. And she'd spun an almost magical spell over Cook with her tales each visit. As a result, Zaira had garnered a promise that the cook wouldn't tell anyone about Alannah skipping her duties.

Now as Alannah halted just inside the doorway, one question clamored in her mind. If anyone could answer it, Zaira would be able to with as insightful as she was. "Has your brother, Mr. Shanahan, been matched with anyone by the matchmaker Bellamy McKenna?"

"Bellamy?" Zaira's brows rose. "That man is a sneaky one, to be sure."

Alannah was tempted to call out that she didn't care to hear Zaira's thoughts about Bellamy. But she swallowed the retort and persisted with her question. "Has he matched your brother with someone yet?"

Zaira lifted the blackened pot from the sink, heedless of the water she was sloshing onto the floor. "From everything I've heard, Bellamy's been busy setting up visits with potential matches for Kiernan. He had a few last week and a couple so far this week."

So the rumors were true. Kiernan was meeting with other women. Lots of other women. To find a match. Particularly one with a sizable dowry. "You're certain?"

"I'm not certain of much." Zaira cast a smile toward Alannah. "But I do know that Kiernan is on a mission to find a bride. And when he's on a mission, he'll stop at nothing to succeed."

Alannah didn't know whether to laugh or to cry. So she did neither and stood mutely.

Bellamy was the one making it all happen. If that was really the case, why had he told her that he wanted to match her with Kiernan? It made no sense. Had she misunderstood the matchmaker? Or maybe he'd changed his mind and hadn't bothered to tell her.

Whatever the case, she'd made a complete fool of herself in spending time with Kiernan. She never would have done so if Bellamy hadn't mentioned Kiernan as a potential match. She wouldn't have been so bold or so forward. And she certainly wouldn't have presumed he wanted to be her friend.

She hung her head. Saints above. How could she ever face Kiernan again now that she knew the truth? That he hadn't been considering her for a match. That he really had only been watching over her because she'd been so insistent on going outside by herself.

She couldn't face him. She would have to avoid him. It was the only way.

12

Alannah hadn't shown up at their usual meeting spot two nights in a row.

Kiernan stared at the ledger on the desk in front of him in his mine office, but the numbers all blurred together. He'd been trying for the past hours to study the financials his accountant had laid out for him, but all he could see was Alannah.

Mostly he pictured her sitting beside him with the stars and moonlight casting a glow over her that made her ethereal. He loved the way she focused completely on him when he was talking, her eyes bright with questions, her head tilted with interest. And he loved the way her expression lit up when she told him about the things she liked doing, her lips curling up with an almost-smile.

He loved when her nose scrunched whenever he said something she didn't like, and he loved that she wasn't afraid to tell him when she disagreed. She had her own opinions about matters, and he'd begun to relish hearing them and sometimes even debating her. Their conversations were never dull, always lively, and yet genuine.

Genuine. Alannah was genuine about everything. She never pretended to be anything she wasn't, was her real self, and never tried to impress him.

Unlike all the women and their families he'd been meeting with where everyone was trying to impress everyone else, especially with what they could offer each other in a marital arrangement.

It felt too much like a business deal, and the longer it went on, the more awkward he was finding it. Of course, he'd always been considered one of St. Louis's finest catches. Although he didn't have a fortune currently, as firstborn he would someday inherit the bulk of his family's estate and wealth in addition to what his da had already given him.

With just the right match, he could rise to the top, farther than Da. But was this whole process worth it?

He clasped his hands to both sides of his pounding temples. If only he wasn't thinking so much about Alannah, maybe he'd be able to think more objectively about his future. But the truth was, he'd missed meeting with her over the past two nights, so much that now he couldn't stop contemplating it. He was actually starting to drive himself crazy with his preoccupation.

"Stop this, Kiernan Shanahan." He shoved away from his desk and stood with such force it sent his chair toppling behind him. He was not only wasting time thinking about her, but he was likely worrying for nothing.

He righted his chair, then stalked around the front of the desk, paused, and shoved his hands into his hair. He stared out the open door that overlooked the area where several men were mixing clay with water in large vats—the last batches of the day before quitting time. Beside them were rows of long wooden boxes with uniformly sized compartments and the edges nailed tight to prevent the clay from seeping out. Several other men were packing the already mixed clay into the molds, while yet another worker scraped off the excess with a level rod.

Kiernan normally took pleasure in watching the creation of the bricks. But not yesterday. And certainly not today.

Expelling a tight sigh, he paced to one side of the cabin and then back.

When he'd stopped by the kitchen to check on her this morning, he hadn't been able to speak to her privately because Cook had been present. For the couple of seconds that he'd stood awkwardly in the doorway, she'd kept her back to him at the worktable, as though she hadn't wanted to see him at all.

He'd been as baffled then as he was now. What had happened to cause the change? It was almost as if she was avoiding him. Was she?

He paced the length of the cabin again. The office was sparsely furnished with only a corner stove, an old desk, and a couple of wooden chairs. Years ago, it had been home to the mine owner, but Kiernan had turned it into the official headquarters.

He didn't spend much time inside the small room, preferred overseeing the various construction sites, talking with the foremen and workers, lending a hand when necessary, and learning all he could about every aspect of the business.

The more he knew, the more he would understand about

the right changes to make and how to innovate and become more efficient. He'd done that with the glass factory and had turned it from a dying business into one of the most profitable in St. Louis.

He'd do the same here too. But according to the ledger his accountant had sent over, he was starting to run low on the capital Liam had invested. They also didn't have enough income yet from sales to cover the expenses. Some purchases had cost more than he'd anticipated, like the beams for the new shaft and the new storage sheds. His accountant had informed him the increase was because the price of lumber had gone up as a result of the fire.

If only the demand for bricks would rise too. But according to Liam's report yesterday, the city council members had decided to leave St. Louis since cholera was worsening. Liam hadn't been sure when the council would reconvene, which meant that for the time being, there was no ordinance in place requiring bricks for the rebuilding projects.

Of course, businesses were still buying bricks even without the ordinance, especially because they didn't want a repeat of the fire anytime soon. But with more people exiting the city every day, some of the building contracts the brickyard had received had been canceled or put on hold.

Kiernan paused and closed the ledger. Even if they were facing some setbacks, he wasn't losing heart, and he wasn't giving up. The cholera wouldn't last forever. In time, people would return to normal life. Sales would eventually increase.

However, since he was falling short on what he needed to pay his workers, he might have to ask Liam to invest more—which would make Liam the larger investor. Would it also technically make him the owner? Kiernan wasn't sure, and he didn't want to find out.

His gut twisted at the prospect of having to sell his glass factory. The loss would be embarrassing, to say the least. Instead of proving he was a good businessman with good investment skills and an eye for the future, he'd end up saddling himself with a business that wasn't going anywhere except downhill, dragging him along with it.

Was that all the more reason to get serious about the women he'd been visiting? Why, then, did the prospect of marrying one of them so he could gain a dowry feel more and more selfish?

Expelling another long sigh, he grabbed his hat from the chair where he'd tossed it earlier, situated it on his head, then stepped outside into the evening sunshine. He might as well head home. He wasn't getting any work done. Besides, he hadn't spent time with his family recently and was due to join them for a meal.

At some point tonight, he'd track down Alannah and find out what was wrong. If he'd done something to offend her, he wanted to know. Or if Mam was threatening her, he needed to know that too.

He locked up and made the rounds through the brickyard to let his foremen know he was going, including Torin at the kiln. Kiernan hadn't talked with Torin about Alannah since the knife incident, but the air was tense between them, and just yesterday Torin mentioned the need to talk to him about Alannah.

Kiernan could admit he was avoiding the conversation because he had the feeling he would only make things worse, especially because Torin was too smart and would figure out he was spending time alone with Alannah.

As he mounted his horse and started down the road north toward Oakland, he couldn't rein in the anticipation. The truth was, he'd begun to look forward to being with Alannah so much that he'd started to cut short his visits with the other women. He spent the previous evening with the seventh of the candidates, and all the while, he kept pulling his watch from his pocket, trying to decide how much longer he had to stay before leaving.

The young ladies had been perfect gentlewomen from among St. Louis's best families. He couldn't find fault with any of Bellamy's choices. He had a final week to go, three more women to meet, and then he would have to decide who he wanted to marry.

But how could he, when he didn't feel anything for any of them? When Alannah was the only woman on his mind?

He gripped his reins tighter and ducked under a branch, the forest growing thick around him with the flowering dogwoods hanging low and full.

The meetings with so many women were apparently causing quite the commotion among the St. Louis elite. Earlier, Liam had informed him with his usual laughter that the women were beginning to fight with each other, competing over who was the best candidate for becoming his bride.

The news had left Kiernan uneasy. He hadn't meant for his methods to cause trouble or to stir up strife. What if he ended up not liking any of them? Then he would have put them through distress and conflict for no reason.

Yet, how could he not conjure attraction for even one of

the women? Maybe he needed to be more invested in the visits instead of wishing he could return home and spend time with Alannah.

Perhaps the break from Alannah was for the best.

At a sudden gunshot in the air behind him, his stallion halted abruptly and almost reared up. Thankfully, Kiernan had quick reflexes, and he grabbed on to the reins more securely.

As he strained to remain in the saddle, the horse shied around, and Kiernan found himself facing three men, the one at the front pointing a gun directly at him.

Was he being robbed?

His hand slid instinctively toward his revolver.

"Halt right there, Mr. Shanahan." The hardened square face with the thin scar above his lips belonged to none other than Shaw Farrell. Not much older than Kiernan's twenty-two years of age, Shaw was thickly muscled with large hands. It was rumored Shaw could strangle a man with just one of those hands in less than a minute.

Clearly, he knew Kiernan's identity. Had the fellow been waiting for him to pass by? Or had he been out in the area already? What if he'd been searching for Alannah?

Kiernan's blood froze at the thought. He'd known there was that possibility. But what if that's why Shaw had stopped him? Because he suspected the Shanahans were hiding her?

"Tell me what you want, Shaw." Kiernan rested his hand on his revolver. Shaw wouldn't get away with murdering a Shanahan. The punishment would be too swift and severe. More likely in Kiernan's case, the fellow would threaten him a little, maybe even bully him, but that's as far as it would go. At least Kiernan hoped so.

Shaw lowered his revolver but didn't holster it. "Should have known you were the one sheltering Darragh."

Kiernan kept his gaze hard and pointed. "He's one of my best employees. I offered him a job at my brickyard."

The two men standing slightly behind Shaw had equally hard demeanors. Though they weren't as broad or strong, they carried themselves with an air of dangerous nonchalance. Kiernan had seen it often in gang members, men who'd become so accustomed to violence and death that they no longer valued even their own lives.

"Torin Darragh's a dead man." Shaw's threat was the same he'd thrown out the day he'd fought Torin in front of the glass factory back in the spring.

Kiernan gave what he hoped was a casual shrug. "If I find my best employee dead, I'll know where to send the police."

Shaw gave a casual shrug too. "The police won't know where to find me."

"I'll make sure they look." It was possible Shaw was bribing some of the police to do his bidding. But Kiernan would find the means to pay them better to do what he wanted.

He hoped the situation didn't come to that with Torin dead and the police searching for Shaw. What Kiernan had really been hoping for was that Shaw would finally give up his vendetta. But was it only a matter of time before Shaw found a way to kill Torin?

Most likely it would take money to get Shaw to leave Torin alone. "How much do you want?" Kiernan didn't have money to spare at the moment. But if paying Shaw would resolve the issue and keep Torin and Alannah safe, then Kiernan would figure out a way to come up with the necessary funds.

Shaw exchanged a glance with his companions, a slight grin curling up his lips. "I like this fellow."

The feeling was not mutual. "How much?"

Shaw's grin inched higher. "I want Torin's sister."

There was no blasted way Kiernan would ever let Shaw have Alannah. "It was clear she didn't want you." He was referring back to the day Shaw had kissed her in front of the factory, a memory that burned through him every time he thought about it.

"She'll have me."

No she wouldn't. Kiernan forced his hands not to fist. "Find someone else."

"Alannah Darragh is the most beautiful woman in St. Louis, and I don't want anyone else."

Why was Shaw being so persistent? "We don't always get what we want."

"I do."

The frustration was only swirling faster inside Kiernan. If he wasn't careful, eventually he would say or do something that would reveal how much he knew about Alannah and how much he cared about her. Because aye, he did care about her.

"I'm planning to marry Alannah," Shaw continued. "I'm ready to have a wife and kids."

The thought of this man doing so with Alannah sent chills through Kiernan. "And bring them the danger of gang life? No."

"I'll be able to give them anything they want."

"They won't ever be free, and you know it."

Shaw's gaze turned sharp, almost lethal, and his grin disappeared. "Ten thousand dollars."

Kiernan released a scoffing laugh. Ten thousand? The amount was exorbitant. Kiernan would never be able to amass that much. He'd never be able to amass even half that amount, not even if he begged his da for it.

"Nobody leaves the Farrell gang without paying." Shaw holstered his gun. "And the cost is always steep."

Too steep. Alannah or ten thousand dollars. If Shaw didn't get his payment, he'd kill Torin. That was becoming all too clear. Kiernan was also afraid that Alannah would give herself over to the gang leader in order to save her brother. She'd suggested it after the threats outside the glass factory. Thankfully, Torin hadn't gone for the idea. And Kiernan hadn't either, and he never would.

The trouble, now that Shaw knew Torin was at the brickyard, was how long before he learned where Alannah was? Even though Kiernan had warned Mam and the other servants not to say anything, how could her presence at Oakland stay a secret forever?

Maybe he'd been foolish to stand in the way of Bellamy matching and marrying her off. At least with another man, she'd be safe from Shaw. And her safety was the most important thing.

Kiernan shifted his horse. "Stay away from Torin and his sister, Shaw."

"Or what?"

"Or you'll wish you would have." Kiernan didn't wait to gauge the man's reaction. Instead, he nudged his horse forward down the road. His back was stiff, and a part of him expected another shot to ring out, one to scare him, maybe even injure him. But after several long moments with nothing, he picked up his pace, his heart thundering with his pulse.

For as much as he wanted to shelter Alannah—and Torin—trouble was drawing closer. He just prayed he would be ready with a solution when it finally caught up to them.

13

At the firm knocking on the front door, Alannah stepped out of the dining room and into the entryway. Mrs. Shanahan, Zaira, and the boys had been gone for most of the day visiting with family friends but would be home in time for the evening meal.

The other maids had been given the afternoon off to do visiting of their own. Since Alannah had no one to visit—except Torin, which wasn't an option—she'd stayed behind. She'd almost finished setting the table and needed to hurry back to the kitchen and help with the final preparations for the meal.

But without anyone else there to answer the knocking, Alannah hesitated.

Torin's warning from two nights ago still rang in her head. *"We got word the Farrell gang is planning to do something soon. No matter what happens to me, you need to promise to stay here and not show yourself."*

Torin wouldn't want her to open the door, would tell her

to let the person come back another day. Kiernan would probably say the same thing.

Not that she was talking to Kiernan.

The knocking resounded again, a wee bit louder. What if the person was bringing a message from Torin? Or Kiernan? Or even Mrs. Shanahan letting them know of a change of plans for the evening?

Alannah started down the hallway toward the door.

She'd open it a crack. That would be safe enough, wouldn't it?

As she reached the door, she stopped and listened. She couldn't hear anything on the other side except the sounds of summer—the rustling of leaves in the breeze and the buzzing of cicadas.

At the tap of footsteps retreating across the porch, Alannah quickly turned the knob and opened the door enough to see the form of a young woman with a fashionable riding dress and brown hair beneath a lovely hat. A beautiful black horse was tied loosely to the hitching post near the stairway.

It was Shelia. The woman who'd once won Kiernan's heart. Alannah had seen her on other occasions but had never spoken with her.

Why was she visiting? Too curious to resist, Alannah swung the door wider. "May I help you?"

With one foot upon the top step, the woman halted, then turned. Alannah could understand why Kiernan had been smitten with her. Shelia was lovely in an elegant, refined way with pale skin, a slender face, and a narrow nose.

Her thin brows arched just a little, as though surprised to see Alannah—or anyone—there.

"The Shanahans will be back soon, to be sure." Alannah

waved at one of the wicker chairs in the shade of the veranda. "You're welcome to have a seat while you wait."

Shelia hesitated. "Kiernan isn't yet home?"

"No, Mr. Shanahan is gone most evenings." Alannah had stayed in her stifling room for the past two nights to avoid him. She'd hoped that would send the message she wasn't interested in spending any more time with him. Unfortunately, he hadn't seemed to accept her unspoken message and had sought her out this morning in the kitchen.

She should have known Kiernan wouldn't be so easily swayed. After all, he believed they were friends for the sake of being friends. He didn't realize she'd offered friendship as the basis of a match that had been one-sided.

She owed him an explanation. But she wasn't sure how she would ever be able to face him without burning up with embarrassment while she explained her mistake. She would blame Bellamy.

Shelia stepped back up on the porch. "I'd actually heard Kiernan wasn't visiting with any of his potential matches tonight, and I was hoping to catch him—well, before the family returns." Her cheeks flushed at her admission.

Shelia had visited only a couple of nights ago and hadn't stayed for long. What if she hadn't come to see the family then either? What if her sole purpose in stopping by on the previous visits had been to see Kiernan?

Something sharp pricked Alannah. The young woman was about to become engaged to Kiernan's best friend, Liam. The party was coming soon, in about a week. Why would she be seeking Kiernan out privately so close to becoming engaged? Unless she was having second thoughts about marrying Liam and had decided she wanted Kiernan after all.

Alannah couldn't stop from studying the woman's face, needing to find the answer—not that it mattered. Alannah wasn't matched with Kiernan anymore, probably never had been. Besides, with as many visits as Kiernan was having with other women, he'd likely fallen for someone else by now, or at least found a woman who would make him happy.

Ultimately, that's what really mattered, wasn't it? He was a good man, and Alannah only wanted him to be happy.

Shelia, on the other hand, had caused him heartache. If she started to take an interest in Kiernan again, what was to prevent her from hurting him more?

Alannah couldn't let that happen. She shouldn't have invited Shelia to stay, needed to get her to leave before Kiernan returned. "If you're hoping to get him back, you're too late."

In the process of heading to one of the chairs, Shelia stumbled to a halt.

"He's already been matched." The lie slipped from Alannah's lips before she could stop it.

Shelia's brows dipped as she studied Alannah. "That's not what I heard."

Of course, Shelia probably knew every last detail of Kiernan's matchmaking efforts from Liam. Even so, Alannah couldn't let the woman upset Kiernan again, not when he was trying to free himself from the past and move on.

She needed to bow her head in deference and walk away. But another lie fell out anyway. "I heard it right from Bellamy McKenna, the matchmaker, so I did."

"Oh. I see."

Alannah finally ducked her chin. Technically, she wasn't telling a lie. She had heard from Bellamy that Kiernan was to be matched. To her.

Before she could think of anything more to say to send Shelia on her way, the thudding of a horse's hooves echoed in the silence of the evening. Shelia crossed to the porch railing and peered down the road at the rider drawing near.

Alannah half prayed it wouldn't be Kiernan, that he would be gone like the previous evenings. But at the sight of his brawny body atop his powerful stallion, her heart gave an extra beat.

He turned onto the gravel lane surrounded on both sides by the towering oak trees. He seemed in a hurry, almost frantic.

Although a part of Alannah wanted to rush off and hide from him as she'd been doing for the past two days, she had the strange sense that something was wrong.

Besides if she left now, Shelia would have him all to herself. The young gentlewoman would discover Alannah's lies and then realize something was going on, at least suspect that Alannah had feelings for Kiernan.

Because she did have feelings for him. There was no sense in denying the truth.

As Kiernan drew closer, the glare in his eyes and the hard set to his jaw were intimidating. His gaze swept past Shelia and landed upon Alannah with an intensity that nearly took her breath away.

He seemed to see only her. Even as he reined in his horse and started to dismount, his dark blue eyes stayed riveted to her.

She quickly backed up, her legs suddenly trembling. As much as she wanted to save Kiernan from Shelia, she couldn't face him. Not yet.

She fumbled to make it through the doorway.

"Alannah, wait." Kiernan was already bounding up the stairs.

"Kiernan." Shelia moved to the top of the stairway, almost as if she was attempting to intercept him.

Alannah quickly closed the door and leaned against it.

"Alannah, please," Kiernan called out again, his footsteps stopping on the stairs.

"I wanted to see you privately, Kiernan," Shelia said. "We need to talk."

"Not now." His tone held a note of irritation.

"Please? Just for a minute? I've been waiting all day."

A second of silence passed.

Alannah pressed her hand to her chest to calm her rapidly beating heart. She willed Kiernan to say no, to rush past Shelia, to come after her instead.

"What is it?" Kiernan asked more politely.

Another moment of quiet passed, and Alannah could picture Shelia moving nearer to Kiernan on the top step above him, eye to eye, mouth to mouth. If she was desperate enough to have Kiernan back, maybe she would attempt to kiss him.

"I've been thinking about us recently." This time when she spoke her voice was decidedly seductive. "And I miss you."

Alannah pinched her eyes closed. How could he resist Shelia now? Why would he want to?

"You have a fiancé. You shouldn't think about me anymore."

"I cannot help myself."

"You have to remain faithful to Liam. He loves you."

"What if I made a mistake? What if I would be happier with you instead?"

What was Shelia saying? That she wanted to call off her almost-engagement to Liam and reunite with Kiernan?

He was silent again, this time longer.

Anger simmered inside Alannah. Why couldn't Shelia be satisfied with Liam? Did she think her happiness was more important than anything else, including Kiernan's? She obviously hadn't cared about how he would feel when she'd rejected him for Liam in the first place.

Kiernan cleared his throat. "There is no more you and me, Shelia. It's you and Liam now."

Heavy footsteps veered toward the door.

Was he done with Shelia? Was he coming into the house?

Alannah's eyes flew open, and she sprang away from the door, both relief and panic mounting inside.

"I know you still want me." Shelia's comment came out certain, almost arrogant.

The footsteps came to an abrupt halt, and Kiernan spoke just outside the door. "I once thought I did. But I don't anymore."

Had he fallen for one of the women he'd been seeing? Was that why he didn't feel anything for Shelia now?

The knob on the other side of the door rattled.

Alannah took another step back.

"Then what your maid said is true?" Shelia persisted. "Bellamy McKenna found you a match?"

Alannah sucked in a sharp breath. Kiernan would learn she'd lied and wonder why. How would she explain herself to him? She would only add to the list of embarrassing misunderstandings.

The turning knob stilled.

Had he heard her sharp intake? She cupped her hand over her mouth—obviously too late.

A strange, charged silence filled the air.

What had she done now? She'd put Kiernan into an awkward situation where he would look foolish if he denied the match. She should have kept quiet with Shelia instead of letting her jealousy get the better of her. Because that's what it was. She was jealous of Shelia having the right to Kiernan in a way a maid would never have.

"Alannah's right," Kiernan said softly. "Bellamy has someone picked out for me."

Alannah startled. Kiernan was agreeing with her? Why?

"Who?" Shelia's tone turned demanding.

"I'd rather not say."

"The news will come out soon enough. You may as well tell me."

"You'll have to wait until I decide to make it public."

Shelia released a scoffing laugh. "I'm not blind, Kiernan."

He didn't respond.

"I know your attraction when I see it, and you're clearly attracted to your new maid."

Alannah drew in another breath, this one covered by her hand, thankfully. Of course she'd sensed Kiernan's desire from time to time, but to have Shelia state it so bluntly made the situation more mortifying.

"Or," Shelia continued, "maybe she's your newest distraction—"

"Don't talk about her that way."

"Once you finish with her, don't come crawling back to me. This is it."

"I agree." Kiernan's voice contained a hard edge. "This is it. Go home to Liam and stay faithful to him."

Alannah was frozen in place in the middle of the entryway. Cook would be wondering what was taking her so long. But she couldn't make her feet move.

After another moment of tense silence, Shelia's footsteps tapped down the stairs. At the jangle of a stirrup, it was clear the young woman was mounting and readying to leave.

"Good-bye, Kiernan," she spoke stiffly a few seconds later, likely in her saddle. "I hope you don't regret not choosing me."

The hoofbeats began to clop away, slow at first and then steadier until at last they faded down the lane away from the house.

As the door handle turned, Alannah spun and started toward the dining room, her heart thudding with the need to hide from Kiernan. Not only had she made incorrect assumptions about them over the past couple of weeks, but she didn't want him to discover that she'd been standing in the hallway listening to his conversation with Shelia.

The door opened behind her. "Alannah, wait," Kiernan called.

She kept going, racing into the dining room. She reached for the door and swung it shut.

But he was quickly on her heels and stuck his boot into the doorway, keeping the door from closing all the way.

She pressed her whole body against it.

"Talk to me."

"No, Kiernan."

"Tell me why you're avoiding me."

14

Kiernan kept his foot wedged in the door, but he didn't force his way into the dining room after Alannah even though he wanted to.

"I've been busy," she said.

He shook his head curtly at her excuse. "You're always busy."

"'Tis too embarrassing, so it is."

Why would she be embarrassed? She'd done nothing wrong. "Did I do something to offend you?"

"Not at all."

"Then what?"

She paused. Was she searching for another excuse?

"Tell me the truth, Alannah."

An exasperated exhalation came from the other side. "I didn't realize you were visiting with so many other women."

Was she jealous? A strange satisfaction twisted through him. "You knew I met with Bellamy to begin the matchmaking process."

"But I thought—I assumed . . ."

"What?"

"I thought you were meeting with just one woman."

Most people did meet with one match at a time—a person the matchmaker picked based on his skills and intuition for matchmaking. But, of course, Kiernan had pushed Bellamy to do things differently.

"I shouldn't have been visiting with you at night," Alannah continued, "not when you're trying so hard to form a match with someone else."

"I've been there to keep you safe." At least that's what he'd been telling himself. But if he was honest, he had to admit that his conscience had been nagging him about their late-night meetings. "Besides, there's nothing wrong with our talking."

"It isn't right for us to sit out there alone."

"As friends. You said we could be friends." It was unnerving just how quickly she'd become his friend. In fact, in the short time he'd known her, she was a better friend than Liam had been during a lifetime.

"I know I said we could have a friendship." Even though her voice dropped, her chagrin was easy to hear. "That was before—well, before I understood everything."

"There's nothing complicated about it."

"'Tis very complicated, so it is."

"It doesn't have to be." He leaned his head against the door, somehow needing to feel connected to her again after the past two days of nothing.

She was silent, as if she was contemplating what he said.

Something deep inside urged him to let her go. It was the same urging he'd felt when he'd been riding home. He'd almost convinced himself that severing their friendship would be best for both of them.

But the moment he'd seen her standing on the veranda speaking with Shelia, an overwhelming need to talk to her had welled up within him. The need had been so strong that he'd wanted to walk right past Shelia and drag Alannah into his arms.

He supposed part of the need had to do with the encounter with Shaw and the threats the gang leader had made regarding Alannah. The rest of the ride home, Kiernan had been anxious about her, almost desperate to make sure she was at Oakland and doing okay.

A quiet desperation still plagued him. He didn't know how much longer Alannah would be safe at his family's country home, and his mind had been rolling through all the possibilities of new places she could go to hide. He'd tossed aside one friend's home after another, none of them safe enough. He'd even ruled against returning her to Enya's city home.

Besides, even if he did find a more secure place, how much longer could she hide? She couldn't do so indefinitely.

He had to come up with a better plan, and the one that kept forcing its way to the front of his mind was Torin's idea to marry Alannah off. Kiernan still didn't like it, but it would put an end to the threat to her.

"I'm sorry, Kiernan," she finally said. "I think it's best if we don't meet any longer."

Why had she agreed before but wouldn't any longer? "I don't understand what's changed."

"I told you. I learned you were meeting with all those women." From the tightness of her voice, she was making it sound as if he was mingling with women of ill repute rather than society's finest.

"So I can only be friends with you if I stop seeing *all those women*?"

"No, I know you have to be finding a match."

"If I need to find a match, then why did you tell Shelia I already had one?" He could almost feel her presence through the door and imagined she was leaning against it the same way he was.

"I'm sorry." Her voice came out a strained whisper. "I shouldn't have done that."

"Why did you?"

"I'm embarrassed to say."

"Tell me."

She was silent.

"If you don't tell me, then I'll have to come in the dining room and make you." He kept his tone light, hoping she would know he was teasing but persisting nonetheless.

"Ach." A thudding came against the door, as if she was lightly banging her head on it. "If you must know, I think you deserve someone better than her, so I do."

"Is that right? Like who?"

"A woman who doesn't toy with your affections but is instead loyal and committed and sees all the wonderful things about you and wants you for who you are." Her words came out in a rush.

Her declaration warmed his heart, and he savored it for a few moments.

"Are you still there?" she asked timidly.

"Aye." Something about Alannah Darragh was delightful

and brought him to life in a way he hadn't felt in a long time, if ever. "*Wonderful things*?"

She gave a huff and pushed against the door. "Go away with you now, Kiernan, and leave me be."

He laughed softly, his muscles relaxing after the past two days of tension from not being with her. "I'll go away, but only if you promise to meet me at our spot tonight."

"I don't know." Her tone seemed to hold a smile. "I don't want to be interfering with your match."

"Interfering?" He guffawed. "It's too late for that, don't you think? You told Shelia I was matched. By tomorrow the word will be all over St. Louis that I've picked someone to marry."

At his statement, the dining room door swung wide, and Alannah in all her beauty stood before him. Even in her simple black maid's attire covered with a white apron, she was more than beautiful. She was breathtaking, and he could do nothing but stare at her exquisite features, drinking her in like a water-deprived man.

Her eyes were round and filled with dismay, her delicate brows furrowed, and her lips pursed in consternation. "Oh, Kiernan." She almost reached for his arm but then seemed to stop herself. "'Tis my fault, to be sure. I blathered when I shouldn't have. I just didn't want her holding on to you and keeping you from having happiness of your own."

Had Shelia been holding on to him?

She certainly had been paying him more attention over recent weeks since they'd all moved out of the city. She was the type of woman who liked attention, and maybe she felt better about herself in trying to command his affection.

Truthfully, he hadn't felt an ounce of affection for her today, hadn't felt affection in a while. In fact, he felt nothing for her other than irritation.

"Can you ever forgive me?" Alannah asked.

"I'm not worried about it." He stuffed his hands into his pockets to keep from reaching for her hand and comforting her. His comfort wouldn't remain platonic for long. After all, he didn't claim to be a saint, not around someone like Alannah.

"But what will we do? Everyone will think you're engaged."

"*We* won't be doing anything." He spoke gently but firmly. "Because it's not your problem, Alannah."

"But I'm the one who got you into the predicament, and I should be the one to help you out."

"I'm due for a visit to Bellamy. I'm sure he'll know what to do." Kiernan knew exactly what Bellamy would say. To burn the list of qualifications.

Was it time to admit Bellamy had won their wager and to let him do his job the way he wanted to?

Alannah was still watching him, her brows crinkled with worry and her nose scrunched in that adorable way.

Although his body suddenly ached to feel her, he forced himself to take a step away from her instead of toward her. "Don't worry about it any more today."

"You'll be letting me worry tomorrow, then?" A small smile played at her lips—with that lovely dip that taunted him with the need to be kissed.

He moved another foot back. "Do you want me to forgive you for the mix-up?"

"Oh aye—"

"I'll forgive you, but only if we can meet again tonight

one last time." This would be it. It had to be. For both their sakes. Because there could never be anything more between them. Could there?

His heart gave a strange flip at the thought.

Her smile tilted higher. "Your demand is fearsome and difficult. But I'll agree to it, Kiernan Shanahan."

"Good." He was grinning now too.

"You never miss the water till the well has run dry."

"Are you admitting to missing me?"

"Maybe."

"Alannah?" Cook's angry shout through the back door echoed down the hallway. "Where are you?"

"Coming!" Still smiling, she scurried past Kiernan.

He couldn't keep from watching the gracefulness of her stride, the way her hips swayed, and the wispy blond strands that had come loose from her coil and now caressed her neck. When she reached the end of the hallway, she paused and glanced back at him, flashing her smile one more time before exiting and disappearing outside.

He expelled a tight breath, not ready to let her go, needing to talk to her longer, needing to be near her, needing to see her smile again.

◆ ◆ ◆ ◆ ◆ ◆ ◆

Kiernan wanted to go on talking with Alannah all night. But she'd yawned at least three times, and he had to bring their time together to a close.

"So that's how my mam got into editing." She stifled another yawn from where she sat on the blanket beside him. "And I learned to love doing it too."

He stared up at the sky, his arms behind his head. "I'm sure your love of reading has lent you a keen eye for mistakes."

"It has. I never can seem to read a book anymore without keeping a mental list of the things that are wrong."

He hadn't known she liked to edit and had aspirations to edit for a newspaper or magazines or journals one day. But for some reason, she'd shared that with him tonight, maybe because it was their last night, and she had nothing to lose by revealing this part of herself.

He was surprised to find himself hoping that someday she would be able to fulfill her dream. It was odd because he had always agreed with his da that women—particularly married women—needed to focus on their household and families without the distraction of employment.

Of course, women in Alannah's poor working class often had no choice but to work even after they were married by taking in mending or laundry or ironing. Some even labored in factories or fields.

But editing? That was different. It was something she wanted to do regardless of whether she had to. It was a passion and a purpose. He'd never thought about women having passions and purposes outside the home. But maybe they deserved to have such aspirations just like men. Why shouldn't they?

"I hope you'll be able to pursue your editing." He pushed up from his reclining position to his elbows.

"Thank you, Kiernan." A cooler night breeze teased at a tendril of her hair that had come loose from her braid. "You're kind to listen and understand."

He wanted to tuck the wayward strand behind her ear, but he hadn't so much as brushed a finger against her, and he had to keep things that way.

The buzz of fireflies melded with the trill of the crickets. The sounds of the night had become like music and from now on would remind him of his time with Alannah.

She yawned again, covering her mouth. Slowly she pushed up until she was standing. She was still wearing her maid's uniform but had discarded her cap. As she picked up the lantern, the glow highlighted the beauty in each line of her face.

"I should go," she said softly.

He wanted to protest, but he nodded. "I'll leave in a minute." It was best if they didn't go together.

She hesitated for a moment before starting forward. "Good night, Kiernan."

He watched her go, his whole body keening for her. He wanted to chase after her and draw her into his arms. But he forced himself to stay where he was, even as his heart beat hard in protest and a strange discontentment sifted through him.

Why the discontent? Was it because his time with Alannah was over? As much as he wanted to suggest another meeting, deep inside he knew he couldn't keep fooling himself into believing they were only friends. His attraction went far beyond friendship, probably always had. Continuing their late nights together was only stirring up temptation.

Besides, he still needed to arrange a new place for her to stay and move her there within the next day or two.

He didn't want to think about the day when she'd no longer be at Oakland. But after his encounter with Shaw earlier, Kiernan knew that day was coming sooner rather than later.

15

All throughout mass, Kiernan had noticed the curious glances he was attracting along with the whispers. Now as he stepped out the doors of the Cathedral of St. Louis, he was still drawing attention.

The Sunday morning was cloudy and the air humid with the promise of rain. The air was also filled with the usual mingling scents of coal dust and smoke, livestock feces and refuse from the slaughterhouses, and the ever-present stench of hot fat from the tallow factories.

A hand clamped his shoulder, and Kiernan turned to find Liam in his fine pinstriped gray suit and top hat grinning at him. His dark hair was smoothed back away from his face. His mother and two young sisters, all attired in their finest gowns and hats, were inside the Cathedral, speaking with another family and casting looks his way.

"You're the talk of town this morning." Liam's hand moved lower and slapped Kiernan good-naturedly on his back.

"It appears I am." Kiernan leaned against one of the tall

Greek revival-style pillars that lined the Cathedral's front portico. The oldest cathedral and largest in St. Louis, the building was an important monument downtown, with its greenish blue steeple and golden ball and cross at the top. Thankfully, the firefighters had worked hard last month to save the Cathedral by demolishing the buildings around it to prevent the spread of the flames.

Blackened ruins still remained along the streets to the west of the Cathedral. Some of the destruction had been carted away to make room for rebuilding—the rebuilding that would hopefully require bricks and turn his brickyard into St. Louis's wealthiest business. If not the wealthiest, then hopefully his venture would prove more profitable than his da's ironworks.

"I'm surprised to see you in the city for mass." Liam released him and checked his pocket watch. "I thought you were going with your family to St. Bridgett's."

The small parish was close to Oakland and where his family attended mass while residing in the country. Everyone else—including his da—had gone there this morning without him. "I have business to attend to."

Liam's brows shot up. "On Sunday?"

Around them, several other families mingling among the tall columns halted their conversations as though hoping to hear his business.

His spine stiffened, and he was tempted to glare back and tell them to keep to their own affairs. But he focused on Liam instead. "It's of a personal nature."

Liam's grin reappeared. "Oh, I imagine it is."

Just as he'd suspected, the news of his supposed engagement had spread to the farthest reaches of St. Louis and beyond. He wouldn't be surprised if everyone west of the Mississippi all the way to California now knew that he was officially matched by the matchmaker.

Except that he wasn't engaged or officially matched. Not even close.

Liam leaned in. "Shelia told me about the match last night while I was visiting her."

"So you decided to shout it from the rooftops this morning?" Kiernan couldn't keep the sarcasm from his tone.

"I may have mentioned it at the pub on my way home. That's all."

That's apparently all it had taken.

"Shelia also told the company." Liam's smile wasn't dimming. His friend was probably just excited about the so-called match and expected Kiernan to be happy too.

But Shelia on the other hand? If she'd sensed any hint of deception from their exchange last evening, it was possible she'd hoped to put him on the spot. More likely, she'd been annoyed by his refusal to tell her anything and decided to exert pressure on him to reveal the name of his match.

No doubt each of her visitors had gossiped about him. Maybe word had already passed among the list of women he'd met with. They would realize they hadn't been chosen, and there would be hard feelings all around for his calloused approach to handling everything.

The muscles in his chest tightened. He'd expected the gossip this morning when he'd ridden into the city but hadn't realized he'd be the center of attention.

At least he could be grateful the city wasn't as busy as it normally was. Fewer people had attended mass, and fewer people were out on the streets. Hopefully, that meant fewer encounters with busybodies today as he tried to figure out what to do about his situation.

Whatever the case, he intended to meet with Bellamy and discuss his options. That's why he'd come to town.

Liam's smile disappeared. "You should also know, Shelia mentioned that you're having a dalliance with one of your new maids."

"Blast it all." Kiernan pushed away from the column and spun toward his friend, anger surging through him.

Liam took a rapid step back and held up his hands as though to protect himself from Kiernan's wrath. "I'm not condemning you."

"It's a complete lie." Kiernan had the sudden need to ride out to the Douglases' and ask Shelia what she'd been thinking to spread such a rumor. If she cared about him the way she'd indicated, then why had she done it? It wasn't like her to be petty or mean-spirited.

Besides, she had Liam which ought to have been enough. But for whatever reason, she wasn't satisfied with that.

Liam glanced through the Cathedral's open doors into the nave at his mother and sisters, then he leaned in and lowered his voice. "I admit to having stolen the virtue of a willing maid from time to time."

"I'm not stealing the virtue of any maid," Kiernan ground out the words. He'd behaved perfectly last night with Alannah when they met in the field after dark.

Liam was watching his face, probably trying to gauge the truth.

Kiernan met his gaze levelly. "I don't sleep with the maids. I never have, and I never will."

"Hey, you'll find no judgment here." Liam waved a hand

at himself. "Whatever is going on, I don't care. But I thought you should know what people are saying."

Kiernan clamped his jaw and peered toward the river unseeingly. What should he do now? Was there any way to make the rumors go away?

He didn't want Shaw to hear and then investigate and realize the maid was Alannah.

Of course, his parents would likely learn about both rumors at their mass. As a result, they would be eager to know more about his supposed match. More than that, they would be dismayed to hear about his indiscretion.

Da would confront him. Not only would Da be disappointed, but he would probably launch into a story about how he'd never once looked at another woman after meeting Mam. He'd boast about how he had the perfect marriage and perfect wife and tell Kiernan he needed to strive to do better. He'd turn it into a competition like he did everything else.

And Mam? She would realize right away that Alannah was the suspect maid. Mam would use the rumor as an excuse to send her away. Of course, Kiernan wouldn't let Mam do that. But it was all the more reason to move Alannah someplace new. . . . Today if possible.

He just hoped Bellamy would have some ideas on how to solve the problems and make everything alright again.

◆ ◆ ◆ ◆ ◆ ◆ ◆

Kiernan stepped into the dimly lit interior of Oscar's Pub, and the waft of beer and tobacco smoke greeted him. The place wasn't open yet, but the door had been unlocked. Although the tables were empty, a lone figure sat on a stool at the bar counter, slurping from what appeared to be a bowl of soup.

Kiernan didn't need to see the ginger-colored hair with a cowlick to know it was Georgie McGuire. The older man was almost always at Oscar's Pub, sitting at the same place in the center of the bar that ran along the far wall. Kiernan wouldn't have been surprised to learn that the fellow slept on a pallet on the floor in the pub at night.

At the sound of the door closing, Georgie shifted around on his stool, the spoon paused halfway between the bowl and his mouth. His purplish nose stood out amidst his pale face, and he flashed a near-toothless grin. "Bellamy said we'd see you today."

That meant Bellamy had heard the rumors too, which didn't surprise Kiernan. The young matchmaker probably heard and knew of every rumor ever spoken in St. Louis, especially among the Irish community.

"Where's Bellamy?" Kiernan wound his way through the maze of tables and chairs, most littered with mugs from the previous night. As always, the paintings on the wall drew Kiernan's attention, landscapes of Ireland that never failed to remind him of Da and Mam's homeland and the fact that they'd had to work hard to make a new life for themselves in America, and if they could do it, so could he.

Georgie finished with his spoonful of soup and nodded toward the kitchen at the back of the pub. "Bellamy!" he called. "You were right. Kiernan Shanahan is here for a visit."

A slight clattering of dishes was the only answer.

Kiernan stopped at the bar even though he was tempted to stalk around to the other side and go directly to Bellamy.

That would probably make him appear desperate and therefore guilty. Instead, he gripped the bar counter and took a deep breath. He needed to be patient, just as he'd been since leaving the Cathedral.

He'd ridden to the Shanahan home on Third Street, hoping to speak with Finola and Riley and to discover what they'd heard about the rumors. But the couple had been gone, apparently having left the city a few days ago for Riley's family farm in the country.

Kiernan hadn't been surprised. Even though the two had been faithfully helping the immigrants all throughout the spring, Finola had recently discovered she was with child. Kiernan had known it would only be a matter of time before Riley took his wife and unborn child away from the reaches of cholera.

Nevertheless, Kiernan had spoken with Winston, their faithful family butler, and had eaten a meal at Winston's insistence even though he was eager to return to Oakland and make sure no one was bothering Alannah. The longer he was away from her, the more he worried about her facing the ramifications of the rumors.

That meant he wanted his meeting with Bellamy to be brief.

"So you're in a bit of a bother, are you now, lad?" Georgie set his spoon down, then picked up the bowl and drank the remainder of the soup.

Kiernan didn't want to be rude, but he had no intention of discussing his business with anyone but Bellamy.

Georgie set the bowl down and wiped his sleeve against his mouth. "Well, now that you've put yourself to sea, Bellamy's no dozer, and he'll have you back on land in a wee minute."

"That he will." Kiernan tapped his fingers against the counter, trying to curb his impatience.

"Bellamy, he'll find you a lass who thinks the sun and moon rise and fall with you, so he will."

Kiernan didn't need a *lass* like that. He'd be happy enough to have a woman who was decent and good, two things Shelia clearly lacked.

"As long as the lass is not named Shelia Douglas, I'll be happy."

Georgie drummed his fingers against the bar counter in time with Kiernan's. "Always did think Shelia Douglas was like a prize hound waiting to get her snout scratched."

Kiernan snorted.

Georgie grinned, his lips pulling over his gums.

"What are you going on about, Georgie?" Bellamy stepped out of the kitchen, a towel tossed across his shoulder and a twinkle in his eyes.

Georgie busied himself dragging his spoon through the last drops of soup in his bowl. "Never said nothin', so I didn't."

"Is that a fact?"

"Oh aye."

Bellamy shook his head, fighting back a smile as he approached Kiernan. "What can I be doing for you today, Kiernan?"

"You're already well aware of what I'm needing today, Bellamy."

"Naturally."

"Oh aye, naturally," Georgie echoed.

Bellamy leaned a hip against the counter and crossed his

arms, a smirk tugging up his lips. "Are you ready to admit you lost our wager?"

"I lost." The confession came out easily.

Bellamy lifted a brow. "Will you finally let me do my job my way?"

"Aye." At least mostly.

Bellamy didn't move except to narrow his eyes.

Did the matchmaker sense his hesitancy? "I need a match, so I'll do whatever you ask." Kiernan tried to make his voice as sincere as possible. Because he was sincere, wasn't he?

Bellamy held his gaze a moment longer before he tossed the towel from his shoulder to the counter. "Good. Then you'll meet me out at Dover's Pond in exactly an hour."

The little park wasn't far from Oakland. Kiernan had fished there as a boy and sometimes had gone swimming in it. The pond likely wouldn't be too busy on a Sunday afternoon and would allow them the privacy they needed for a discussion.

Kiernan nodded at Bellamy. "An hour will give me time to go home first."

"Ach, no. You'll not speak to anyone until we meet. Not family. Not friends. And not even acquaintances." Bellamy leveled him a stern look. "You'll go to the pond and stay there until I arrive."

"But I need to talk to my parents—"

"Remind me again. Who won the wager?"

Kiernan pushed down a swell of frustration. He needed Bellamy's help and had to do what the fellow was asking, even if he didn't like it.

Was it too late to throw away caution and responsibilities and all rationality and go to Alannah and propose to her?

His heart thumped hard at the prospect. What would she say? How would she react? It was an impulsive idea, and she would oppose it. After all, since she'd been reluctant to meet with him, she'd probably be even more so to spend the rest of her life with him.

After a beat of silence, Georgie cocked his head with his cowlick toward Bellamy. "The matchmaker won."

"That I did." Bellamy pivoted and began to walk back to the kitchen.

Which meant Kiernan had to follow through on his part of the wager, had to give Bellamy's choice some consideration.

But that didn't mean he actually had to marry Bellamy's match, not if he didn't like her, did it? Would Kiernan ever like anyone else besides Alannah? At the moment, he couldn't imagine it.

"I've errands to be running before the meeting," Bellamy called. "See that you're there at the pond on time, and not a minute late." He disappeared into the kitchen. Then a few seconds later, the back door opened and closed, leaving silence behind.

Kiernan turned on his heels and started toward the exit. He needed a miracle today. Hopefully the matchmaker could give him one. If not, Kiernan didn't know what he would do.

16

Something had happened. Alannah hadn't been able to figure out what except that it had to do with her.

With her legs dangling off the edge of the pier, she swished her toes in the water. The coolness was soothing and, in a small way, reminded her of standing on the beach near Tralee and letting the waves wash over her bare feet.

She bunched her skirt up and dipped her feet in farther, nearly touching a bright orange fish circling under the pier. Only a short distance away on a log half in and half out of the water, a turtle the size of a pinecone seemed to be staring at her, as though asking her what she was doing there.

"I don't rightly know," she answered and then sighed.

Bellamy had shown up a little while ago at Oakland, where she'd been finishing washing dishes from the noon meal. Since the servants were given Sunday afternoons off, Cook had granted her permission to go when Bellamy said he needed to see her. The matchmaker hadn't disclosed the nature of his visit, only that it was important. He'd hauled her up onto his mount behind him and then had brought her to the secluded area. He'd told her to wait here for him to return, that he was going after Torin and would be back soon.

She had a feeling the meeting had to do with whatever had happened to cause such a stir, which she hadn't noticed until the walk home from mass. The other maids had been whispering and tittering, and Mrs. Shanahan's face had been ashen.

Upon returning to Oakland, the matron had closed herself away with her husband in the library. Not long after that, Mrs. Shanahan had approached Alannah, her expression stern and her lips pinched tightly. She'd asked Alannah to meet with her once she finished her kitchen duties.

The request had filled Alannah with foreboding. She'd guessed the meeting wouldn't be pleasant and had been all too happy to avoid it.

A lone drop of rain fell onto Alannah's hand, and she glanced up to the dark clouds. Hopefully, the rain would hold off for a little longer. But Bellamy had nodded at the covered pavilion off to the side of the pond where she could take cover if necessary while she waited for Torin and him to return.

Another raindrop plopped onto her, this one on her nose. She never should have agreed to spend time with Kiernan again last night. But he'd been so difficult to resist yesterday in the front entryway when he'd pleaded with her, had claimed it was the last time. She hadn't been able to tell him no, even though something had warned her that she should.

Someone must have witnessed their nighttime meeting and reported it to the matron. That had to be what was wrong. Now she would have to face Mrs. Shanahan's wrath.

Alannah released a shiver. What if the matron fired her?

No matter how much Kiernan might protest, they couldn't plead innocent. Not when they were guilty of being together.

Maybe Bellamy and Torin were aware of the imminent dismissal from her position and were anxious of what was to become of her.

Had Bellamy come up with another plan since he'd obviously realized his proposition of matching her with Kiernan wouldn't work? Maybe this time he had a match that would be more realistic and viable. Would she consider it?

"No, I'll not be marrying a stranger," she whispered, kicking the water and sending a spray into an arc. Yet, she'd made a wager with Bellamy and had promised she would consider his candidates.

"Alannah?" a familiar man's voice called from across the pond.

She glanced up to find the imposing Kiernan Shanahan standing on the other side and attired in his Sunday best, a sharp black suit and hat. He'd tethered his horse a short distance away from the pond's edge under a silver maple.

"What are you doing here? Alone?" His tone contained an edge of worry, and he started toward her through the long rushes and cattails.

She gave her feet one last splash, then climbed up so she was standing on the pier as he rounded the edge of the pond. Her heartbeat accelerated like it did every time she saw him. He held himself with such certainty and strength that it was hard not to admire him. And, of course, his broad shoulders and bulky arms and long legs were easy to admire too.

His eyes were dark within the shadows of his hat, but it

was easy to see that they were riveted to her. His jaw was clenched. And his chiseled features hardened.

Was he upset to see her here?

She took a timid step back.

"You shouldn't be by yourself." This time his voice was angry.

She rolled up her backbone, her resistance stiffening. "I'm perfectly fine, and I don't need you to be telling me what to do."

"I ran into Shaw Farrell yesterday on my way home from the brickyard just a couple miles from Oakland. So aye, I am telling you what to do."

Shaw had been that close? "Why didn't you say so last night?"

Kiernan started down the pier, his footsteps *thunking* against the planks. "He still wants you."

"Oh bother." So this must be what the meeting was about. To protect her from Shaw. "Whyever can't he let the matter with Torin go?"

Kiernan came to a halt a foot away, his jaw still rigid. "He'll look weak if he allows someone like Torin to break away from his gang. If he doesn't punish Torin in some way, then he'll risk other men defying him."

Torin had already explained all of that to her. In fact, she'd learned through some of the people she'd shared the tenement with during her first days in St. Louis that no one left their gangs. It was seen as disloyal, ungrateful, and even traitorous. Those who tried to break away didn't last long. Their bodies were usually found drowned in the Mississippi.

She couldn't let that happen to Torin. If it was within her power to keep him from danger, then she had to do it.

"Is there anything we can be doing to keep Torin safe?" She threw the question out to Kiernan even though she already knew the answer.

She'd either have to marry Shaw or someone else. Even that was no guarantee of saving Torin.

Kiernan latched a hand on to her arm. "You can do your best not to be seen until I find another place for you to hide." He started to tug her off the pier.

She held herself back. "I have to wait here for Bellamy."

Kiernan released her as if she'd suddenly turned hot to the touch. "Why are you waiting for Bellamy?"

"He went to get Torin so we could have a meeting. I don't rightly know why. But with Shaw in the area, maybe they're wanting to speed up the plans to get me married."

Kiernan peered around the perimeter of the pond, his eyes narrowed upon every detail. "It's possible." He took off his hat, ran his fingers through his auburn hair, then rubbed at the back of his neck.

He was silent for a moment as more raindrops plopped against the pier. His expression held an unusual gravity that sent a strange tremor through her.

Finally, he dropped his hand and blew out a tight breath. "It could also be because of what happened last evening."

"What happened?"

He didn't meet her gaze. "When Shelia came over and we told her I was matched."

"You mean when *I* told her."

"I didn't disagree with you." He waved a dismissive hand. "Regardless, she went home and spread the news, so now everyone believes I have a match."

"I'm sorry, Kiernan."

His eyes flashed to hers, the dark blue turbulent. "I'm meeting with Bellamy today, too, so he can help me figure everything out."

What would Kiernan do next? The question begged to be asked, but although she'd grown more comfortable around him after spending so much time with him recently, she still wasn't bold enough to pry into his plans with Bellamy. Or maybe she was a coward and afraid of what Kiernan might say.

He palmed the back of his neck again and stared out over the pond, the smooth surface broken by the raindrops. "I'm afraid that's not the worst of the rumors."

She swallowed the lump in her throat. "Someone saw us together last night, didn't they?"

His eyes held an apology. "No. It's worse than that."

"Worse?"

"Shelia also spread the rumor that I've been . . ." Kiernan's expression became pained. "That we've been . . ."

Her stomach clenched at what she knew was to come.

A flush worked its way up his neck. "She told everyone that I've been having a dalliance with you."

"Mercy." Heat surged into her face too. "Whyever would she do such a thing? 'Tis malicious. Cruel, even."

"She's not usually a malicious person." His whisper was laden with distress. "But she also likes to have her way."

"She's wanting you to keep loving her even though she has Liam?"

"Maybe."

Clearly, that's why Bellamy was in such a hurry. He needed to find her a match right away before her reputation was so irreparably damaged that no man would want her.

"I should have been more careful around Shelia yesterday, shouldn't have drawn her attention to you."

More sprinkles pelted her. "Now I understand why your mother wanted to speak with me." Mrs. Shanahan had no doubt heard the rumor about Kiernan compromising Alannah and had every intention of firing her whether the rumor was true or not.

"I'll explain everything to Mam and clear up the confusion."

"It won't change the rumors, though. She'll have to let me go."

"You'll stay until I can line up another place of employment."

"I really have no choice but to be marrying the person Bellamy picks for me." It was the only way.

He clasped her arm. "Don't say that."

"Doing so will protect me from ruin and from Shaw."

"You can go back to Enya's and hide there again."

"For how long?" She swiped at the drops now hitting her cheeks. "I can't keep running and hiding forever, can I?"

"Shaw will tire of the game eventually."

"Until then, I can't be relying on you for help, Kiernan. I've already relied on you too much."

"I want to help."

"You're a good man, to be sure. But I'm not your responsibility."

The rain was coming faster and wasn't showing any sign of going away. As if noticing the same, Kiernan glanced around. His sights snagged upon the covered pavilion. "Let's get out of the rain."

She didn't resist as he hurried them off the pier and through the long grass, the rain growing in intensity with each step they took until it was downpouring, forcing them to run the last of the distance.

As they ducked under the covered area, the wind picked up and the rain seemed to chase them, spraying a mist at them. The bench at the center was already wet, and Kiernan tugged her around it to the other side where finally they were mostly away from the deluge.

But they were already wet. She wasn't drenched, but she was damp enough to feel the heaviness of her lacy cap and hair and the weight of her skirt.

Kiernan took off his hat and shook the rain off it. "Looks like we're stuck here for a few minutes until this passes."

The drops splattered hard against the surface of the pond and the clearing around it. It was beginning to run in rivulets off the slanted roof above them. The temperature had also decreased, and the wind brought a chill with it.

She huddled beside Kiernan, trying to avoid any more encounters with either the rain or wind, which was nearly impossible. "At least we don't have to worry about anyone riding about the countryside and seeing us together."

"It doesn't matter what people think." Kiernan sounded as though he was trying to convince himself. "We know the truth."

The truth was, even if they hadn't been having a *dalliance*, they had been secretly meeting after dark, sitting together on a blanket, and spending hours of unchaperoned time together. They were guilty of at least that.

"We're not exactly innocent."

"There's nothing wrong with talking." He set his hat on

the bench and then combed the damp strands of hair at the back of his neck.

"Most people wouldn't understand that a man and a woman can be together without—you know." Her voice trailed off, embarrassment once again rising to clog her words.

He paused and slanted a glance at her. "Without what?"

"You know what, so you do." The flush moved into her cheeks, and she wanted to lift her hands to cover them but also didn't want to bring attention to her discomfort.

"Enlighten me."

"I'll be doing no such thing."

He chuckled low.

She swatted his arm. "You're a beast, Kiernan Shanahan."

"You like me anyway."

"Aye, so I do." The admission slipped out before she could stop it. When he grew silent, she crossed her arms over her chest and tried to ward off a shiver.

In the next instant, he shed his coat and then draped it across her shoulders.

She sidestepped away from him. "I can't be taking your coat."

He gently pressed her shoulders from behind. "Keep it, Alannah."

Though the outside of the coat was damp, the interior was warm from his body heat, enveloping her with the scent of his aftershave that was woodsy and heavenly all at once. She could only resist a moment longer before wrapping the coat around her more securely. "I thank you."

He squeezed her shoulders, seeming to linger a few seconds longer than necessary. Or maybe she was only imagining it.

When he let go, she slowly exhaled. But as his fingers pulled at one of the pins holding her cap in place, her breath caught.

"Your cap is wet." He spoke matter-of-factly, tugging the pin all the way loose. He didn't give her time to protest before moving on to the next pin.

She stood motionless as he nimbly pulled out the rest of the pins holding her cap in place.

He dropped the lacy material onto the bench, where it sat in a soggy lump beside his hat.

A strand of her hair fell over her ear.

"Looks like I took out one too many pins." He reached for the piece and lifted it back toward the knot holding together the rest of her hair.

She raised her hand to take care of the errant strand, but her fingers brushed against his, and she quickly lowered her hand to her chest, feeling the increasing thud of her heartbeat.

He fidgeted a moment, shifting another pin, but in the next instant, more of her hair tumbled free.

"I can see that you're doing a lovely job fixing it," she teased. "Are you sure you don't want to be a lady's maid?"

"If the brickyard fails, that will be my backup plan."

She laughed lightly, and more hair fell, toppling over the other shoulder.

He gathered the long tresses as though he had every intention of winding it up and returning it to the remainder of pinned hair. His fingers wound through the long locks. But instead of twisting, he only seemed to be unraveling it all.

"Do you need some help?" Her question came out slightly breathless.

"No." His one-word answer rumbled all too close to her ear, sending tingles over her neck.

He plucked another pin out and then another.

"You're only making more of a mess," she softly chided.

"There. Better." He bent and placed all the pins on the bench beside her cap.

She started to reach for the pins, needing to sweep her hair back up. She'd only worn her hair down once during their nightly meetings, and that had been the first time when he'd caught her unaware. Every night after that, she'd gone prepared with her hair plaited.

Before she could gather the pins, he wrapped an arm around her from behind and pulled her back. One of his hands was still in her hair, but the other flattened against her waist so she stumbled a step and bumped into his body.

He didn't move away, but he loosened his hold on her stomach, almost as if he was giving her the chance to break free of his touch.

A part of her cautioned against reveling at being so close to him, even if only for a few seconds. But it was as if she'd been waiting for him to hold her, and now that he was, she couldn't fathom being anyplace else.

So instead of pushing away from him, she leaned back.

The acquiescence on her part must have been the permission he'd been seeking because he tightened his hand on her stomach, drawing her nearer, before digging his other hand deeper into her hair.

Just for warmth. That's why she was staying against him. And to keep away from the spray of the rain.

"Your hair needs to dry." His voice was low behind her, his mouth against her head, his nose burrowing into her hair.

More warmth cascaded through her heart and over the edge like a rushing waterfall that couldn't be contained.

He pulled back just slightly, as though once again giving her the opportunity to put an end to the closeness. "Do you agree?"

"Oh aye, I wouldn't want to be catching a chill on account of wet hair." She slid her hand over his—the one resting on her stomach. She glided over every inch of his fingers, wanting to explore this new terrain. Was there anything wrong with taking this detour with him, letting herself have a few moments of forbidden pleasure? What harm could come from it?

As her fingers caressed him, his arms turned more rigid on either side of her, and he seemed to be restraining himself. She would have believed he wasn't enjoying this moment, but in the next instant, his lips pressed against the back of her head.

Was he initiating a kiss?

His lips were firm and almost possessive.

Aye, he was most definitely kissing her.

Her heart spurted, sending her blood humming through her veins.

His kiss didn't mean anything. It couldn't. They were just friends who were a little attracted to each other, and this sweet embrace would soon be forgotten once they returned to reality.

With the hand that was still in her hair, he swept the locks to one side, baring her neck. In the next instant, the warmth of his breath caressed her throat just behind her ear.

What was he doing? He wouldn't kiss her neck, would

he? That would be taking this rainy interlude too far. Yet if he did kiss her, she wouldn't stop him. Not for anything.

Because the longer she was against him under the pavilion, the more she wanted a kiss from him. They would have to part ways once Bellamy returned, so why not steal a kiss, here and now?

17

Kiernan was desperate to kiss her. His body was tight with the need. Especially with the elegant stretch of her neck practically begging him for a kiss.

But he couldn't start taking advantage of her, not when he'd worked so hard to respect her. He hadn't done what Shelia was accusing him of. He hadn't used Alannah to sate his own needs.

Because that's what this would be if he kissed her neck—he'd be using her, proving himself to be nothing more than a selfish idiot. He'd already brought her enough trouble with the rumors that were circulating, and he didn't want to chance hurting her any further.

He swallowed hard, drew in a deep breath, and forced himself to inch back. He did so slowly because desire stretched through him like a tight fuse just waiting to be detonated. One wrong move, and he wouldn't be safe. And neither would she.

Never had a woman been as difficult to resist as Alannah,

not even Shelia. And never had a woman made him want to forget about everything else and just be with her, except Alannah.

She was very special, and he couldn't think of anyone else who could measure up to her, not even close. Not only was she vibrant and caring and interesting, but she made him smile like no one else ever had.

Was he falling for her? Maybe even falling in love?

Blast. He couldn't let that happen.

With a spurt of strange panic, he released his hold on her waist and took a step away from her.

Before he could put more distance between them, she pivoted and snagged his shirt and part of his vest into a fist. Her long lashes dropped halfway, but not before he caught a glimpse of the desire in her eyes. He doubted she was falling in love, but she obviously wasn't put off by his attention to her. Did she want to kiss?

The fuse inside him flared to life with sparks and sizzles. He wanted to kiss her more than anything.

But no. He couldn't let anything happen. It wouldn't be fair to her. And it wouldn't be fair to the young woman Bellamy was picking out for him today. He didn't want to enter into a new relationship while harboring feelings for someone else.

Her fingers dug into his shirt more firmly, as though she heard his protests and wouldn't let him get away.

He didn't want to go anywhere. This was right where he wanted to be. With her. Like this.

Even so, he forced himself not to move. If they were going to share a kiss, she had to be the one to initiate it. He didn't want any confusion about his motivations. He wouldn't take advantage of her, wouldn't put any pressure on her for more.

As if he'd spoken the words aloud, she used his shirt to drag herself closer, until she stood facing him with only a hand's distance separating them. She angled her face up, her lips parted in readiness.

Her half-lidded eyes danced around his face before locking in on his mouth. He felt the heat of her gaze as if it was her touch, and it sent the flames scurrying along the fuse line throughout his body, making him combustible.

He almost groaned with waiting for her to initiate the kiss. But he waited, the air charged between them.

Finally, she lifted to her toes and touched her lips to the corner of his mouth, a gentle nibble, giving him a taste of what was to come.

Although he didn't want nibbles and wanted to devour her in return, he closed his eyes and let her move at her own pace.

Her next kiss was against his top lip. She captured it, tugged it, then released it to do the same to his bottom lip. Each tug undid his mind, so when she reached the other corner of his mouth, he was lost in a haze.

By the time she finished her tantalizing kissing, as if she had all the time in the world, she placed a kiss against his mouth fully and completely. In that instant, he opened for her, fusing their lips, taking control of the kiss with a strength and power that catapulted them swiftly to heights he'd never gone before—heights that made him instantly breathless and weightless.

As she joined in the passionate melding, her hand continued to twist tightly into his shirt, winding the fabric until the buttons strained. She wasn't afraid to show her desire, wasn't afraid to be passionate, wasn't shy about expressing herself. And with those qualities, the kiss was nothing short of life-altering, setting his axis off-center.

He became aware that one of his hands was snagged in her hair, keeping her in place against him. His other hand was splayed across her back, pressing her closer, except that her arms were still between them, her fists on his chest and in his shirt.

Regardless, he could feel her body and knew that if he wasn't careful, he could easily go on kissing her. While stealing a forbidden kiss at the pond in the rain was one thing, he couldn't let himself get carried away with any more than that. He had to keep the boundaries up between them somehow. . . .

With a strength he didn't know he possessed, he broke the connection between them. He was loathe to release her mouth, hungered for her even more now that he'd tasted her, but he took a rapid step away.

Wearing his dark suit coat over her uniform, she was practically engulfed in it. Her damp hair was stuck to her face, her cheeks were flushed, her blue eyes lighter than a sky at dawn, and her lips . . .

Heat stabbed him low and hard. Her lips were swollen, and the little pucker in her upper lip was too hard to resist. He didn't ask her permission. He stooped down and tasted that dip with his tongue and then followed with a short kiss.

As he pulled back, she gave a soft sound of complaint in her throat, one that nearly sent him to his knees. He had to put a barrier between them before he grabbed her and ravished her mouth again.

With an unsteady gait, he rounded the bench until he was

on the side with the blowing rain. She was watching him, her fingers touching her upper lip where he'd just kissed her. Her beautiful eyes were filled with both wonder and questions.

Likely questions about what it all meant.

What exactly did the kiss mean?

He'd never approved of men—not even Liam—having relations with their maids. The women were vulnerable, perhaps even felt helpless and feared for losing their jobs if they didn't cooperate with the men of the house.

Kiernan didn't want to be like that, but was he becoming like Liam anyway?

"Forgive me, Alannah." He jabbed his hands into his hair. "I overstepped myself just now, and I apologize."

"'Tis not your fault, to be sure." She let her hand flutter away from her mouth. "I was too forward with you. And I apologize."

"You do?"

She nodded and turned partially away. "I think we should agree to put the moment behind us and never think on it again."

Oh, he'd think on it again, probably for the rest of his life. But could he put it behind him, at least for now?

Frustration shot through him at the prospect of moving on from the kiss and acting like it didn't happen. In fact, he wanted to kiss her again.

His attention slid to her lips, rounded and full and soft. He wanted to spend every day, all day kissing those tantalizing lips. Was that a possibility?

He'd never imagined he'd be so attracted—even in love—with a woman like Alannah, someone from a different echelon of life, someone who didn't fit into his world.

But after the past few months of getting to know her, especially after her move to Oakland, he had to admit he didn't want to lose her. He wanted her to be a part of his life. But how would such a union work? Especially one without a dowry? Or without his parents' approval?

Bellamy had agreed to assist with a match today. But what if he didn't need Bellamy's assistance? What if he considered Alannah? Would she be agreeable? She needed a match as soon as possible too. He could help her with that. They could help each other. A union would be mutually beneficial.

Should he bring up the possibility?

She didn't move from behind the bench except to huddle deeper within his coat. Her long hair cascaded in disarray around her, and he wanted to plunge his fingers back into the silky strands and lose himself there.

"Can we agree to forget all about what just happened?" she asked again.

"No—"

At a call from near the pond, he swung his attention away from her to find Bellamy leading his horse with Torin trailing after him. The rain was still falling steadily, and both men were plodding forward regardless. Apparently, they were serious enough about getting Alannah matched that they weren't taking the time to wait for the rain to pass before meeting.

Kiernan didn't blame Torin for the rush. If their roles had been reversed, he would be doing his best to marry Alannah off before Shaw could get his hands on her. What would Torin say if he offered himself as a match for Alannah?

A scowl formed on the young man's face as he took in Kiernan. Clearly, Torin hadn't been expecting him to be at the pond, probably thought Bellamy would have Alannah's match there.

Bellamy's hat was pulled low, and he was wearing an oiled cloak, well prepared for the rain. He stopped at a nearby tree to secure his horse, looking as calm and unruffled as always.

What would the matchmaker think about matching him with Alannah? No doubt Bellamy would be surprised at the suggestion, but if Kiernan explained how he'd grown to care about Alannah, maybe Bellamy would agree to the proposition and help to convince Torin. Together, the three of them could persuade Alannah.

Kiernan squared his shoulders, letting determination rise within him—the same determination he'd fostered for his business enterprises. He was a driven man and almost always got what he wanted. In this case, he wanted Alannah. He was smart and savvy, and if he put his mind to it, could he win her over?

As Torin ducked under the roof of the pavilion and out of the rain, he didn't remove his glare from Kiernan. "What are you doing here?"

"It's lovely to see you too, Torin," Alannah said wryly.

Torin tore his attention away from Kiernan, removing his dripping hat and drying his rain-streaked spectacles before focusing on Alannah. "Are you okay?"

"I'm fine." She offered her brother a smile.

He didn't smile in return. Instead, he turned toward Kiernan again. Before Kiernan could brace himself, Torin plowed into him, slamming a fist into his gut, knocking the wind from him. Kiernan was unprepared for the hit, and the momentum threw him backward out of the pavilion into the rain.

Torin followed after him, sending another punch against his chin.

Pain ricocheted through Kiernan's head, but at the glint of a blade slicing through the air, Kiernan spun away from Torin. The knife missed him by mere inches.

With murder flashing in his eyes and hardening features, Torin came after him again.

Alannah was shouting at Torin, but the rain and the pounding of Kiernan's heart kept him from hearing what she said. He was too focused on the knife Torin was holding out.

"I told you I'd kill you if you used her." Torin's voice echoed with anger.

Had Torin heard the rumors? In particular the one about Alannah and him? "I didn't sleep with Alannah."

"He didn't, Torin!" Alannah had stepped out into the rain now, too, and was crossing toward her brother.

Before she could reach Torin, Bellamy barreled into the young man with his shoulder. Although Bellamy wasn't an overly muscular fellow, the power of the slam sent Torin flying so that he landed on his backside in the grass. Torin didn't immediately move, as though the blow had stunned him.

Bellamy caught up to Torin and stomped on his arm, pinning the hand with the knife to the ground.

Torin started to reach for his boot where he kept his second knife, but Bellamy's other foot came down hard on Torin's arm, halting him and forcing his hand to the ground.

"Doncha be doing anything stupid now." In his long black oiled cloak and black hat, Bellamy looked more like the grim reaper coming for a soul rather than cupid sowing seeds of love.

"He used Alannah." Torin's expression was tortured as he stared up at Bellamy.

Kiernan wanted to deny the man's accusation. But a part of him knew he deserved Torin's wrath. He might not have slept with Alannah, but he had kissed her just a few moments ago. And he shouldn't have done so, not without some kind of promise to her for their future.

Alannah stood in the middle of the fray, the rain beginning to plaster her unbound hair to her body. "Mr. Shanahan hasn't used me, Torin. He's not that kind of man."

Kiernan wanted to believe she was right. But now that they'd kissed, would he be able to resist kissing her again if the opportunity presented itself? He liked to think he could, but what if he was too weak?

The truth was, if he wanted to stay strong, he had to stop putting himself into situations that might cause him to stumble. Or maybe he needed to push forward with considering a match with her.

Without his hat, Kiernan became conscious of the rain pelting his head and soaking his hair, penetrating through the layers of his garments, splattering against his face. It was the punishment he deserved for kissing Alannah. Now he had to make amends.

"I have a solution to our problems," he stated more calmly than he was feeling. "Not only with the recent rumors but also with Shaw Farrell's threats."

Bellamy glanced at him expectantly. Torin, still locked into place on the ground by Bellamy's boots, turned his angry gaze to Kiernan.

"I realize Bellamy probably has other candidates in mind

for Alannah." Kiernan forced himself to speak. "But I'd like to be considered as her top match."

Her eyes widened at his declaration, her long lashes damp with raindrops he wished he could kiss away.

Torin only stared, his mouth stalling around a response. And Bellamy shifted away from Kiernan, but not before he glimpsed a small, satisfied smile on the fellow's lips.

Why was Bellamy acting as though he'd gotten what he wanted? Had he planned this match between them all along? Was that why he'd proposed the wager?

Bellamy had certainly seemed to think something was going on that day at Enya's house. Maybe he'd intended to use all the other women as a way to open Kiernan's eyes to the kind of match he really needed: a woman like Alannah.

If so, it had worked.

"I need an urgent match and so does Alannah." Kiernan spoke the logical conclusion aloud, hoping everyone else would agree. "So why not consider the option?"

Bellamy didn't remove his boots from Torin's arms, but he slipped his hand inside his coat pocket and pulled out a folded piece of paper. He held it toward Alannah.

She took the sheet from Bellamy and swiftly stepped into the confinement of the pavilion, her back facing them as she unfolded the paper.

Bellamy cocked his head at her. "Alannah knows you were the man I picked for her."

"I was your candidate?" Kiernan couldn't hold the question in.

"Oh aye." This time Bellamy didn't hide his smile.

Torin, still unmoving on the ground, leaned his head back and seemed to relax, the fight gone.

Kiernan leveled a glare at Bellamy. "Why didn't you say so from the start?"

Bellamy gave a one-shouldered shrug. "If you hadn't been so stubborn, you would have figured it out earlier."

Was the matchmaker right? Bellamy had wanted to do his job without interference. But Kiernan had insisted on his way, as usual.

"I admit. I was stubborn." Kiernan supposed he wouldn't have been able to acknowledge that stubbornness unless he'd gone through the process of visiting with all the women and discovering for himself that none of them could ever compare to Alannah. Even though it had taken time and effort, he'd learned his lesson well—that his list of qualifications was superficial and selfish and stupid. Bellamy had seen that from the start.

If Bellamy had told Alannah about their match, why hadn't she brought it up?

Kiernan's mind spun back to all the times they'd met at night. Had she been agreeable to spending time with him because she assumed they were courting? Most likely when she'd heard about him seeing all the other women and realized he wasn't courting her after all, that had been why she'd stopped visiting with him.

He'd been a fool not to consider her from the moment he'd met her. He supposed in some deep place in his soul, he'd already known how special she was, but he'd been too consumed with making himself important, too focused on what he could gain, too caught up in becoming better than his da.

But couldn't he have her and still make everything else work?

Kiernan hungrily took her in again. Safe from the rain beneath the roof of the pavilion, she was reading whatever was on the sheet. Was it some kind of agreement for their match?

"Mr. Shanahan wants to marry Alannah?" Torin rolled out from underneath Bellamy's boots and sat up.

"Why else do you think I arranged this meeting today?" Bellamy glanced to the sky overhead as if grateful for the rain.

It was Kiernan's turn to gape. Bellamy had purposefully orchestrated the time together alone at the pond. No doubt he'd hoped the rain would force Kiernan and Alannah to talk, maybe even confess their feelings to one another.

Torin was staring at Kiernan, amazement softening his features. "Mr. Shanahan cares about Alannah? Enough to marry her?"

Bellamy nodded. "Oh aye. He does. And he's finally admitting it."

Kiernan couldn't respond, was still speechless over Bellamy's cleverness. He should have seen it, especially after watching him match his two sisters. But he'd underestimated the fellow.

On the one hand, Kiernan didn't want Alannah having to learn about his true feelings for her this way, secondhand from Bellamy. On the other hand, he was relieved he no longer had to deny to himself and everyone else that he liked Alannah.

The question was, did she like him enough to marry him?

Alannah's shoulders had stiffened, and her body had turned rigid.

"I thought it was only fair," Bellamy continued nonchalantly while nodding toward the paper Alannah was holding, "that Alannah knew your list of qualifications for a wife before she agreed to the match."

Kiernan's heartbeat slammed to a halt against his chest. What was Bellamy doing? The list wasn't for Alannah. He didn't want her to see it, not even a single line of it.

Kiernan darted forward. He needed to get the paper from her, needed to throw it away. Because that's where the list belonged—in a rubbish heap.

18

Alannah's chest squeezed painfully.

Kiernan had a list of qualifications he wanted in a wife. And she didn't meet a single one of the items written in his bold handwriting:

Qualities Needed in a Wife:

1. *From high society*
2. *Well-bred*
3. *Educated*
4. *Manage a large house*
5. *Host parties to entertain business associates*
6. *St. Louis native*
7. *Familiar with important people*
8. *Polished*
9. *Poised*
10. *Pretty*
11. *From a wealthy family*
12. *Substantial dowry*

Ach, maybe she did meet a couple of his prerequisites. She was pretty. She knew that well enough from the compliments and attention she drew from men, even from him.

She was also educated. She might not have gone to a school for long, but her mam had made sure she could read and write from an early age. She'd loved reading and so had made sure Alannah and her siblings had loved it too.

But the rest of the list? Alannah fell short in every area that was important to Kiernan. She wasn't from the same social class, had grown up in a laboring family, had never managed a home or hosted parties, wasn't from St. Louis and didn't even like the city, had no notion of who was important in his social circles, nor did she care. She wasn't polished or poised, was instead herself, flaws and all. Her family had no wealth and therefore would never be able to give him a *substantial* dowry.

Before she could tuck the list away in her pocket, it was ripped from her grasp. She spun to retrieve it only to find Kiernan under the pavilion, backing away from her with the sheet.

His face was etched with embarrassment. "The list isn't important."

"Whyever did you make such a list if 'tis not important?" The question fell out as an accusation, one laced with disappointment.

She'd been near heaven's door when she'd kissed Kiernan. The moment had gone from blissful to utterly heavenly in the span of a few seconds, especially as he'd kissed her back. Oh aye, she'd had pleasant kisses before. Those kisses were a part of her past that she wasn't proud of when she'd pushed God away and lived by her own standards.

But Kiernan's kiss? Saints above. It couldn't even begin to compare with anything she'd ever experienced. His kiss was in a universe of its own.

The trembling inside flared again, and she hugged her arms to keep her body from quavering from need.

His kiss had awakened something inside her, something she didn't understand. Was it love? She wasn't sure, except that the strength of the emotion had been so consuming and so powerful that she'd wanted to launch herself against Kiernan, wrap her arms around his neck, press her body and lips to his, and never stop being with him.

If he hadn't ended the kiss and put the bench between them, she probably would have grabbed him again and kept kissing him.

Good thing she hadn't.

Her gaze dropped to the sheet he was gripping. It didn't matter if he tried to take it away and destroy any evidence his list had ever existed. She would know the truth about the kind of woman he wanted. And it wasn't her.

Why, then, had he offered to marry her?

Bellamy had agreed that Kiernan was finally admitting to caring about her. And Kiernan did care. She couldn't ignore all the things he'd done for her over the past weeks—sheltering her, giving her employment, keeping her safe, even bringing her books.

She also couldn't ignore the attraction that had been simmering below the surface all along. And she certainly couldn't deny his passion from moments ago.

But all of that wasn't enough to form the basis of a marriage. She wouldn't marry him just because in the heat of the moment he felt something for her, liked their kiss, and had been enjoying spending time with her.

Eventually all that would go away because a marriage didn't always have heat and kisses and joy. Sometimes it was hard and full of pain. What would he do in those moments when the feelings disappeared and he was left holding a tattered list of qualities he'd wanted in a wife but would never have?

"Listen, Alannah." Kiernan was crumpling the sheet. "The list is invalid."

"What list?" Torin stepped up behind Kiernan and snatched the paper from his hand.

Kiernan lunged after it, but Torin was holding it high and pushing Kiernan away at the same time while he was glancing at what was written.

After a moment of struggling, Kiernan stopped and lowered his head, as though in defeat. His hair was wet and dark, and strands stuck to his forehead. Even so, he still radiated with the power and purpose of a man born into privilege . . . a man who was so different than her with a life she wouldn't fit into.

If only she could be everything he wanted and needed.

The truth was, she'd never expected to rise above her station, never even wanted to . . . until this very moment, until knowing everything that was important to him. If only she'd been born wealthy and well-bred. If only she was from high society. Then she could be the kind of woman Kiernan deserved.

Torin finished reading from the paper and shoved it into Kiernan's chest.

Kiernan hesitated, almost let the sheet drop, but then grabbed it.

"That list is a load of—" Torin glanced at Alannah, then fumbled for a respectable word rather than a curse—"you-know-what."

Bellamy had joined them under the pavilion, the only one who was still mostly dry in his cloak. He leaned against a beam and was watching as though he was enjoying a theater production. The drama was indeed more than she'd bargained for.

The hurt and disappointment were much more too.

She pressed her hand against her aching heart—an ache that went deep and thudded with the reality of the situation: Even if she spent a lifetime striving to become everything on Kiernan's list, she'd never measure up.

Kiernan ripped the sheet of his qualifications in half, then in half again. "I was foolish to make the list. Bellamy tried to warn me, but I didn't listen."

"What does that mean?" Torin's voice was belligerent. "Are you looking for a woman with a dowry?"

"I thought I was," Kiernan said quietly, still tearing the paper. "I thought I could use the dowry for my business."

Torin opened his mouth to retort, then stopped.

"Now I realize I can't—don't want—to marry a woman for my own gain."

Torin's brows furrowed. "But you're needing the money, aren't you now?"

Kiernan halted his tearing but didn't respond.

"A couple fellows were talking yesterday," Torin continued. "They said you might not be able to pay workers next week."

"I'll pay." Kiernan's tone and expression turned hard. "I'll make sure everyone gets what they deserve."

Behind his spectacles, Torin's eyes remained troubled.

Alannah felt that trouble settle in her stomach. Clearly, Torin was concluding the same as her—Kiernan was having financial struggles with his brickyard, and he'd hoped to use his dowry to ease the strain.

He was within every right as a wealthy gentleman to require a dowry that could benefit him. And if he needed it for his brickyard, then all the more reason to marry a wealthy woman who could help him.

Even if he was ripping up his list and claiming it no longer mattered, the dowry was important. She wouldn't stand in the way of that, regardless of how much he might try to persuade her.

Her attention shifted to Bellamy where he was leaning against the beam. Maybe he'd changed his mind about the match. Why else would he give her Kiernan's list? He could have thrown it away. At the very least, he could have kept it private between him and Kiernan.

By showing it to her, he'd surely realized she wouldn't want to be with Kiernan, that if she'd felt anything, she would do her best to squelch those feelings. "Do you have someone else for me, Bellamy? Tell me you have another man in mind."

"No." Kiernan thrust a halting hand out toward Bellamy. "Don't say anything."

Bellamy's brows rose.

Alannah waved at Bellamy to speak. "Go on with you now. Tell me."

Torin shook his head. "I want Alannah to marry Kiernan."

She glared at him. "It's not your choice."

Torin frowned back. "Bellamy told me the man of his choice was waiting at the meeting place. There's no one else but Kiernan."

"It doesn't matter. Bellamy needs to find me someone else."

"We don't have time to waste," Torin insisted. "Not with the rumors."

"I agree." Kiernan leveled serious eyes upon Torin. "It's because of me that Alannah's reputation is sullied. Now I intend to do the right thing and marry her."

"No." The word slipped from Alannah almost harshly. "I won't be marrying someone because he's pitying me or feeling sorry for me."

"It's not pity—"

"And I won't be marrying a man who's wanting a different woman altogether than me."

"I've realized I don't want anyone but you." Kiernan's voice dropped and held an earnestness that tugged at her heart.

She wanted to stop her protest and let him convince her. It would be easy to do so. But she'd only come to regret giving in, and someday so would Kiernan. "No, 'tis clear I'll never be living up to what you want in a wife."

"I don't want those things anymore." He ripped the list again, this time ferociously and into tiny pieces. "I'll show you what I think of my list." He stalked out from underneath the pavilion and over to the pond. As he reached the edge, he tossed the pieces into the water. Within seconds the steady rain drenched them, taking them out of sight below the surface.

Kiernan turned and faced her, the rain still pelting him. "There. Gone."

If only that were really true. "You might be able to make the paper go away. But I'll know the list is still there inside you." No matter how much he might care about her and be attracted to her, she would always feel inadequate.

Torin was studying Kiernan carefully. "The dowry is the main thing you want, isn't it?"

"I want Alannah." Kiernan's voice held a note of stubbornness. "She's more important than a dowry or anything else on the stupid list."

"You say that now," she cut in, "but what happens in a few years when you wish I was more polished and poised? Or could host better parties? Or impress your friends?"

"That doesn't matter," he growled. "It's all shallow."

"The dowry does matter," Torin insisted.

"I will never have a dowry." Just like she would never have anything else Kiernan needed.

"I'll find you one." Torin pushed his spectacles up and met Kiernan's gaze. "If I give you a dowry, will you marry Alannah?"

"I want to marry her without one."

"But I don't want to marry you." Alannah couldn't stop from lifting her chin and turning her glare upon Kiernan. "I refuse to consider it."

"Alannah," Torin scolded. "He cares about you."

"I kissed her," Kiernan blurted.

The world went silent except for the rain pattering on the pavilion roof.

"Today. Before you and Bellamy arrived." Kiernan pulled back his shoulders and seemed to brace himself for another attack from Torin.

Bellamy scrubbed a hand over his mouth and ducked his head. Was he smiling?

Alannah gave a huff of frustration. This was no smiling matter, not when Torin would now kill Kiernan for certain this time.

But Torin didn't move, not even to stiffen. Instead, he nodded, as if the matter were settled. "Aye, then you'll be marrying her. I won't have it any other way."

Kiernan expelled a taut breath, almost as if he was relieved.

What had just happened? Had Kiernan used their kiss to gain Torin's support for the match?

Alannah huffed again. "I'll be the one deciding this, Torin. Not you."

Torin didn't bother to look at her, was instead focused on Kiernan. "I vow I'll get a dowry for Alannah. I don't know when I'll have it, but I promise I will."

Kiernan just shook his head. "That's noble of you. But I don't need it."

"'Tis my responsibility, and I'll do it." Torin's face took on a haggard look, one that reminded her of Da during his last days—those turbulent times when he'd been worried and exhausted.

She appreciated that Torin wanted the best for her, but a dread filled her anyway. What would her brother do to get a dowry for her? There was no telling. He wasn't a criminal. That's why he'd left the Farrell gang. But if he was desperate enough, she suspected he'd do whatever he had to in order to get what he needed. He was already in enough trouble, and she didn't want him to get into any more.

She shrugged out of Kiernan's coat. "You may as well save yourself the effort. I'm not marrying Kiernan."

"Please, lass?" Torin's voice softened. "Please. For me? So that I know you're safe?"

Should she agree so that she wouldn't have to be a burden to him any longer? No, then she would only burden Kiernan instead.

She shook her head and started to hand Kiernan his coat.

Kiernan folded his arms, refusing to take the coat, his eyes dark and almost dangerous. "Don't say no yet. Think about it."

Time wouldn't change her mind, but with Torin's pleading eyes still upon her, she couldn't make herself say so. Instead, she swallowed the emotion clogging her throat. "I won't be needing to think long."

"One week." The stubbornness was back in Kiernan's tone. "We'll go to Liam and Shelia's engagement party next weekend, and we'll announce our match there."

Go to a high society party? She almost scoffed at the notion. She wouldn't have anything to wear, wouldn't fit in, would never be accepted.

She would only hurt Kiernan's reputation all the more.

Bellamy pushed away from the beam and straightened. "Sounds like a fine plan if I ever heard one."

It didn't sound fine to her. But at the moment, she was outnumbered, the three men watching her and waiting for her acquiescence. What else could she do but give Kiernan a week? At the very least, she would have time to come up with a better plan—one in which she didn't have to marry a man who deserved a much better woman.

19

"This is madness." Da's voice boomed through the parlor. "I expected more from you."

Kiernan perched on the edge of the settee, his head down, his face buried in his hands.

Da was pacing the length of the carpet in front of the settee. Mam sat in one of the wingback chairs and hadn't said much so far. She hadn't needed to. The disappointment etched into her face spoke loudly enough.

The Shanahan reputation was sacred, especially after Da had worked so hard to build it. They'd already had one scandal earlier in the year with Enya. Thankfully, everything had worked out. Even so, they didn't need another situation to deal with.

During the short walk back to Oakland from the pond, Bellamy had offered to stay for the meeting with his parents. Kiernan and Bellamy had led their horses by foot with Alannah and Torin walking behind them, the two arguing in hushed tones the entire way. Even though Kiernan had wanted to have Bellamy's support while talking with his parents, he'd also known that wouldn't make things any better.

Kiernan had wanted to ask Bellamy the reason behind bringing up the list to Alannah. But a part of him already knew why. Bellamy was forcing him to be honest with her so their relationship wasn't based on any pretenses.

Somehow over the next week, Kiernan had to prove to her that the list didn't matter to him anymore, that he cared about her above all else and was ready to marry her no matter what anyone else thought. Because he didn't care about the opinions of others, did he?

Da stopped his pacing and stood in front of him. "What were you thinking, Kiernan? I raised you better than to take advantage of a maid, so I did."

Kiernan sat up, flinching at the despair in Da's green eyes. With his broad shoulders, stocky body, and muscular build, James Shanahan was an imposing man. Everyone said Kiernan looked like his da not only in body but with the same wide cheekbones, dimple in his chin, and thick brows. The only difference—besides twenty-five years in age—was that his da had bright red hair and green eyes instead of Kiernan's muted auburn hair and blue eyes.

Kiernan shoved a hand through his still-rain-drenched hair. "I told you I didn't sleep with her, that we did nothing more than talk." At least until today.

"And I told you it doesn't matter." Exasperation filled Da's tone. "People will be thinking what they will about it. Believe me, they're already assuming the worst."

"I'm marrying her, so it doesn't matter."

Kiernan didn't know where Alannah had gone after they'd returned home and she'd said her good-bye to Torin. Maybe she'd retired to her room. After all, it was still part of her afternoon off, for another hour at least, and she could go anywhere or do anything.

A strange mounting anxiety urged him to seek her out and try to set things right between them, the way they'd been before she'd learned of his list. She'd kissed him without reservation, had wanted him as much as he'd wanted her. If only they could go back to that.

As it was, with Da's fiery temper, the entire household was likely hearing the conversation. He just hoped Alannah was back in the summer kitchen and wasn't being subjected to his parents' comments.

Mam sat with her hands clenched in her lap. She was still attired in her best Sunday gown, everything about her lovely and graceful. "You should have let me send her on her way when I first wanted to. I knew she was trouble from the moment you brought her out here."

"She's not trouble." Kiernan's spine prickled. "Since arriving in St. Louis, she's faced difficulties that aren't of her own making."

"Everyone faces difficulties, and we can't be taking responsibility for hers."

"Some people face more than others, and we need to help."

"Not her." His mam's tone was stubborn. "Not any longer."

Kiernan couldn't keep to his chair. He shot up, forcing Da to take several steps back. "I am marrying Alannah." His voice came out low, almost menacing. "And you need to accept it."

His da's eyes widened.

Kiernan couldn't let them disparage Alannah. She didn't

deserve it. Even if he didn't marry her—which he would—she was one of the sweetest, kindest people he'd ever met. She deserved to be treated with the same kindness in return.

His da was watching him, his thick brows quirked high. For a moment he didn't say anything. Then he spoke quietly. "You care about her."

"Aye." Kiernan's chest swelled almost painfully with his longing for her and the possibility that he might have ruined things between them.

His mam rose now, too, smoothing down her wide silk skirt. "It doesn't matter how Kiernan feels. That woman has been manipulating him all along, trying to wheedle her way into his life so she can secure a future for herself."

"You're wrong. She doesn't want to marry me."

Mam opened her mouth, but her response stalled. She was probably relieved to learn the news. At the very least, she wouldn't have to try hard to get Alannah to reject him since she already had.

Da watched him a moment longer, then lowered himself to the closest chair. With the rainy afternoon, a cooler breeze wafted through the windows that were open and protected by the covered veranda. Even so, Da took out a handkerchief and dabbed at the perspiration on his forehead.

As he did so, he remained quiet, the sign he was contemplating the new information and trying to make sense of it. Although Da was a driven man, he was fair. He wouldn't demand that Kiernan marry someone else if he was in love with Alannah.

"Let me see if I have my information correct," Da finally said. "You've been helping to protect Alannah from her brother's rival gang. In the process, you've fallen in love with her. And now with the rumors, you want to do the honorable thing and make her your wife."

"That's it." Kiernan couldn't have summed it up more concisely if he tried. "If that isn't enough, Bellamy chose us for each other."

"Did he now? Above any of the women you met with over the past two weeks?"

"I didn't know it until today. And now I understand why. She's the only one I can truly be myself with, and she's genuine with me in return." Among all the other things he liked about her, he appreciated that he didn't have to strive to be more or do more or be successful. She liked him for who he was.

Or at least, she used to like him before she saw his list.

Da finished wiping his forehead, then tucked away his handkerchief. "Bellamy's a good matchmaker, so he is."

Mam snorted softly. "Matchmakers aren't the Almighty himself."

"If anyone has the Almighty directing him," Da countered, "that's Bellamy McKenna. He worked miracles for both Finola and Enya, so he did. And he'll work a miracle again for Kiernan."

"She's a nobody and not suitable, James." Mam raised her voice, as though she was hoping Alannah—wherever she was—would hear her. "At least with Finola and Enya, Bellamy found young men who are their equals."

"She's my equal." Kiernan was growing more ashamed of his list the longer he thought about what he'd written. "In fact, she's better than me." She wasn't as selfish and arrogant and shallow as he was.

"Not only is she a nobody," Mam protested, "but she has nothing—"

"What about you when you disembarked from your ship, and Da walked up to you?" Kiernan had heard the story of how his parents met dozens of times over the years. Da liked to say that he'd been doing business down at the levee and noticed Mam walking off the steamship gangplank and thought she was the prettiest Irish lass he'd ever seen. He hadn't cared about anything else and had gone right up to her and proposed on the spot. She'd slapped him on his cheek and told him to go away. They were married three months later.

"I wasn't a poor domestic." Mam's da had been a tailor, a respectable trade. He'd had a difficult time garnering business and had decided to emigrate to St. Louis where a brother lived. He'd sent Mam and one of his sons ahead to prepare the way for the rest of the family. But then her da changed his mind and decided to stay in Ireland after all. Although Mam hadn't been as helpless and destitute as the immigrants fleeing from the Great Hunger, if the times had been different, she very well could have been.

Da was looking at her with a gentle rebuke in his eyes.

Mam lifted her chin.

"We didn't have much in those early days, Lucinda." Da crossed to her and reached for her hand. "But we had each other, and that was enough, wasn't it?"

Her expression softened, and she raised a hand to his clean-shaven cheek. She was quiet for a moment, then sighed. "Fine. I won't say anything more about the girl."

"Alannah." Kiernan could be just as stubborn as Mam when he chose to. And in Alannah's case, he wanted his family to respect her as they would any gentlewoman he might have decided to marry.

"Very well." Mam released a sigh as if it was costing her greatly to acquiesce. "I won't say anything more about *Alannah*."

"You'll be kind to her?" Kiernan persisted.

"Aye, I'm kind already."

Kiernan narrowed his eyes at Mam, but she didn't meet his gaze. He'd made strides with her today, but maybe it would take time for her to accept Alannah. It would likely take time for many within his social circles to accept her. But he was a determined man, and he'd make sure it happened eventually.

"So," Da said. "You're set on marrying her?"

"I won't be swayed." It was the right thing to do. He knew it. Torin knew it. And Bellamy had always known it. Now he just had to convince Alannah.

"But she doesn't want to marry you?" Da asked, clearly reading the direction of his thoughts.

"I've persuaded her to take a week to think about it. I'd like to announce our match at the end of the week."

"And if she still doesn't agree at that point?" Da persisted.

With Shaw's threat hanging over him, Kiernan knew he couldn't wait longer than a week. A week might even be too long. In fact, if Shaw made any more threats, Kiernan would have to persuade Alannah to get married right away. Or he'd have to move her somewhere else. Maybe he would relocate her anyway, just to be safe.

Whatever the case, he was willing to do anything to have her as his wife, and he had to assure her of that. "I'll figure out something. I always do."

Da grinned. "I found a way to win my wife. Now it's your turn to step up and do the same."

As his da clamped him on the shoulder, Kiernan couldn't muster a grin. He already had enough pressure to prove himself with his businesses. But apparently now his da wanted him to prove his skill in wooing women.

After Kiernan left the meeting with his parents, he went to his room and changed into dry clothing. Then he searched for Alannah in all her usual spots. When he couldn't find her, he tiptoed up the servants' stairway to the dormer. Upon reaching Alannah's room, he tapped against the door lightly, not wanting to draw attention to his presence in the servants' quarters, especially not with the rumor that was already circulating. If someone saw him there, they'd most certainly assume the worst and add to the speculation about Alannah and him.

But he was willing to take the risk. A strange desperation was pulsing through him, one driving him to tell Alannah he'd been an idiot to write that stupid list of requirements and to assure her that he didn't care anymore about those things.

He also wanted her to know their kiss meant something to him, that it hadn't been just a casual or fleeting moment of passion. Instead, he hoped it was the beginning of more such moments—after they were married, of course.

With his back and head hunched against the low ceiling, he waited and listened for any movement inside her room.

Silence was all that greeted him.

He knocked again, but still no one answered.

He inched the door open and peeked in. She wasn't there.

The room was tidy, the narrow bed neatly made, clothes put away, an extra pair of shoes tucked under her bed.

She'd stacked her books on the dresser. It wasn't a large collection, about a dozen along with the couple he'd given to her. Most were well worn, the covers tattered and the pages frayed. Someday, maybe he could give her a whole bookshelf full of books, even an entire library. But for now, he had only one more book for her.

He tugged it out of his pocket, this one *The Pirate* by Sir Walter Scott. Kiernan wasn't sure if she would like it. But the selection at the mercantile hadn't been large this morning when he'd stopped by after meeting with Bellamy at the pub. Even though the store had been closed on Sunday, he'd asked a favor of the store owner to let him purchase the book. And now he was glad he had and that it had stayed dry in his saddlebag.

Hopefully, it would go a little way in softening Alannah's heart and making her more willing to forgive him.

He laid it on her pillow, then backed out of the room and closed the door. As much as he wanted to see her tonight, she obviously didn't want to be found, which meant he'd have to wait until tomorrow to make her realize they belonged together.

20

Alannah turned the final page of Zaira's manuscript and read the last line. Then she set the sheet on top of the rest of the pile she'd kept neatly piled on Zaira's desk.

"Well?" Zaira asked from the bed behind Alannah.

Zaira's bedroom was decorated in light green and white, giving it the feel of a moonlit garden, with the wallpaper containing an ivy pattern, the bed canopy made of wispy white tulle, and the comforter patterned in white-and-green stripes with a dozen lacy white throw pillows in all shapes and sizes. The potted plants around the room added to the garden-like feeling, as did the plush light green rugs.

Alannah peered out the window. The darkness of the night prevented her from seeing outside. Was Kiernan still home, or had he left?

The very thought of never meeting with Kiernan again made her heart ache. In fact, everything inside her ached. But she'd weathered losses before, and she could do so again. She had to.

She pivoted in the chair until she was facing Zaira.

The young woman was lying stomach down, elbows bent, and her chin resting in her hands. Her big eyes were wide and beautiful in the low lantern light, loose wisps of red hair framing her high cheekbones. Her face was etched with uncertainty as she waited for Alannah's pronouncement.

"You're a fantastic storyteller." In editing for Hugh, Alannah had learned to start with the positives first. "It flows well, the writing is smooth, and the plot is exciting."

"You're not just saying that to make me feel better, are you?" Another stack of papers sat on the bed beside Zaira, another book she'd started writing. An ink pen lay abandoned on a half-finished page, and crumpled papers littered the floor.

"I would never say something that isn't true." Alannah reached over and squeezed one of Zaira's ink-stained hands.

"Then tell me what I need to work on." Zaira squeezed back and pushed herself up so she was sitting cross-legged, her long skirt tangled in her legs.

Alannah gathered the manuscript into a neat stack, grateful she'd had the opportunity to do the editing and get more practice. In addition to taking over her kitchen duties on occasion to allow her to edit, Zaira had invited Alannah to come to her room to edit at the desk whenever she wanted. Doing so was much more comfortable and allowed for more privacy.

Tonight, after the rainy afternoon at the pond with Kiernan, Bellamy, and Torin, Alannah had hardly been able to wait to visit Zaira's room and lose herself in the manuscript.

Even if the problems were still awaiting her when she finished, at least she'd been able to escape for a couple of hours.

She opened the manuscript to the middle where she'd marked several places. "I really like how the character is learning so much about herself here, but for a couple of chapters, we lose sight of the plot."

Zaira's brow furrowed.

Alannah waited for protest or denial. She'd argued enough with Hugh to know that most writers had opinions that were difficult to change.

Zaira reached for the manuscript, and Alannah relinquished it.

As Zaira read through the notes in the margin, Alannah's stomach tightened. She hadn't overstepped, had she? She'd learned a lot about editing in those couple of years before leaving home, and she had a good sense for stories and characters and plots.

If only she had a good sense for real life. But somehow she'd made a mess of everything with Kiernan.

Alannah hadn't wanted to listen to the conversation between Kiernan and his parents earlier. But she'd heard it all from where she'd stood just outside the back servants' door, sent by Cook to tidy the dining room for the simple Sunday evening meal. Portions of the discussion had grown loud, including when Mrs. Shanahan had made the declaration that Alannah was a nobody and not a suitable match.

The meeting had made it all too clear that Mrs. Shanahan hadn't changed her opinion about Alannah, was still opposed to Kiernan having anything to do with her. As much as Alannah wanted to object to the matron's declaration that she was unsuitable, she couldn't. Not after seeing Kiernan's list. The list of requirements was likely the same that Mrs. Shanahan had, that any mother or father in a family like the Shanahans would have.

Alannah couldn't hold back a sigh.

Zaira glanced up from her manuscript. "What's wrong?"

"Nothing. I'm fine."

The young woman placed the manuscript on the bed, then sat up on her knees, giving Alannah her full attention. "You're not fine."

Zaira's tone was so gentle and kind that tears stung the back of Alannah's eyes.

"You're thinking about Kiernan, aren't you?"

"Of course not."

Zaira tsked. "You don't need to pretend with me, Alannah. I heard my parents and Kiernan today just like everyone else. And I know he cares about you."

Alannah reached for the pencil on the desk and twisted it in her hands.

"I also know he's been meeting with you after dark out beyond the garden."

Alannah's gaze shot up to Zaira. "You do?"

"I do now." A self-satisfied smile curled up her lips. "I thought I heard him coming and going late, but I wasn't sure what he was up to."

Guilt knotted in Alannah's stomach. "It's not what you're thinking—"

"I didn't think you were having illicit relations, if that's what you mean."

"We weren't, to be sure. I vow it." Alannah pushed up from her chair, needing to hide from the never-ending embarrassment today had brought.

Zaira jumped up from the bed. "Don't go."

Alannah halted. Even though she wanted to rush from the room, she obeyed Zaira like a good servant would do, poised for the next command.

As if sensing Alannah's subservience, Zaira waved a hand toward the door. "You don't have to stay if you don't want to talk. But I thought that since we're becoming friends, you might like a listening ear."

After how much Zaira had entrusted to Alannah, shouldn't she trust Zaira in return?

Zaira sat back down on the edge of the bed. "I will say that I've never seen Kiernan as taken with a woman as he is with you."

"I don't think so."

"I know so. He never fought to keep Shelia the way he's fighting to keep you."

"He fought to keep me?"

"Aye, silly. Today in the meeting with Mam and Da. He wants to marry you and doesn't plan to let them change his mind."

Alannah's thoughts whirled again with all the things she'd overheard. *"She's the only one I can truly be myself with, and she's genuine with me in return. She's my equal . . . in fact, she's better than me."*

Zaira was right. He'd said he wouldn't be swayed from marrying her, that he was determined to win her.

But that was precisely the trouble. He might have this momentary attraction to her, think he wanted to marry her, believe they were right for each other, but ultimately, she would do him more harm than good.

"Do you care about him too?" Zaira's tone wasn't pushy or even nosy.

Alannah hesitated. Did she dare admit she liked Kiernan so much that at times the desire scared her?

She swallowed the reservations holding her back and nodded. "Aye, I've never cared about a man the way I do for Kiernan."

Zaira gave a bounce and a clap. "I knew it!"

"But I can't have him, Zaira," Alannah quickly protested. "I'm not the right woman for him."

"Who says?"

"Everyone."

"It doesn't matter what anyone else thinks about the two of you."

"But it does. And I'll only cause embarrassment to him and your family."

Zaira reached for Alannah's hand and dragged her to the bed beside her. As Alannah sank into the mattress, Zaira laid her head on Alannah's shoulder in a sisterly way—or at least as sisterly as Alannah had imagined since she'd never had one.

"You're a wonderful person, Alannah. And people will see that the same way Kiernan has. The same way I have. Eventually no one will think about all the rumors and how you and Kiernan met. All that will matter is that you're together."

If only that were true. But nothing ever seemed to work out in her life so perfectly. God didn't look with favor upon her the way He did others.

Besides, even if Kiernan cared about her, she had to do what was best for him. And the best thing was for him to have a woman who could help him succeed in life, especially in giving him a dowry that would help him with his brickyard.

Before she could formulate a response, the pounding of hooves resounded in the lane coming toward the front of the house. It was a pounding so furious that the bearer could only be bringing bad news.

Zaira sat up, and Alannah did too.

What could it be? Had something happened to Riley and Finola? Or perhaps there was news of Sullivan and Enya. What if one of them had succumbed to the cholera?

Alannah grasped Zaira's hand at the same time the young woman clasped hers, as if they'd both concluded the same thing at the same time.

They remained stiff and unmoving on the edge of the bed until the horse halted. A moment later, footsteps thudded up the stairs, across the veranda, to the front door, and a rapid pounding reverberated through the house.

Responding footsteps came from the hallway outside Zaira's room, probably Kiernan's or his da's.

Zaira scrambled off the bed and crossed to the door. She opened it a crack and peeked out.

"Mr. Shanahan?" a man shouted from outside. "You've got to come right away."

The footsteps on the interior stairway leading down to the entryway hastened.

"It's urgent!" the man called. "The Farrell gang is at the brickyard causing havoc."

Alannah jumped up now, too, and gasped. The Farrell gang? There was only one reason the Farrell gang would be threatening the brickyard. And it was because of Torin.

Shaw was probably hunting for him and hoping to destroy him.

Zaira threw open the door the rest of the way and headed out into the hallway. Alannah followed, her heart pounding.

The house door banged open, and the voices resounded throughout the entryway, hurried and grave.

At the top step, Zaira halted, and Alannah did likewise. Darkness engulfed the stairway and even the hallway below, but the light of the moon outlined Kiernan in the doorway as he conversed with a man on the threshold.

James Shanahan stood behind Kiernan, in his night clothing, including a long nightcap. Kiernan was still attired in his clothing, missing only his coat and vest. He was holstering a revolver, one he'd obviously brought to the door in case he needed the protection.

"I'll be right there," Kiernan said. "Ride into town and alert the police and then tell Liam."

The messenger gave a curt nod before he spun on his heels and crossed the porch.

Kiernan closed the door and then stalked past his da down the hallway.

Mr. Shanahan grabbed on to Kiernan and tried to stop him. "You can't be going and trying to fight them yourself."

Kiernan shook off his da's hold. "I won't sit back and let them destroy my brickyard."

Mr. Shanahan lumbered after Kiernan. "At least wait for the police."

Kiernan paused at the back door. "I can't wait. My workers, my buildings, everything I've invested in the business is at stake."

"Your life is more important than the business."

"My workers' lives are important too."

The frustrated voices of the father and son carried up the stairway where Alannah huddled next to Zaira. Madigan and Quinlan had gathered behind them. And Mrs. Shanahan was making her way down the stairs in her nightgown while still donning her robe.

Kiernan stepped outside, letting the back door slam behind him. The noise reverberated through Alannah, setting her world off-kilter.

Mr. Shanahan threw the door open and called, "Be careful, son. Please don't do anything rash."

If Kiernan responded, Alannah couldn't hear him. A moment later, Mr. Shanahan stepped back in, his shoulders sagging. When he turned, Mrs. Shanahan was on the bottom step.

"Blessed Mother, help us." Mrs. Shanahan's whisper was grave.

It sent chills up Alannah's backbone.

The question was, did she have the power to stop Shaw and his attack? If she handed herself over to him, would he call off the fight at the brickyard? And would he finally leave Torin to live in peace?

She hesitated a moment, then swallowed her reservations. She had to go to the brickyard now. She had no other choice, not if she wanted to save Torin and protect Kiernan from danger.

21

Alannah tiptoed down the servants' stairway, her cloak on and the hood up. As she stepped out onto the main floor, the light from the parlor illuminated the hallway.

The whole family had congregated in the front room while Mr. Shanahan had gone up to his room to change. He'd just returned and was speaking to his family while waiting for the coachman to bring around his horse so he could ride to the brickyard.

Could she go with him? Dare she ask?

If she attempted to travel by foot, she wasn't sure she'd be able to find her way in the dark. And she would be much too late to intervene and possibly too late to prevent Torin from being hurt since at least fifteen if not thirty minutes had elapsed since Kiernan had left.

Even now, if she rode with Mr. Shanahan, the damage might already be done. What good would she do then? Was she being foolish to think she could rush off to the brickyard under such circumstances?

Torin had warned her that if anything happened to him, she wasn't to go out. Besides, if she showed herself there, she would only distract Torin and Kiernan and make them angry after how hard they'd worked to keep her safe and out of Shaw's hands.

Her heart sank low.

Madigan and Quinlan were sharing every detail they'd ever heard about the Farrell gang—the cockfighting in basements, the knife brawls in alleys, men losing fingers and toes and even eyes, and more.

Alannah had already learned enough during her time living in the Kerry Patch, had witnessed the brutality and fighting between the rival gangs. Now she whispered a prayer for her brother's safety and for Kiernan's, but like so many prayers, they seemed to hit the ceiling and fall back down upon her shoulders.

"Let me go with you," Madigan insisted. "I know how to handle the rifle."

"I do too," Quinlan's younger voice chimed in.

"No, you'll be staying home." Mr. Shanahan spoke firmly.

Before they could protest or say anything else, another knock came against the front door, this one less urgent but still firm.

Alannah slipped out the back door. She wouldn't go to the brickyard, but she couldn't stay at Oakland. She didn't want to risk the possibility of bringing danger to the Shanahans' doorstep. She'd been thinking about it all the while she'd gone up to her room to get her cloak.

If Shaw and his gang could do something like that at the brickyard, who would stop them from attacking the

Shanahans' home too? Especially if they realized she was there?

"May I help you?" Mr. Shanahan asked to whoever had just been knocking.

What if a worker from the brickyard was bringing an update? She couldn't go until she learned the latest news. She paused and listened.

"Oh aye, you can be helping alright." The voice, with its Irish brogue, was familiar, but she scrambled to place it.

"Oh?" Mr. Shanahan's tone took on a chill.

"I'm here to collect Alannah Darragh." The demand carried through the entryway and out the back door. The voice most certainly belonged to Shaw.

Her pulse raced forward, and she pushed farther back against the house. She was too late. The danger had already arrived.

Silence settled over the entryway, and Mr. Shanahan didn't respond right away. Did he know who Shaw Farrell was? Would he recognize him?

"I'm sorry," Mr. Shanahan said. "Mind you, who did you say you were? And why exactly are you here for our maid?"

"Go get her," said another voice, this one gruffer.

"Now hold on, Charlie," Shaw said. "Let's be polite about the matter."

"Get us the girl," the second man—Charlie—said again, this time slower, as if that proved he was polite.

Alannah shuddered. After weeks of hiding successfully from Shaw, all it had taken was the rumor today to give away where she was. He'd probably heard of Kiernan sleeping with her the same way every other person in the countryside had. Now that Shaw finally knew where she was, he'd come after her.

Should she just step inside and hand herself over?

She reached for the door handle. But even as she tightened her grip, she couldn't make herself open the door. Torin would rather die than sacrifice her to Shaw. She suspected Kiernan would feel the same way.

"What business do you have with our maid?" Mr. Shanahan asked again, and this time, his voice dropped to a dangerous level.

A beat of silence ensued.

"You cannot be threatening me with your gun," Mr. Shanahan said, "and expect me to allow you access to one of my hired staff."

Had Shaw or Charlie pulled a gun on Mr. Shanahan?

Alannah was tempted to peek through the back door to find out what was going on. But she held herself stiffly against the house, her mind starting to whirl. Why wasn't Shaw at the brickyard with the rest of the gang? Why set the destruction in motion and then come after her? Maybe he figured no one would be able to oppose his taking her, especially if Kiernan had already dashed off to rescue his brickyard.

"Put the gun away, Charlie." Shaw again spoke smoothly, almost diplomatically. "I'm sure Mr. Shanahan doesn't want any violence tonight. Not with his family watching."

"You wouldn't dare." Mr. Shanahan's tone remained hard. "You'll never get away with harming me or my family."

"Just go get the girl, Mr. Shanahan. Then we'll return to the brickyard and put an end to the fighting."

"She belongs to my son Kiernan, so she does. He's intending to marry her."

"She belongs to *me*." Shaw gave up the last pretense of friendliness. "Kiernan has known she's mine all along, and he's been trying to keep her from me."

"Is that right, now?" Mr. Shanahan's question dripped with disbelief. "What would the young woman say if we questioned her?"

"She'd choose me."

Mr. Shanahan didn't respond immediately. "Very well. Let's bring her down and ask her which man she prefers, you or Kiernan. If she wants Kiernan, then you leave her and go on your way."

"Fine," Shaw stated, almost as if he already knew who she'd choose—him.

But could she? She shook her head. Ach no, she never could, not even for a wee minute.

Mr. Shanahan called out an order to one of the maids. Footsteps hustled down the hallway toward the back servants' stairway.

Before anyone opened the door and happened to see her standing there in the darkness, Alannah ducked into one of her hiding spots behind the big potted plants—the place she used from time to time during the day when she took a reading break.

With the large fern leaves hanging down over her, she slid the wicker chair in position to cover her the rest of the way. It was difficult enough for someone to see her there during the daylight. She guessed it would be harder in the darkness, even by lantern light.

As she huddled low, her heart thudded so loudly, she feared it would give her away.

She waited tensely for someone to step outside and call her name, but as the moments passed, the door remained closed. Worry continued to beat a steady tempo against her chest. All the while, her mind scrambled to find a solution to the conflict with the Farrell gang. Was there a way to keep those she loved safe?

Those she loved.

A sweet but piercing ache sliced through her. Oh aye, she loved Kiernan. She could deny it all she wanted, but she'd been falling in love with him since he'd helped her find shelter at his sister's home.

He'd been so kind and considerate from the first moment she'd met him. And his concern for her the night of the fire in St. Louis—her pulse always raced whenever she thought of how he'd acted. He'd come stomping into the O'Briens' house calling for her, his voice frantic.

She'd been in the dining room packing valuables for the O'Briens to save from the fire. When she stepped into the hallway and Kiernan's eyes landed upon her, the relief in his expression had been so unexpected that she had the wildest desire to rush to him and bury her face against his chest.

Of course at the time, she'd been embarrassed by the strength of her desire for Kiernan, had known it was inappropriate to be thinking of him so informally. But as he stalked down the hallway toward her, all brawny and handsome and intense, she hadn't been able to resist him when he scooped her up and carried her through the house, out the back door, and directly to the waiting carriage.

That was the trouble with their match. He was still very much irresistible. Which was why she'd kissed him.

She let her fingers linger over her lips, the memory of Kiernan's mouth upon hers earlier in the day. He'd kissed her as if she was the most precious thing he'd ever touched. He wanted her as much as she wanted him. The kiss impacted him just as it had her. She couldn't forget that he'd even met with his parents and convinced them to agree to the match with her.

A man's call resounded from the side of the house nearby. "I'll check the kitchen and the other buildings. You look around the grounds."

It was Shaw and Charlie. They'd apparently moved their search outside.

Maybe she should have left while she could still make her escape. Even though she was mostly hidden behind the plant and chair on the porch, if they examined the area thoroughly, they might spot her.

"If she really did leave," Charlie called, "my guess is she went to the brickyard."

Rays of light began to penetrate the darkness of the backyard, and a moment later, the two men, each carrying a lantern, stepped around the house. One of them made his way across the yard toward the summer kitchen. The other veered near the veranda, holding his lantern low and shining it underneath the porch.

She tried to scoot farther behind the plant and chair. There was a crack between the two, and if the light hit her just right, he'd probably see her face or possibly her hair.

The light bobbed closer.

She scrunched her eyes closed, as if somehow that could

keep her hidden. All she could do was pray fervently that Charlie wouldn't decide to come up on the veranda.

At the squeak of the back door, her eyes shot open. More light spilled outside, which was not what she needed.

"You're trespassing, Mr. Farrell!" Mr. Shanahan stepped outside. "I suggest you be moving on your way if you don't want to make more trouble for yourself."

"If you've got nothing to hide," came Shaw's response by the summer kitchen, "then you won't mind us taking a look."

Mr. Shanahan started to say something else, but a woman's voice cut him off. "'Tis alright, Da." Zaira. She'd followed Mr. Shanahan out onto the porch. "Alannah went to her room and got her cloak the moment she heard about the attack at the brickyard. She's probably halfway there by now."

"They have no right to take her." Mr. Shanahan's reply was low and angry. "She's Kiernan's."

Alannah hugged her arms around herself more tightly. Under any other circumstance, Mr. Shanahan's words would have warmed her. But at the moment, all she could think about was figuring out how to get Shaw and Charlie to leave without harming any of this dear family and their property.

Footsteps padded down the veranda her way along with a small light.

Had Charlie come onto the porch now?

As the light drew nearer, she stiffened and waited for a shout that would alert Shaw of her whereabouts. But at the sight of a full skirt and Zaira's womanly figure, Alannah breathed out her relief.

Zaira ambled over to the wicker chair, placed a candle on the side table, then began to lower herself.

What was the young woman doing? She needed to find

a different spot to sit, a spot that wouldn't be so close to Alannah and wouldn't draw unwanted attention.

As Zaira reclined, she scooted the chair closer to the plant. Then she spread out her skirt, drawing one side over her crossed leg in such a way that it blocked the opening between the chair and the pot.

Alannah could no longer see anything. But that also meant neither Shaw nor Charlie could see her. Had Zaira guessed she was hiding on the veranda and purposefully positioned the chair to conceal her even more?

There was no other explanation.

Zaira was so sweet. Alannah wanted to reach up and squeeze the young woman's arm to silently communicate with her, but she couldn't risk moving. She also wanted to ask Zaira how she'd known about the hiding place. Maybe Zaira had passed by when Alannah had been so engrossed in a book that she hadn't realized anyone had noticed her.

Some of the tension in Alannah's body eased. Even so, as the two men continued to call out to each other, she waited, unmoving.

After a few moments, the lantern light grew brighter, and Zaira drew herself up and flounced her skirt.

"Did you find her, Mr. Farrell?" Zaira's tone held a note of accusation.

"Any more buildings on the property?" His reply was curt, almost frustrated.

"I guarantee if there were more, she wouldn't hide in any of them, not if she knows you're coming after her."

The gang leader was intimidating, and Alannah was surprised at how composed Zaira was remaining while talking to him.

Even so, the young woman was playing a dangerous game with one of the most notorious men in St. Louis. Alannah couldn't let her come to harm. But she had the feeling someone was going to get hurt, maybe even killed. And there would be nothing she could do to stop it. . . .

22

Flames greeted Kiernan as the brickyard came into view. The fire roared into the dark night sky above the drying sheds, above the cabin serving as his office, and above the wooden frame of the new tenement that was half-way built.

With dread coursing through him, he kicked his stirrups against his stallion, urging it faster.

During the ride over, all he'd been able to think about was Torin. That's why Shaw had come out to the brickyard—to finally capture Torin and make him pay for leaving the gang. From the extent of the destruction, it was clear that Shaw was also punishing Kiernan for sheltering Torin.

Kiernan's pulse thundered in tempo with his horse's hooves, and he prayed that Torin had escaped Shaw's clutches.

Blast. Why hadn't he taken better care since meeting Shaw in the woods to warn Torin, to even encourage him to go into hiding? Now, maybe it was too late.

A gust of smoke hit Kiernan in the face, and he ducked his head. But his eyes were already stinging, and he coughed.

This was madness. Did Shaw think he and the rest of his gang could get away with this kind of destruction? Kiernan would hire the best lawyer in St. Louis—or beyond, if necessary—to take up a case against the gang leader.

Shouts rose into the air, and men were racing everywhere. Were they still battling against the gang? Or were they only fighting the fire now?

As his horse pounded past the worker tents and low campfires, now deserted, he was grateful the men had risen to the challenge and rushed out to save the brickyard, but how many had been hurt?

As he reached the new tenement, he reined in his horse a safe distance away and dismounted. Men formed a line from the nearby well to the building, and they were passing buckets to one another as fast as they could work. But it wasn't enough. The fresh wood frame, even if damp from the rain earlier in the day, was alight with dozens of small fires.

If they had a fire crew with hoses spraying the framed building down, maybe they would be able to save it. But from what he could tell, it was a lost cause.

"The Farrell gang?" he called to the closest fellow, one of the miners.

The man paused and nodded at Kiernan. "Took us by surprise, that they did. But they're gone now."

"Anyone hurt?"

"Few gonna have some bruises. But reckon we held our own."

Kiernan swept his gaze over the toppled piles of bricks that had been awaiting transport—some were crushed, others broken. The glow from the flames also illuminated equipment destroyed and supplies overturned.

He motioned to one of his foremen who was directing the water brigade.

"The tenement can't be saved!" Kiernan tilted his head toward the opposite side of the brickyard. "Put your efforts into saving the sheds and bricks."

The foreman nodded, then gave a few curt commands at the fellows he'd been working with, and they began to jog toward the drying sheds.

Kiernan picked up a bucket, filled it with water, and joined them. But as they reached the open sheds with the bricks underneath, he stopped short and his heart plunged hard.

The roofs on all the sheds were already collapsing onto the bricks underneath. Since the bricks hadn't been fired, they were too weak yet to withstand the pressure and were cracking and falling apart under the fiery boards falling on top of them.

Some of the men were attempting to rescue the bricks, dragging loads away from the flames. But the bricks were heavy and difficult to maneuver, and they wouldn't be able to save many. Even so, Kiernan called out instructions, and the rest of the men joined in trying to salvage what they could. All the while, he searched each face for Torin's.

"Torin?" he finally called to one of the other foremen.

The man was hauling an armful of bricks away from the burning shed. "Haven't seen him."

A sick knot formed in Kiernan's gut. Torin wouldn't have run off or hidden away in the middle of a fight. And he certainly wouldn't neglect to help put out the fire. So where was he?

Kiernan headed toward the kiln, the knot inside cinching tighter. If Torin died, Alannah would be devastated. She'd lost everyone else in her family, and she didn't deserve to lose Torin too.

As he neared the kiln, his boot kicked at something lying in the gravel. He halted and picked it up. It was a knife—Torin's—and it was coated in blood. A second knife sat only a few feet away, the blade crimson. Not far from the knives a pair of spectacles lay on the ground, the frames bent and the glass crushed.

He grabbed the spectacles and stuffed them into his pocket even though they were likely irreparable. Then he crossed the final steps to the kiln. A stairway led down to an underground chamber, and through the open door, the glow of light inside illuminated a man kneeling beside an outstretched body.

Kiernan descended the steps two at a time and paused at the doorway.

The room allowed the workers to feed the fire, keep control of the temperature inside the kiln above, and monitor the progress of the firing process. To one side was a fan of sorts that Torin had been tinkering with—a new machine he'd built but hadn't finished. Elaborate charts were tacked to the walls, and papers filled with diagrams were scattered over a standing table against another wall.

As Kiernan sidled through the doorway, he confirmed what he'd already guessed. The injured man was Torin. He was on his back with his eyes closed—one swollen shut and the skin already turning blue. His lips were busted, his nose bleeding, and his jaw cut.

The middle-aged, hefty fellow kneeling beside Torin

was Donahue, Torin's assistant. The other was Donahue's brother, and Kiernan couldn't remember his name. They were both frantically trying to staunch the blood flow from what appeared to be at least a dozen stab wounds over Torin's now bare torso. Some were surface wounds, but others looked like the blade had penetrated deep.

"He's still alive?" Kiernan asked.

"Barely, boss." Donahue wrapped linen around Torin's lower arm. With a droopy eye and mustache that also drooped, Donahue was weaker on one side of his body but had always been a stellar employee at the glass factory and had come over to the brickyard upon Torin's request. He was reliable and liked fidgeting with machinery as much as Torin.

Kiernan crouched, his hands itching for something to do. Desperation prodded him to help Torin, who was no criminal but instead a hard worker, intelligent, helpful, and caring. In addition, he was fiercely loyal to Alannah and wanted the best for her. "He needs a physician."

"Oh aye," said Donahue's brother, who had a swollen eye and a bleeding slash on his cheek. He was pressing tightly against a wound in Torin's side. "They cut him up bad. No telling what's damaged inside. But if we can keep him from bleeding to death, then he'll need plenty of sewing up."

Kiernan swiped up the discarded shirt lying on the floor, in shreds from where the men had been tearing it and forming strips to stop Torin's bleeding. Kiernan cut a slice, then pressed it gently against another wound, this one in Torin's shoulder.

The young man shifted his head and moaned.

Blood began to seep through the linen in Kiernan's hand.

"Find a wagon that wasn't torched. We'll put him in the back and haul him to the city."

Donahue's brother tore a piece of linen. "The Farrell gang left him for dead. If they catch us trying to save him, they'll come and finish him off and us too."

Donahue nodded. "No doubt they're still out there close by, watching us."

Kiernan didn't disagree with either of the men. But he wouldn't neglect getting Torin to a doctor, not if there was still a chance of saving him.

He wrapped the linen around Torin's shoulder, securing it in place at his armpit. "I'll take him. By myself."

The two fellows halted their ministrations.

Kiernan could feel their stares. They were probably wondering what made Torin so special that Kiernan would put his life at risk for him. Or maybe they'd heard the rumors about the relationship with Alannah and were well aware of his connection with Torin.

Regardless, Kiernan had to come up with a plan to save the young man. His mind raced with all the possibilities, and he landed on the only thing he could think of. "We'll build a casket. If they want a dead person, that's what we'll give them."

23

Alannah didn't move from her hiding spot on the veranda. As far as she could tell, Shaw and Charlie had left Oakland. Zaira had also gotten up and disappeared inside, taking the light with her and leaving Alannah in the dark.

Even with the yard and house now quiet, an unease prickled the back of her neck, almost as if someone was still out there in the dark, watching and waiting for her to step out of her hiding place. Or maybe she was just imagining that Shaw and Charlie had walked off a short distance but were lingering nearby, intending to capture her the moment she made her presence known.

She'd been certain Zaira had known she was hiding behind the plant and chair and had positioned herself there to keep anyone from seeing her. Once the danger was gone, surely Zaira would come out and talk to her and let her know she was safe to emerge.

But only Mr. Shanahan had stepped through the back door and had met the coachman on the lane as he'd been bringing the horse up to the house. Mr. Shanahan hadn't wasted any more time. He'd mounted and left Oakland, taking the road to the south in the direction of the brickyard.

Alannah shifted, one of her legs numb from sitting in the same place for so long. Had she been here an hour? Maybe not quite so much time had elapsed, but she was ready to stand and stretch.

What had become increasingly clear as she'd waited was that as kind as Kiernan had been all this time trying to help her and Torin out of their predicament, it wasn't his problem to solve, especially not by marrying her.

She expelled a taut breath. She had to go. But where? She didn't have enough money saved to return to Ireland. Did she even want to go back anymore? Since moving to Oakland, she'd hardly considered the possibility.

Where else could she go? She didn't have any friends in the city. She didn't have any family here except for Torin.

She didn't know what to do. The only idea she'd had over the past hour was returning to the O'Briens' for a day or two, just until she could find other employment.

"Alannah." A whisper came from the open window above her. Someone was in the library, attempting to communicate with her.

She held herself motionless and waited.

"It's me, Zaira," the whisper continued.

Alannah's chest squeezed at the kindness of the young woman. "Zaira, I'm so sorry about all of this."

"Hush now. You're not to blame."

"I am, to be sure. And so is Torin."

"Your brother?"

"Oh aye. He's in trouble with the Farrell gang."

"If you bat an eyelash the wrong way at the Farrell gang, you'll be in trouble with them."

If the moment hadn't been so serious, Alannah might have smiled. As it was, she fought back tears. "Shaw wants me as payment for Torin leaving the gang."

Zaira released an indignant huff. "I won't let them have you, and neither will Kiernan."

"I don't want Kiernan to be involved any longer."

"That man wouldn't be able to keep away from you if someone chained him up and locked him away."

Leave it to Zaira to be dramatic. Even so, Alannah couldn't put him in more danger. "I have to figure this out on my own."

"I'll help you."

"No—"

"Yes. I already have a plan."

"I won't involve you either."

Zaira was silent for several seconds. "You won't deny me this adventure, will you? I need it as research for my next book."

"I'm not daft, Zaira. I know you're making an excuse."

"I'm not. This is the most fun I've had in ages."

Alannah bit back her whispered retort. How could she turn down the offer when the fearsome truth was that she didn't have a way to sneak back into the city without help.

As if sensing her victory, Zaira spoke again. "I've put on one of your black skirts. All I need now is your cloak."

"You cannot pretend to be me."

"I can, and I will. I'll ride out disguised as you—"

"I don't ride well." She'd only done it a few times in her life, had never needed a horse in Tralee.

"They won't know that. Besides, I can pretend to be awkward if you think that would be best."

Alannah scrambled to come up with a different plan than the one Zaira was concocting.

"Once I leave," Zaira whispered, "if anyone is waiting in the woods or on the road, they'll follow me for a ways."

"I don't like this idea at all, so I don't." Alannah didn't want Shaw and Charlie to get near Zaira. What if they did something to harm her?

"You'll wait until I'm gone, then you'll ride my horse and head out the other way on the eastern road back to St. Louis."

"I won't take your horse."

"You have to. You'll ride as fast and hard as you can straight to Oscar's Pub."

"To Bellamy?"

"Aye. Bellamy might be annoying and arrogant, but he'll shelter you. I know he will."

A flicker of hope fanned inside Alannah. If Bellamy hid her, that would give her more time to figure something else out.

"Do you know how to get to Oscar's Pub?"

"I think I can find it."

"You'll need to stick to the alleyway behind the pub. There's a stable there where you can tie up my horse. Then you can go into Bellamy's studio."

"His studio?"

"'Tis a little storage shed behind the pub."

How did Zaira know so much? And what did she mean by studio? Now was neither the time nor the place to ask.

"I'll go to Bellamy," Alannah whispered. "But I don't want you to be riding out pretending to be me."

"I'll be fine." Zaira's response contained too much confidence. And perhaps a wee bit of naïveté. "It'll be a grand adventure."

Alannah wanted to argue further, but Zaira was already lowering a cloak out the window. "Here's mine. Now hand me yours."

Alannah managed to somehow shrug out of her garment. If someone was watching the window, the shadows of the slanted veranda roof would likely keep them from seeing the exchange. But she pushed hers swiftly toward the window anyway.

A moment later, Zaira spoke again. "As soon as I've been gone about five minutes, go to the barn. The coachman will have my horse waiting for you."

Alannah clutched Zaira's cloak, a fine light linen that wasn't as heavy as a winter coat but would provide covering for the cooler temperatures that had blown in with the rain. It was soft, almost velvety, and smelled of roses. Even though she couldn't see the color in the darkness, she knew it was a rich plum that contrasted Zaira's red hair.

Zaira was so pretty and sweet and innocent.

'Twas a bad idea to involve her, especially with how dangerous Shaw and Charlie were. "Zaira, wait."

Only silence came from the library.

"Zaira?" Alannah whispered louder.

After a moment with still no response, she sank back against the wall and closed her eyes. Zaira wasn't like most women, was more determined, more adventurous, and more cunning. Alannah suspected that even if she tried, Zaira wouldn't be swayed from this mission.

A hooded and cloaked figure raced past the veranda from the direction of the servants' entrance at the side of the house. As the person started across the backyard, Alannah held her breath. Wearing the ragged cloak and simple black skirt, Zaira looked like a poor maid, to be sure.

Alannah was tempted to call out and put a stop to the plan, but Zaira was hurrying too fast. All Alannah could do was wait.

After disappearing into the barn, Zaira rode out a few minutes later. She bobbled her reins, slipped down one side, and then led the horse the wrong direction before seeming to struggle to rein the horse the opposite way.

Zaira was not only a good writer, but she was also a good actress. Of course, Alannah wasn't quite so terrible on a horse, but Zaira was at least making her lack of experience believable.

As soon as Zaira disappeared from sight, Alannah counted the minutes. When at least five had elapsed, she crawled out from her hiding spot, sidled off the porch, and then darted toward the barn. She kept to the shadows, not wanting the moonlight to illuminate her if by chance anyone from the Farrell gang was staking out the place.

When she reached the barn, a horse stood just inside the entrance. The coachman was nowhere in sight, which meant Zaira had saddled both horses, likely because she'd wanted to keep their plans as secretive as possible, and probably because she didn't want the fellow to try to stop her from going.

Alannah hesitated a moment, then she hoisted herself up into the saddle. As she started out of the barn, her gaze settled on Kiernan's bedroom window at the back of the house. It was dark.

This was it. The last time she would see Oakland. The last time she'd have anything to do with the Shanahans.

"Good-bye, Kiernan," she whispered. "I thank you for everything you've done for me."

A lump pushed up into her throat. She would miss him. She couldn't deny that. In fact, she couldn't imagine she'd ever want another man again, not after getting to know Kiernan. No one else would be able take his place in her heart.

She slid her hand into her pocket and fingered the newest book he'd given to her. It had been lying on her pillow when she'd rushed up to don her cloak. The sight of it had brought tears to her eyes, especially at the realization that he'd placed it there after everything that had happened at the pond, after she'd turned down the match and walked away from him. He'd still been as kind and giving as always.

"Good-bye," she whispered again. "You're a wonderful man."

As several tears spilled over and slid down her cheeks, she urged her horse to move onward. Shaw and Charlie would learn soon enough that the woman riding south wasn't her and only a decoy.

She had to push herself hard, just as Zaira had instructed. She couldn't let the young woman's efforts and sacrifice be for nothing.

With a shake of the reins, the horse began to gallop. It moved past the house, circled around front, and then headed down the lane without Alannah having to do anything but hang on.

As she guided the creature onto the road and toward town,

she lifted two prayers heavenward—the first for Torin, that he was safe, and the second for Kiernan, that he wasn't in any trouble.

She hoped this time God would find favor with her and not let anything happen to the two men she loved.

24

Kiernan sat stiffly on the wagon bench. He didn't know if any Farrell gang members were closing in, but he was prepared, his revolver in hand and at the ready on his lap.

Donahue sat beside him, driving the wagon as it jostled over the rutted lane leading to Wayfair Cemetery, a graveyard where the poorest immigrants of St. Louis were buried. Kiernan had learned Donahue's brother's name was Dustin, and the fellow sat in the back, holding the casket steady.

Apparently, the archbishop of St. Louis had recently authorized the expansion of the graveyard into the nearby woodland and was no longer requiring burial payments from the very poor who could instead obtain a Poor Ticket that would allow for a free burial.

Located on the outskirts of the city, Wayfair Cemetery was the best cemetery for the plan—the only plan Kiernan had been able to devise in so short a time.

The carpenter in charge of making the brick molds had been able to rapidly construct the casket from one of the stacks of lumber that had survived the burning. After loading the casket into the back of the wagon, no one had questioned their hasty departure or the explanation that they were taking Torin to the graveyard and then going to the police to report the murder.

Kiernan glanced behind him at the man-sized wooden box Dustin was sitting against. As with the half a dozen other times Kiernan had wanted to open the lid and check on Torin, he refrained and instead surveyed the shadows of the thick forest that surrounded the cemetery.

He had to stay vigilant just in case the Farrell gang was still following them.

As the wagon came to a halt, Kiernan stood and raised his lantern. A chill raced up his spine as he took in the new unmarked graves. They went on endlessly, at least a hundred, if not two hundred freshly dug sites—likely all victims of cholera.

The recent report he'd read in the *Republican* indicated that over one hundred had died in the past week alone. He'd supposed the number to be an exaggeration, but if each of the many cemeteries in St. Louis looked like this one, then maybe the news was true.

If he hoped to prevent Torin from adding to the death tally, then he couldn't stand there gawking. He had to hurry.

"Look there." Donahue pointed to a mound beside the gravediggers' shed that bordered the older area of the cemetery.

Kiernan shifted his light and then almost recoiled at the sight that met him. The dead were stacked beside the shed, most wrapped in blankets but a few without, revealing pale, stiff corpses.

"Is this the brink of hell itself?" Kiernan whispered, unable to tear his gaze from the bodies piled so casually, as if the people hadn't mattered and their lives hadn't counted. Where was the dignity and respect they deserved, even in death?

"Heard the gravediggers died," Donahue spoke solemnly. "The superintendent of the cemetery had to hire boys to bury the dead, and still they can't keep up."

Kiernan lowered himself to the ground, his muscles tense with the need to do something more, anything, to help the poor people of St. Louis survive the disease that was killing so many. But what else could he do?

He'd thought the brickyard and the new tenement would provide fair wages and employment along with a safe place for young men to live. But his brickyard was in shambles. All his hard work, plans, and dreams meant nothing now.

Though the loss weighed heavily upon him, he didn't have the time to feel sorry for himself. He had to put into motion the rest of his plans for saving Torin.

Kiernan grabbed a shovel out of the wagon bed, then headed toward the graves, carrying the lantern with him and leaving the wagon shrouded in blackness. He surveyed the closest mounds, which weren't more than a foot apart. There wasn't enough room for a new grave nearby. They'd have to go farther out.

He didn't want to take the time to bury the casket, but if they didn't, they wouldn't be able to save Torin.

Without waiting for Donahue and Dustin, Kiernan wound his way through the graveyard. When he reached the back corner near the woods, he was relieved to find a hole that had already been partially dug. He set the lantern down and set to work shoveling out more dirt.

A few minutes later, Donahue and Dustin arrived, carrying the casket between them, two more shovels lying on top. They placed the casket on the ground carefully and then helped with the digging.

Less than five minutes later, they had a space big enough. It wasn't deep, but it would suffice. They lowered the casket, settled it into place, then shoveled the dirt back on top. Once it was completely covered and packed down, they bowed their heads for a moment of prayer. Then with shovels in hand, they returned to the wagon, Dustin sitting in the bed again and Donahue settling into place as the driver.

As the wagon rattled back down the lane, Kiernan kept his head bowed, hoping to look like a defeated man. It wasn't hard to do since the defeat was growing heavier with every passing moment. He'd let down all the workers depending on him. He hadn't kept them safe, certainly hadn't kept Torin from harm.

In addition, his effort to become a prosperous businessman like his da had been unsuccessful. In fact, not only had he failed, but he'd failed miserably. With the extent of the damage tonight, he'd likely lost too much at the brickyard to be able to recover. Even if he hadn't already been in financial difficulties from overextending his finances, the losses would be too widespread to overcome.

What would he do with a brickyard that lay in ruins? He could sell it to repay Liam for his investment in it. But who would want it? Not with so much needing to be repaired and rebuilt. And not when purchases had all but screeched to a standstill over recent days.

Was it finally time to admit he wasn't like his da? That no matter what Kiernan did, he'd never surpass his da? Even though Da had started with less, had known fewer people, and had faced more opposition, he'd driven himself and proven himself to be a man of power, ability, and savvy.

Kiernan couldn't begin to compare to that.

He pressed his lips together to keep from cursing himself for being such a failure. That's what he was, a failure. He couldn't even get the woman he loved to agree to marry him the way his da had his mam. Now that Torin was hurt—possibly even dying—his gut told him she'd be even less interested in a match.

"I think we're still being followed," Dustin said from the wagon bed.

Kiernan glanced behind them into the dark shadows of the night from the trees and shrubs on both sides of the road. He couldn't see anything, but he didn't want to take any chances. The Farrell gang had already proven they had no regard for his business, livelihood, or his workers. He wouldn't underestimate them again.

As he peered ahead at the winking of lights that revealed the outline of the city, he braced his shoulders. He'd failed at everything else, but he couldn't let himself fail at saving Torin.

25

Alannah crouched in the alley behind Oscar's Pub. The shed had been locked when she'd arrived a short while ago. With the pub still lit up and busy with patrons, she couldn't simply enter through the front entrance and ask for Bellamy.

As she'd tried to decide what to do next, the back door of the pub had opened, and Bellamy's sister, Jenny, had stepped outside to dump out a basin of slops. Alannah had quickly approached, given her name, and asked for Bellamy.

Now as she waited for the matchmaker, her pulse kept bolting at every sound. She didn't think anyone had followed her to town. But once Shaw and Charlie realized they'd been fooled, they might try to track her. She hoped they would give up the hunt, but she had to remain vigilant just in case they hadn't.

At a shout from down the alley and the thudding of running footsteps, she flattened herself against the shed's splintery wood.

If Bellamy didn't come soon, maybe she would return to

the stable where she'd tied the horse and find a dark corner to hide in.

The night sky was hazy, as it often was in the city with so much coal dust from the factories and steamboats. Even so, the air was fresher after the recent rain, the stench of sewage and garbage not as nauseating as she usually found it.

If only she were in Tralee, standing on the beach, listening to the waves. As she waited for the usual stab of homesickness in her chest, it didn't come. If anything, there was only a dull ache.

Was that what time away did? Or was she less homesick because of something—someone—else? The truth was, with each passing day, she longed less for her homeland and more for Kiernan. It was almost as if he had become her new home, that she was content as long as she could be near him.

She knew it couldn't be that way, that she had to resist those feelings—for his sake. Even so, she wished he were right beside her with his strong and steady presence. He would know what to do and how to get her out of the danger with Shaw. Not that she couldn't figure it out for herself, because she could. And Zaira was helping, so she wasn't alone.

It's just that Kiernan understood her like no one else ever had.

She pressed a hand to her pocket and the outline of the book he'd given her. Her heart swelled with an aching need for him. She could only pray again that he'd remained safe and that Torin had too.

The back door of the pub swung open, and Bellamy stepped outside. He held several bottles in each hand and carried them to a crate next to the rubbish bin. He deposited them, then stretched and started to cross the alley toward the shed.

She didn't realize she'd been holding her breath until he neared the shed door. Should she make her presence known yet?

He opened the shed, then stepped inside, leaving the door open a crack.

Without waiting for an invitation, Alannah pushed up and glanced down the alley both ways. Seeing no one, she sidled along the shed wall until she reached the door. As she slipped through into the dark interior, Bellamy was beside her in an instant and closing the door.

"What happened?" His voice was more anxious than she'd ever heard it before.

"The Farrell gang attacked the brickyard."

"Ach, tell me it isn't so."

"'Tis so, and I'm sorry it is."

He muttered through the clanking as he locked the door. A moment later, the striking of a match was followed by a small flame. He worked quickly to light a lantern and then turned to her.

"Kiernan rode out to the brickyard," she whispered. "And so did Mr. Shanahan."

Bellamy's brows were furrowed above his dark eyes. "And then someone from the gang tried to kidnap you?"

"Oh aye, Shaw himself."

"The devil."

"Zaira took my horse and cloak and rode out toward the brickyard, pretending to be me. And she sent me to town."

Bellamy released an exasperated breath. "That girl. She'll be the death of me yet."

Alannah could understand Bellamy's frustration with Zaira's recklessness because it mirrored her own. "She told me to find you and stay in your studio."

"Did she now?"

Alannah still didn't understand what Zaira had meant by *studio*, but from the crease in Bellamy's forehead, he obviously wasn't pleased with the pretty redhead.

"I'm sorry to impose, Bellamy." Alannah glanced around the shed for the first time. It was filled with shelves of supplies, casks of beer, and crates of other liquor. She wasn't sure what a *studio* looked like or what it was for, but the shed didn't appear any different than other storage units she'd been in. "Can I stay here until the morning?"

"You can come inside and upstairs to our living quarters."

"I'll not be putting anyone else in danger more than I already have."

He started to protest again, but then his jaw ticked. "Zaira. She's in danger, isn't she?"

Alannah tried to swallow the lump of fear that had lodged in her throat ever since Zaira had ridden away.

Bellamy didn't wait for her answer and began to fumble at the lock. "I'm going after her."

"Hopefully, no one bothered her, and she made it to the brickyard."

Bellamy was already opening the door. "Turn off the light and latch the door so that no one can get in. You'll be safe until I get back."

"I thank you, Bellamy."

He stepped out and closed the door. His rapid footsteps headed toward the stable.

Alannah locked the door, extinguished the lantern, then lowered herself to a crate.

A minute later, the clopping of a horse's hooves passed by the shed. The pace picked up into a gallop and a moment later faded into the distance.

Alannah released a tense breath, then settled in to wait. And to pray that no one would get injured. Surely God wouldn't allow any more bad to happen in her life, not after letting her suffer so much already. She'd had her lifetime quota. It was time for something good to happen for once.

◆ ◆ ◆ ◆ ◆ ◆ ◆

At a rattling of the door, Alannah jerked her head up, and her eyes flew open. She hadn't meant to doze, had tried to stay awake and prayerful. But as the minutes had passed and then an hour or more, her eyes had grown heavy.

The stress of the night had exhausted her more than she'd realized.

At a soft knock, Alannah stood and fumbled through the darkness to reach the door. The only person it could be was Bellamy. He had to be returning with news.

"Alannah?" came a woman's soft whisper. Zaira.

"Oh aye." Alannah unlocked the door, and Zaira pushed inside. "Whyever are you here? You didn't get into trouble now, too, did you?"

Zaira closed the door behind her. Then without answering, she stepped to Alannah and drew her into a hug.

Alannah could feel the young woman trembling. Her hair had come loose, and the hood was down. "What's wrong?"

Zaira just squeezed her tighter.

Unease prickled Alannah's spine. Had Zaira gotten into trouble with Shaw and Charlie? Maybe they'd harmed her. Or Bellamy.

Alannah pulled back. "Did they hurt you?"

In the dark, only Zaira's outline was visible, but it was enough to see the young woman shake her head. "No. I'm unharmed. Shaw and Charlie stopped me on the road to the brickyard, but when they realized I wasn't you, they let me go."

"Is Bellamy okay?"

"He's fine. I was already at the brickyard when he found me." Even with the positive news, Zaira's voice contained a grave note.

A vise wrapped around Alannah's throat. She couldn't keep from reaching out and gripping Zaira's hands. "Kiernan?" *Oh please, God above. Not Kiernan.* If something had happened to him . . .

"Kiernan had left for the city by the time Da and I got there."

"You're sure he's okay?"

"'Tis Torin—" Zaira's whisper broke on the edge of a sob.

Alannah's body stiffened for what she knew was to come.

"I'm sorry, Alannah," Zaira choked out the words. "Torin was killed."

Alannah could only picture her brother as he'd been earlier that day at the pond, his blue eyes wide behind his spectacles as he'd gazed between her and Kiernan. His kind eyes had pleaded with her to accept Kiernan. Had he known that he didn't have long to live? Maybe he'd wanted to make sure she was taken care of when he was gone.

Torin was gone.

He'd never walk up behind her and surprise her. He'd never give her one of his easy grins. He'd never wrap his arms around her in a hug.

Tears sprang into her eyes, and a sob clawed at her throat.

As Zaira pulled her close again, Alannah fell against the young woman and buried her face, letting the sorrow rise up and spill over. Although she wanted to rail and cry out, she let the cloak and Zaira's shoulder muffle her sobs.

It hadn't mattered how much she'd prayed or pleaded with God. He hadn't answered her and had taken the last of her family from her anyway.

26

The wagon rumbled to a stop at the rear of the Shanahans' St. Louis mansion. Kiernan was already bounding down from the seat before it came to a complete halt. He hurried to the back and climbed into the wagon bed.

His pulse thundered with dread as he tossed aside the few boards and tools Donahue and Dustin had placed over Torin's body. The brothers had used the few minutes of darkness to take him out of the casket while Kiernan had been searching for a grave site. Then they'd carried the empty casket to the grave.

If anyone had been watching, they would have seen Torin's casket being lowered into the ground and buried. And if anyone had followed them into the city, they would have seen an empty wagon bed, save for the shovels and an assortment of boards in a pile next to Dustin. Hopefully, they hadn't seen the body underneath that pile.

They'd halted two blocks from the doctor's house, and Dustin had set out on foot to secretly ask the doctor to come to the Shanahan home with all haste. Now Kiernan hoped they weren't too late to save Torin after so much time had elapsed.

He yanked back the cover to find Torin's pale face. His eyes were closed and his body motionless.

Was he dead?

Kiernan lifted a hand to Torin's mouth, and a soft exhale warmed his fingers.

Kiernan's shoulders deflated in relief. "He's alive."

Donahue was waiting at the end of the wagon bed. "Praise be."

"Grab his feet, and I'll hold his head." Kiernan was already lifting Torin's head as gently as he could.

As Kiernan crawled forward holding Torin's upper body, and Donahue moved slowly with Torin's legs, a light sprang to life in a window in the house.

Several moments later, Winston, their butler, opened the back door. The tall silver-haired man was attired in his usual black trousers and white dress shirt, which was untucked and only half buttoned. He wore his slippers and not his shoes. While he'd somehow managed to hastily don his clothing, he'd forgotten to take off his nightcap.

Winston hurried to the wagon and positioned himself at Torin's midsection, slipping his arms underneath and holding the body steady while Kiernan descended.

Silently they made their way through the house, up the main stairway, and down the hallway to the family bedchambers, to Kiernan's room.

The chamber was dark, and the mustiness of the room, having been closed off, greeted him along with the familiar waft of lemon oil used on the walnut furniture.

They carried Torin to the bed and laid him down. Winston lit the globe lantern on the bedside table, then moved to the lantern on the reading table near the hearth, flanked on both sides with wingback chairs.

Everything about the room was masculine and tasteful—

the light blue wallpaper patterned with gray and white vines and leaves, the large chest of drawers, and the elaborately carved headboard.

Kiernan didn't like knickknacks and had only one picture on the wall, a cityscape with the glass factory in the center. He'd had the portrait commissioned to remember his first step in what was to have been his long list of accomplishments. But now, with the damage and losses he'd incurred at the brickyard, maybe the glass factory would be his only accomplishment.

"How is he?" Donahue was watching Torin, his droopy face sagging more than usual.

Kiernan again tested Torin's mouth and nose. "Still breathing."

Winston started toward the door. "I'll heat some water, find some fresh bandages and ointment, and then we'll care for his wounds until the doctor arrives."

Kiernan wasn't an emotional man. But his chest constricted with gratitude for this old butler who'd served the Shanahan family so faithfully and was doing so again without any questions asked.

Donahue didn't linger for long. Kiernan sent him on his way so they didn't draw attention to a lone wagon parked at the house. Then Kiernan helped Winston with cleaning the wounds, and they were tending them when the doctor arrived.

The doctor set to work on Torin's deepest cuts, cauterizing some of the smaller ones and then using ligatures to close off two more serious spots of bleeding that had slowed but not stopped.

All the while he reassured Kiernan that none of Torin's internal organs had been hit—at least that he could assess.

The doctor also was confident Torin would live as long as none of the injuries became gangrenous.

Kiernan didn't have to explain much about the nature of the gang fight for the doctor to easily agree not to mention anything about Torin to anyone. The fellow likely guessed that if word got out that he'd helped save Torin, he would be putting his own life at risk.

As the doctor was finishing stitching one of the last gashes, the bedroom door opened, and Da stepped inside. With his face and clothing blackened with smoke and his hair a dusty gray from ashes, James Shanahan looked as though he'd spent the night fighting fires.

Had he gone out to the brickyard and helped?

"It's a mess." Da came farther into the room. "But we salvaged what we could."

Before Kiernan could think of a response, his da was staring at Torin on the bed, bandaged and bruised—and naked except for a sheet now covering the lower half of his body. "Who's this?"

"Alannah's brother."

Da's eyes rounded. "We were told he was dead and that you were taking him to the cemetery on your way back into the city."

"We did. As far as everyone else knows, he's dead and buried."

Da scanned Torin's motionless body.

With as much morphine as the doctor had administered for pain, Torin wouldn't waken for some time.

"'Tis a smart idea, Kiernan. But there's just one problem."

"There's no problem." He'd been thinking through all the options. "Once he's better, I have a plan."

"Oh aye, you haven't been considering Alannah in all this, have you?" Da's voice was grave, so grave that Kiernan's muscles tightened. When Da motioned to the hallway, Kiernan followed him out of the room, dread building inside him. He'd left Alannah safe and secure at Oakland. If something had happened to her . . .

"What about Alannah?" he demanded as he closed the bedroom door. Winston had lit one of the gilded sconces on the wall, and Kiernan could see the serious lines furrowing in his da's forehead.

"Shaw and one of his men came to Oakland looking for her not long after you rode off."

Kiernan's pulse pattered to a halt. That meant Shaw probably hadn't been at the brickyard when the gang had come to destroy it, or at least hadn't stayed long. What if he'd intended it to be a diversion so that when he arrived at Oakland, no one would be there to defend Alannah?

His heart picked up its pace again, this time slamming hard against his chest. "You didn't let them take her, did you?"

"Of course not. They searched the place and couldn't find her."

"Where did she go?" Kiernan felt as though he was standing on the edge of a precipice about to fall off with one wrong answer.

"Zaira helped to hide her. Then later, Zaira said she exchanged her cloak with Alannah's and rode down to the brickyard to distract Shaw."

"Did he hurt Zaira?"

"Thankfully, they didn't touch her."

Although Kiernan was grateful to his youngest sister for

her assistance, next time he saw her he intended to scold her for getting involved. He hated to think what might have happened if Shaw had realized Zaira's part in the deception.

"She sent Alannah away on her horse, though."

"What?" Kiernan began to fall, plunging down the precipice, with nothing to grab to stop him. "Where to?"

"She's at Bellamy's."

Kiernan snagged on to the words of hope and clung to them. "Then she's okay? Shaw hasn't found her?"

"Not that I'm aware of."

Kiernan spun on his heels and stalked down the hallway. He had to go to her, had to make sure she was safe. The pounding of his heart and the pounding of his blood reverberated through his body. His need for her was almost painful.

"Wait, Kiernan," his da called.

"I'm going to her." Kiernan wouldn't have been able to slow his steps, not even if someone had chained him.

"You should know something first."

Kiernan glanced over his shoulder.

"She probably thinks Torin is dead," his da finished. "That's what everyone at the brickyard believes. That's what we believed, and Zaira and Bellamy went to tell her."

Kiernan picked up his pace and started down the stairway, taking them two at a time. He had to get to her before Zaira and Bellamy did. He wanted to spare her some heartache, at least temporarily. Because in the long run, she would lose Torin anyway. There was no other choice.

27

Torin was dead. Alannah leaned her head on Zaira's shoulder. In the darkness of the shed, she couldn't see the young woman sitting beside her, but her presence was comforting nonetheless.

Even though Bellamy had offered to ride with Zaira back to Oakland, she had decided to remain with Alannah. Bellamy had also wanted the two of them to stay in the apartment above the pub for the night. But Alannah had insisted on keeping to the shed, not wanting to put Bellamy and his family in more danger than she was already bringing them.

Tears filled Alannah's eyes again, and she sniffled, trying to hold them back.

Zaira squeezed the hand she was clasping in her lap.

Alannah was thankful to have such a sweet friend at her side during this terrible time when all she could think about was that she'd lost everyone and everything. First Cagney and now Torin. And she had no job, no place to live, no money, no hope.

At a jerk on the door of the shed, she sat up stiffly. Beside her, Zaira straightened too.

Was it Shaw searching for her? The fellow had gotten Torin. Why wouldn't he leave her alone?

A knock resounded against the door. "Open up." The commanding but low voice belonged to Kiernan.

Alannah's heart sped, and she climbed to her feet at the same time as Zaira. The young woman was the first to reach the door, unlocking it and opening it before Alannah could completely process that Kiernan was here.

The darkness of the night shrouded him as well as Bellamy standing just beyond. But there was still enough light from the stars and moon to see the outline of Kiernan's strong frame.

"I need to speak with Alannah," he whispered. "Alone."

Zaira hesitated. "Alone isn't a good—"

"Go. Now." Kiernan ducked his head, then gentled his tone. "Please, Zaira?"

"Fine, but I'll be waiting just outside the door."

He didn't respond as his sister sidled past him. Instead, he entered the shed.

As he closed the door, Alannah felt his presence, as intense and overpowering as always. He was near enough that she could reach out and touch him if she wanted to.

And, oh saints above, she wanted to. She wanted his comfort, wanted his touch, wanted everything about him so she could lose herself with him and forget all her problems and the loneliness threatening to engulf her.

But she clenched her hands together to keep from using him so selfishly. She couldn't hold on to him, not when she had to let him go.

"Alannah," he started softly, apologetically.

That's why he'd come. To tell her about Torin. "I already know." Unbidden tears pricked her eyes again.

He glanced over his shoulder at the door, then took a step toward her, lessening the gap so that he was standing only inches away. "I have something to tell you." When he clasped her shoulders, she didn't pull away.

Instead, she finished closing the distance between them and pressed her body against his. The hard, brawny length of him was solid and sturdy—everything she needed in this moment.

He didn't hesitate and slipped his arms around her, wrapping her up in his embrace. The tenderness was in stark contrast to the magnitude of his power. And as she rested against him, she couldn't hold back her tears.

"It's alright," he whispered.

It was, at least now. All her problems seemed to fade away, and she felt as though she could face anything and do anything as long as she was with him.

He bent his head, and his lips brushed against her ear. "What I'm about to tell you has to stay a secret. From Zaira and even from Bellamy."

Something in his tone halted her tears.

"Promise me."

She nodded.

His lips moved to the center of her ear, and his soft breath sent tingles over her skin.

Desire rippled through her again. She wanted his kiss, wanted to feel his mouth on her ear and on her lips.

"Torin is alive." His whisper was so low, she almost wondered if she imagined it. "He's injured, but the doctor says he'll live."

"What?" She forgot to whisper and pulled back, her pulse jumping erratically.

He immediately tugged her back, his mouth against her ear again. "Shaw can't know. Everyone has to think Torin's dead."

For a moment, the words *he'll live* raced through her head, and relief so overwhelming filled her that she sagged against Kiernan, clinging to him, tears heating her eyes. Torin was alive, had somehow survived the attack. But how? Where was he? Could she see him?

She pushed back again, lifting her face and trying to study Kiernan. "What happened? How did you—"

He cut her off by dropping his mouth onto hers.

The touch was gentle and filled with warning not to say anything else. But it was also filled with something else . . . assurance and compassion and even love?

Whatever the kiss contained, she suddenly needed it more than she needed to breathe. She closed her eyes and pressed back. There was no gentleness in her kiss. It was hard and demanding all at once.

She lifted her arms around his neck, drawing him down, locking him in place, giving him no choice but to kiss her in return. This time not to silence her, but because there was no other place for him to go.

He half lifted her from the ground, as if he needed her even closer, couldn't get enough of her, wanted all of her. The heat of his mouth melded against hers with a hunger—even desperation—that hadn't been present for their first kiss.

This man. He didn't have to command her with words.

All he needed to do was kiss her and she was his, all of her heart and soul. She was utterly and completely his. There was nothing she wouldn't give him.

One of his hands slid up her back to her neck to her hair that had come loose long ago and that she hadn't bothered to bind, and he dug his fingers into the depths.

The kiss was as intense as he was, and she was dizzy with a tangible current drawing them together, as if they were made for each other and this moment was inevitable.

But it wasn't inevitable . . . ?

What was she doing? With all the trouble she'd already brought upon Kiernan, how could she let this exhilarating moment continue?

With fresh resolve, she pushed against his chest. She shoved hard even as she continued to kiss him, loathe to bring the kiss to an end, devouring him with the same extravagant kisses that he was giving her.

Finally, she gave a thrust that separated them, or at least wakened him to her attempts to bring the kiss to an end.

He halted and broke away, his labored breathing bathing her lips as if begging her for more.

She couldn't. She had to put an end to whatever was happening between them.

She released her hold around his neck and lowered her feet back to the shed floor. Her body felt like it had liquified, and her legs could hardly balance her weight. Her fingers wanted nothing more than to grasp his shirt into a fist and let him be her support.

But if she did so, how would she be able to leave him when the time came?

Drawing in a steadying breath, she took a step back

and then two, until she bumped into a crate. Even with the distance, the air between them was filled with energy that threatened to draw them together again.

She closed her eyes briefly, trying to rein in her emotions. "I'm sorry—"

"No apologies this time." His whisper was gruff, almost angry.

"But we can't—"

In one long stride he spanned the space between them, and his lips crashed into hers once more. He was like a ray of intense sunlight searing into her, burning her up, sending heat deep inside. She was instantly on fire, her protest scorched into ashes.

This time she couldn't hold back a small cry of pleasure, which he captured hungrily, as if it was the fuel he needed for life itself.

Before she could wrap her arms around him, he ended the kiss abruptly. "No more apologies," he whispered again.

She could only nod mutely, too lost to remember where she was and what was going on in the world around her. All that existed in that moment was Kiernan.

He stepped backward, latched on to the door, and then tossed it open.

Outside, Bellamy and Zaira stood nearby. She was staring at her shoes, toeing the gravel and twisting her hands in her skirt. Leaning against the shed, Bellamy just grinned, almost slyly, as if he'd planned the reunion himself.

It was obvious the two had heard the passionate kissing. And perhaps Zaira had been right to protest their being alone together.

Alannah almost sighed. It was too late to change what

had happened. But there couldn't be a next time. No more kisses with Kiernan.

She straightened her shoulders, glad the darkness of the night would hide her swollen lips and flushed face—at least she hoped it did.

Kiernan stepped out of the shed first, and she followed him. As he closed the door, he reached for the reins of his stallion that he'd left standing in the middle of the alley. "Alannah is going home with me." His whisper punctuated the uncomfortable silence.

Was he taking her to Torin? Alannah's heart thudded with a burst of hope. She could hardly believe her brother wasn't dead, and the need to see him flooded her—the need to find out for herself how he was faring.

When Kiernan reached for her hand and guided her to the horse, just the touch of his fingers against hers sent off an avalanche of desire.

"You can't," Zaira whispered, "not until you're married."

Did Zaira think she intended to sleep with Kiernan tonight? "Mind you, I have no intention of—of . . ."

Zaira was leveling a stern gaze at her brother. "Kiernan?"

He hoisted Alannah up to the saddle. "She'll stay in your room."

"And I'll be there too," Zaira spoke firmly.

"Da is there." Kiernan finished situating Alannah. "You have to go back to Oakland."

"But—"

"We don't want Shaw to suspect anything."

Zaira fell silent.

"I'll take Zaira home." Bellamy pushed away from the shed.

"I can go back on my own, Bellamy." Zaira glared at him. "I don't need a nursemaid again."

"Is that a fact?" Bellamy started toward the stable.

"Aye."

Bellamy threw a comment over his shoulder. "If you stopped acting like a wee child, maybe I would believe you."

Alannah could only watch the strange interaction between the two. Bellamy was normally a relaxed fellow. Why was Zaira able to ruffle him so easily?

Kiernan thrust his foot into the stirrup and climbed up behind Alannah. The moment he settled into the saddle with his body against hers, all coherent thought fled. When he reached around her for the reins, boxing her in, she had the urge to rest herself against his chest, lean her head on his shoulder, and bask in his closeness.

But she couldn't. She had to stay strong. Had to do this for Kiernan.

He gently began to tug up her hood, then leaned forward and whispered, "So that no one recognizes you."

"Oh aye."

His nose brushed her ear. "And so that I'm not tempted to kiss you again."

Tingles raced along her spine. Saints above. Just the mention of his kissing made her want to shift in the saddle and pull him down for another kiss. But she finished pulling up her hood and forced herself not to give in to the need to fall against him.

Thankfully, the ride to the Shanahan home on Third Street wasn't long, even though Kiernan explained that he was going a roundabout route through the side streets that were deserted at the late hour, so that hopefully no one would see them.

When they arrived at the back door, Kiernan dismounted first, then helped her down. As he situated his hands on her waist, her blood began to hum with warmth, especially because she felt the pressure of his fingers as if he were touching her skin without her wearing anything at all.

She didn't want to envision herself in such a state with Kiernan. It was lustful and wanton and shameless of her. If a few simple kisses could turn her head so quickly, she had to be more careful.

The back door opened to reveal an older servant. Kiernan introduced him as Winston the butler. As Winston ushered her inside, she was once again loathe to leave Kiernan's side, but he didn't follow and instead guided his horse toward the coach house.

Winston led her quietly through the Shanahan home. With each new room they passed, she was in awe of the grandeur. Although Oakland was spacious and elegant, the city home had clearly been built to impress and entertain guests.

As Alannah started up the grand marble staircase, Kiernan's list of requirements for a wife pushed to the forefront of her mind. He wanted a well-bred, poised, and polished woman who could manage a home like this and who would be able to impress and entertain his important friends.

The truth was, she fell completely short of his standards and would never be comfortable overseeing a large household. In fact, she shouldn't be trailing after Winston as if she were a gentlewoman. She ought to be using the servants' staircase and offering to help him since he was her superior.

The old proverb said it best: Put silk on a goat, and it is still a goat.

She didn't belong here in the Shanahan mansion, and she

couldn't stay in Zaira's room as if she were one of the family. Maybe she would suggest remaining with Torin and taking care of him until he was healed.

When Winston stopped at one of the family chambers, he opened the door for her and then waved for her to precede him into the room. She hesitated a moment until her gaze landed on the unmoving form of Torin on the bed.

Right now, nothing else mattered except seeing her brother and making sure he survived. She would have time later to sort out everything else.

28

Kiernan sat by Torin's bedside, elbows on his knees, head bent.

He'd been praying for God to show mercy on the young man. But the fever had been taking its toll—a fever from one of the wounds that had become infected. For the past three days, Torin had wavered in and out of consciousness. No matter what anyone had done, he'd slipped further into delirium.

Alannah kept a vigil over Torin, sleeping in the chair and tending to him day and night. Finally last night, Kiernan had threatened to pick her up and carry her away. Only then had she gone to Zaira's room and slept in the bed.

She'd been asleep for over twelve hours, and Kiernan didn't intend to wake her, not unless Torin worsened significantly.

Kiernan whispered another prayer, this one for Alannah, that she wouldn't blame herself as she'd been doing the past few days. She wouldn't have been able to stop Shaw, even if she'd handed herself over. The gang leader had made that clear enough by coming after her even though he'd tried to have Torin murdered.

At least Shaw didn't know Alannah was staying with him here at the house. Kiernan had done his best to go on with his life as normal, heading out to the brickyard every day, overseeing the cleanup, and meeting with his accountant about his options.

The only option he had was the one thing he hadn't wanted to do—sell his glass factory. He would have to take whatever he could get and then invest it into the brickyard. Even then, it was doubtful the brickyard could ever be successful the way he'd hoped.

The fixing and rebuilding would take time. Even if they got everything back in working order soon, how would they be able to sell enough bricks to compensate for the losses? Especially with most businesses in St. Louis remaining at a halt.

Kiernan had tried to figure out how to salvage the predicament, but he always seemed to arrive at one conclusion—he'd failed. He'd been too ambitious, hoping he could make a name for himself and make his da proud. But he would end up looking like a fool instead.

With a sigh, he sat back in the chair. Morning light filtered in from the slit between the curtains. He would need to go soon.

At a rustling from the bed, Kiernan stood and reached for the glass of water. He started to bend over Torin to encourage him to drink only to find the fellow's eyes wide open and staring up at him.

Without his spectacles, Torin's eyes were more visible.

They seemed clear and lucid, the glassiness from the past few days gone. His face was pale and scruffy from the lack of shaving. A deep gash on one cheek with the sutures was a ghastly purple, and the skin under an eye was bruised a faint black.

"Mr. Shanahan?" Torin croaked the words as he gazed around at the bedroom.

"Kiernan. Call me Kiernan." He placed the glass back on the bedside table and rested a hand on Torin's forehead. The skin was clammy to the touch, slightly damp, but the heat was gone. Had the fever broken?

"Where am I?" Torin tried to lift his head, winced, then ceased his efforts, no doubt from the pain since the wound in his shoulder had been one of the deeper stabs, likely intended to hit his heart.

"You're at my family's house in the city." Kiernan reached for the glass again and brought it to Torin's lips. "Take a drink." He gently held up Torin's head while he drank.

Torin managed a few sips before he laid his head back. "How long have I been here?"

"This is the morning of the third day."

"Alannah? Is she safe?"

"Shaw tried to get her, but we're hiding her here too." Kiernan set the glass aside, then towered above Torin. Should he go after Alannah and let her know Torin had awoken? She would want to hear the good news. At the same time, he wanted her to sleep as long as possible.

Torin tried to push up again and this time made it to his elbows. "You need to marry her. It's the best way to keep Shaw from having her, and you know it."

Kiernan nodded. He'd had plenty of time to think about

not only what Torin needed to do, but also how to keep Alannah safe. And marrying her was still his goal.

"You love her, don't you?" Torin's voice was weak and gravelly.

"You should go back to sleep."

"I need to know."

Kiernan sat back down. That night when he'd learned Shaw had almost kidnapped her, he'd been tortured the whole time he'd ridden to Oscar's Pub, needing to see her and hold her and know for certain that she'd survived.

When he stepped into the shed, he had no doubt he loved her. He just hoped that he'd get to spend the rest of his life showing her how much he cared about her.

His whole heart, soul, and body burned for her in an almost painful way. He couldn't fathom losing her, and the possibility of Shaw going after her again nearly killed him.

"Aye, I love her," he whispered. "She's my whole world, and I don't want or need anything but her."

Torin's body seemed to relax. "Send for a priest and marry her now."

Kiernan hadn't brought up marriage to her over the past few days, although he'd wanted to. She'd been too worried about Torin. But even if Torin had been well, Kiernan had sensed her pulling away from him, almost as if she was preparing to reject him again. He wasn't sure his heart could withstand another crushing blow from her.

"Please?" Torin's voice dropped to a pleading whisper.

Kiernan met the young man's gaze. "I would if she'd let me."

"You can convince her. Oh aye, tell her what you just told me."

Even if she'd already made up her mind not to marry him, Kiernan could do nothing less than try to keep winning her.

Torin pushed up from his elbows until he was sitting. His face was etched with pain, and he pursed his lips together. "I have to be going. If Shaw hasn't already figured out I'm here, he will soon enough."

"Don't worry." Kiernan pressed Torin's uninjured shoulder to keep him in bed. "Everyone thinks you're dead."

Torin ceased his efforts to get up. And for a few minutes, Kiernan explained their rescue efforts that night of the attack at the brickyard.

"Besides my da and the doctor, Donahue and Dustin are the only two workers who know you lived."

Torin was silent a moment, probably trying to comprehend everything. "Do you really think the Farrell gang believes I'm dead?"

"Either way, after you recover, you have to leave St. Louis."

"I'll go as soon as I'm able to get out of bed."

"You need to move to California."

Torin didn't immediately protest the idea.

Kiernan took some hope from that and decided to share more of his plan. "You'll leave on one of Captain O'Brien's steamboats. My brother-in-law will hide you so that no other passengers see you. When you reach New Orleans, he'll find passage for you on a steamboat bound for California."

"I can go overland—"

"No. It's too late in the year to start the trip by land. Then you'll have to winter in Independence, and that's too risky. Too many people from St. Louis end up there."

Before they could discuss the matter further, the bedroom

door opened, and Alannah stepped inside. She was still attired in her simple maid's uniform but without the apron or cap. He'd told her she could wear anything in Zaira's closet, but she was obviously still refusing.

Even so, she'd never looked more beautiful with her sleepy eyes and flushed cheeks. Her fair hair was brushed back and tamed in a simple braid that now hung over her shoulder.

As she took in Torin, she released a cry and then raced across the room. She looked as though she wanted to fling herself across him and draw him into a hug, but she stopped short at the edge of the bed, her eyes glassy with unshed tears. "You're awake."

"You couldn't get rid of me that easily." Torin attempted a grin and held up a hand.

As she lowered herself to the edge of the bed, she took his hand and pressed a kiss to the back of it, her tears spilling over and sliding down her cheeks. "Don't you ever be scaring me like that again, do you hear me?"

"I'll try not to." Torin's eyes brimmed with so much love for his sister that an ache formed in Kiernan's chest. Maybe someday Torin would be able to come back to St. Louis and be with Alannah if he changed his appearance and name. Even then he'd always risk discovery and danger.

Kiernan left the two to converse while he went into the guest room where he'd been staying. He changed into fresh clothing and groomed with Winston hovering nearby. Then Kiernan stepped back into the sick room, tugging at his cuffs.

He glanced up in time to see Alannah watching him, her eyes wide upon him with admiration. And desire. The blue of her eyes was like a deep pond beckoning him to dive in and lose himself there.

His muscles hardened with the need to cross to her, pick her up, kiss her, and forget about everything else in his life.

As though reading his thoughts, her lips parted slightly.

What he wouldn't give to be able to trace her mouth and that seductive dip of her upper lip. She was truly the most beautiful woman he'd ever met, the most beautiful in all of St. Louis, and he wanted her to be his without question and without any more hesitation.

Her gaze dropped to her hands in her lap, her fingers laced tightly together, as though she was refraining from her need to touch him.

"Oh aye," Torin said with a weak laugh. "We'll be needing the priest today, so we will."

Kiernan tore his attention from Alannah to find Torin watching them, his mouth tilted up in a wide grin.

Alannah didn't respond except to lift a brow in question.

"I want you to be marrying Kiernan," Torin explained. "Before I leave for California."

"California?"

"Kiernan's worked out the details for me to go away. But I won't be doing it until I know you're married and situated."

Alannah stared at her brother for several long heartbeats.

Kiernan stiffened as he waited for her response, but even as he braced himself for the worst, he prayed for the best.

"I'll be going with you, Torin," she said. "I'd surely like California better than St. Louis."

The hope Kiernan had been grasping started to slip away.

Torin reached for her hand and clasped it between his. "I want you to marry Kiernan. He'll give you a life I won't be able to, a stable home, safety, and happiness."

She pulled away from her brother, stood, and braced her

hands on her hips. "You'll not be planning my life for me, Torin Darragh. I'm old enough to figure it out for myself, so I am."

"Blast." Torin scowled up at her. "Kiernan loves you and wants to marry you. Don't you be throwing that away on account of your stubbornness."

Alannah's gaze shot to Kiernan's, her eyes full of questions. He hadn't declared his love to her yet, hadn't known when the right time was, hadn't wanted to scare her.

But now that she knew, he had to say something. His mind scrambled for an explanation, but at the lines beginning to crease her forehead and the panic filling her eyes, he had the sense that he was losing her again, perhaps losing her for good.

Before he could say anything, she spun and began to cross the room to the door.

He had to talk to her. She was attracted to him. That was obvious. And she enjoyed kissing him. There was no doubt about that. Maybe she didn't love him yet, but with time, he could earn her love, couldn't he?

As she exited and closed the door, he finally bolted into action. He raced across the room, threw open the door, and stepped into the hallway to find that she was already nearing the door to Zaira's room.

"Wait, Alannah."

She didn't listen and instead seemed to hasten even more. He lunged for her, and as she opened the door, he grabbed her by the arm and swung her back around.

"I love you." The words spilled out before he could stop them.

She hung her head. "Don't say it, Kiernan. Please."

"Why? It's the truth."

"It doesn't matter. It can't lead anywhere."

"I know you feel something too."

She hesitated.

He could pull her into his arms and kiss her to make his point. His dreams had been filled with visions of kissing her again, and so had his waking moments, if he was being honest with himself.

But could he really use a kiss to win her? Wouldn't that be the same as seducing or manipulating her into doing his bidding?

He released his hold of her arm. "I want you to be mine, Alannah. But I won't force you to be with me."

She kept her head bowed and her hand on the doorknob but didn't move. "I knew at Oakland I didn't belong in your world," she said softly. "But now after staying here in your city home, I'm understanding more completely that I'll never belong in your world. In your life."

"That's not true—"

She tugged at her black skirt. "I'm a maid, not the lady of the house. I'll not be pretending otherwise."

"I don't care about that."

"You deserve a woman who meets your list of requirements. And someday you'll thank me for keeping you from making a mistake and marrying me."

With that, she slipped into Zaira's room and shut the door, leaving him alone in the hallway.

He stared at the dark wood paneling and lifted a fist to pound against it but then stopped himself.

He'd failed again. This time at love. And all because of that stupid list he'd given Bellamy.

Digging his hand into his inner coat pocket, he retrieved the book he'd purchased for Alannah yesterday. He bent and placed it against the door so she wouldn't miss it when she came back out. Then he turned and forced himself to walk away.

29

Alannah's heart ached as she listened to Torin talk about California and the possibilities that awaited him there.

She was thrilled he was alive and was getting stronger. The doctor had come by at midday, examined his wounds, and had assured Alannah that her brother had gone through the worst and the healing would get easier now. He'd even gotten out of bed a couple of times throughout the day.

Yet as happy as she was that his fever had vanished and that he was mending, the turmoil inside her was only getting worse.

"Who knows?" he said from where he was propped up against the headboard by half a dozen pillows. He'd cast off his sheet since the room was stuffy with the heat of the summer day, with only a low breeze laden with the suffocating scents of the city. "I might even give gold mining a try. Wouldn't that be something if I found gold?"

"Oh aye, that would be something, to be sure." She sat in

the chair beside the bed, a pair of his socks in hand as she mended the holes caused by his toes and heels.

Torin paused. "Don't sound so excited for me."

"I am excited. For *us*."

"For *me*." Torin's tone was firm.

She lowered the sock and needle and thread and met Torin's gaze, the bruises and cuts on his face a constant reminder of how close she'd come to losing him. "I meant what I said this morn. I'm going with you. You're the only family I have left, and I want us to stay together."

"Kiernan wants to be your family now too."

"He can't be!"

"Whyever not?"

She stood quickly, dumping her sewing supplies to the floor. "I don't need to explain anything to you."

Torin was watching her through narrowed eyes behind his spectacles—a new pair that Kiernan had purchased. "You don't have to explain." Torin's voice was clipped. "I already know you love him, too, but you're scared to lose him."

She released a scoffing laugh but then bit it back as the reality of Torin's words hit her. Was that what it was? Was she resistant to loving Kiernan because she'd lost so many people she loved and now was afraid of losing him too?

"I admit I am scared. But can you blame me? I almost just lost you."

"But you didn't. Here I am, thanks to Kiernan."

"Aye, it's a good thing Kiernan was there. God must like him better than me."

"That's the most ridiculous thing you could say."

"'Tis not."

"Oh aye, it's a bunch of—dung."

"Then why did God take Mam and Da and Cagney—everyone I loved?" Her voice cracked, and she cleared her throat. "And He would have taken you, if not for Kiernan."

Torin still wore a scowl. "We human beings make our own mistakes and cause our own problems through our own hate and selfishness. We cannot be blaming the problems we create on God."

"What mistake did Cagney make to die on the ship? It wasn't his fault."

"We all know the British could be doing more to provide relief and employment." Torin's voice was as bitter as always when he talked about the British who had discriminated against the Irish Catholics for years, preventing them from owning land or even going into trades. "If our princely overseers were showing more compassion, maybe things wouldn't have gotten so bad. Maybe we wouldn't have had to leave. Then maybe Cagney wouldn't have died."

"Maybe . . ."

Torin sighed. "Listen, I take responsibility for my mistake in getting involved in a gang when I first came to St. Louis. I brought the problems on us. I only have myself to blame. Not God."

As usual, Torin was correct. They existed in a sin-filled world with imperfect people who made poor choices, lived selfishly, and sometimes hurt others. So maybe she hadn't been fair to accuse God of problems human beings had created.

"The way I see it," Torin continued, "God could turn His nose up at us for all the times we think we know best and go our own way. But He doesn't. Instead, He's there offering to help clean up our problems and walk with us through them."

She knew something about going her own way. She'd done her share of that.

With a groan, she buried her face in her hands. "I know you're right. But why do I feel as if God is always so distant, that He's punishing me by not answering my prayers?"

Torin sat forward and patted her shoulder. "Maybe you're expecting God to answer your prayers the way *you* think He should when He's actually answering the way *He* knows is best."

Was it possible she'd been viewing God wrong because of her own anger and grief? Not just with the cause of the problems but in His answers to them? What if she'd been the distant one, and He'd been there all along?

Her heart swelled with the longing to let Him walk with her through her problems instead of pushing Him away. Could she do it even now? As she tried to sort out what to do next?

Torin's voice turned gravelly again. "I felt God near to me the past few days because of you and Kiernan. Thank you for being here."

She lifted her head and met his gaze. This dear brother who'd made mistakes and faced hardships was perhaps growing through them, would hopefully be stronger because of them.

"But now," Torin continued, situating himself against his pillows, "it's time for me to move on, to start over someplace new, and hopefully not make the same mistakes again."

She reached for his hand and squeezed it. "You won't."

"And you have to stop making the same mistakes too." His tone was gentle. "Stop being afraid to love Kiernan."

She clasped his hand harder, as if she could cling to him and never let him go. "It's more than just being afraid to love him." Although she was sure that was a big part of it.

"I realize you don't think you can be what he needs in a wife. But I know you, so I do. And you are more than enough for Kiernan."

More than enough? Was she really? A part of her knew that even though Kiernan had created the list, he could change his mind about what he wanted in a wife. Maybe their relationship had helped him grow and learn to see life a different way.

Torin smiled. "I think Bellamy saw that Kiernan needed someone exactly like you—someone who accepts and admires him for who he is inside and not for what he accomplishes."

Oh aye, she admired him for the man he was inside more than anything else. She'd rejected him again that morning in the hallway when he told her he loved her and wanted her to marry him. And, like past rejections, he'd still given her another new book.

"He's a good man," she whispered.

"I agree." Torin fell silent for several heartbeats. "That's why you would make me very happy if you would marry him before I leave for California."

Could she really consider the option?

"It would put my mind at ease, knowing you're wed to a man who adores you."

"He doesn't adore me."

"Oh aye, he does. Whyever do you think he went to so much trouble to save me?"

"He would have helped you regardless of me."

Torin gave a one-shouldered shrug. "So you'll marry him?"

"You're sure you don't want me to move to California with you?"

"No, lass. Your life is here, with Kiernan." The steadiness and certainty in the depths of Torin's eyes assured her that he'd be okay without her, as long as he knew that she was happy.

A sudden keen longing swelled inside her. She would be happy with Kiernan, of that she had no doubt. But how would she ever adjust to the life he led?

She didn't know how she would ever fit into his world. But the truth was, she loved him too much not to try.

At a knock on the bedroom door, she shot out of her chair and fidgeted with her hair, twisting a loose strand back on one side and then smoothing the rest.

Torin chuckled. "You're more than in love with him. You're crazy in love."

She scowled at Torin over her shoulder as she approached the door. "Hush now." Straightening her shoulders, she swung the door open wide, her heart pattering hard. What would Kiernan say now?

An unfamiliar man stood in the hallway, middle-aged and rotund, with a mustache and one drooping eye. He tipped the brim of his cap at her, then peered past her.

She stepped into the hallway and snapped the door closed, hoping he hadn't already caught sight of Torin.

Even if Torin wasn't fully healed, maybe the sooner he left town the better. It would be difficult to keep his presence a secret at the house for much longer, especially if any of the other Shanahan family came to visit. Thankfully this week, except for Kiernan's da, everyone was gone.

The fellow took a step back. "Mr. Shanahan said Torin wanted to see me."

"Torin is dead." Had Winston let this fellow in the house, and if so, why?

"Who is it?" Torin called. "Is it Donahue?"

The rotund man nodded vigorously and leaned toward the door. "It's me, boss."

"Let him in, Alannah. He's the one who brought me here from the brickyard and knows everything."

Alannah hesitated. She'd learned that the brothers who helped Torin with the kiln had defended him and quite possibly saved his life by tending to his stab wounds so quickly after the attack. They'd also helped Kiernan stage the burial at the cemetery.

This man deserved her gratitude.

"Donahue?" she spoke tentatively as she opened the door for him. "I thank you for all you did to save my brother."

Torin interrupted before Donahue could answer. "He'll be saving more than just me if we can get some things figured out."

As Donahue slipped past her and into the room, she shot Torin a narrowed gaze. "You'll not be overexerting yourself."

In the big bed, Torin still looked frail and weak, but already his energy was increasing. And his determination.

As she closed the door on the two men, she let her fingers graze the book in her pocket, unable to stop the flutter in her stomach at the prospect of letting herself dream about a life with Kiernan. Was that really possible? Could she give herself permission to consider a match with him?

She wasn't sure. But maybe it was finally time to get serious about the matchmaker's wager and trust his choice for her.

30

Nothing at Oakland was the same without Alannah.

Kiernan reclined on the blanket and peered up at the stars, the trill of the crickets his only company. He shouldn't have come out, should have stayed in his bedroom. But he'd ventured to the field anyway, hoping to think, hoping to find peace, hoping to figure out what to do next.

The lantern light glowed on the book he'd brought to read. But he hadn't opened it and hadn't enjoyed the beauty.

He'd thought staying away from Alannah would help him gain perspective and figure out what to do next. So he'd returned to Oakland three days ago. Instead of the distance helping, he was growing more restless, and the ache inside his chest was sharpening.

Should he ride to town and talk to her again? But what could he voice that he hadn't already said? He'd told her he loved her, wanted to be with her, and that nothing else mattered. If he manipulated her into being with him, she'd only come to resent him and their marriage. And he didn't want that.

No, she needed to want the match as much as he did, or it wouldn't work.

Besides, he figured if he stayed at Oakland, he'd draw less suspicion to the city house. Not that the Farrell gang was suspicious. Like everyone else, they believed that Torin was buried in Wayfair Cemetery. Besides, they were too busy dealing with the charges of vandalism and arson to his brickyard as well as the charge of murder.

Of course, he hadn't been able to press charges against Shaw specifically, since no one had seen him at the brickyard the night of the attack. But the investigator Kiernan had hired was compiling evidence that Shaw had been behind everything. It would only be a matter of time before the gang leader was arrested.

Regardless, Kiernan didn't want to take any chances that Shaw would learn where Alannah was staying, at least not until after the man was safely behind prison bars.

As much as Kiernan hated to admit it, if she refused to marry him, then maybe she would be the safest going to California with her brother. There she could take on a new name and identity, and she'd be far, far away from the Farrell gang.

He closed his eyes against a sudden rush of pain in his chest at the prospect of her leaving and not being able to see her ever again. He couldn't bear it.

"I see you can't stay away from Alannah's and your secret meeting place."

His eyes flew open to find Zaira smiling down at him.

She was wearing a nightgown and wrapped up in a robe. Her single red braid fell over her shoulder, making her look younger than her nineteen years. But she'd proven herself to be a mature and capable woman this past week in her quick thinking, daring deeds, and compassion for Alannah.

He'd been tempted a time or two to tell her about Torin still being alive, but already too many people knew, and he didn't want to risk anything, not until Torin was out of the city.

He'd learned that Enya's husband, Sullivan, was due back in St. Louis any day. Until he arrived, there was still time for Alannah to change her mind. And if she didn't, would he be able to let her go with Torin?

He wasn't sure he could.

Zaira's smile faded. "Sorry I'm not Alannah. I didn't mean to disappoint you."

Were his emotions that readable? Kiernan pushed himself up until he was sitting, then patted the spot beside him. "Join me."

She hesitated a moment before she lowered herself. She tucked her legs up and wrapped her arms around them, staring into the distance at the dark woodland that bordered the meadow.

"Don't worry." Zaira bumped his shoulder with hers. "You'll be able to sit here again with Alannah someday soon."

He'd explained to his family that he was keeping Alannah at the city house in order to hide her. He hadn't told them she'd rejected him again and wouldn't be coming back. He could at least admit it to Zaira, couldn't he?

He released a tight breath. "Alannah doesn't want me, Zaira."

She snorted a laugh. "Oh please. I was there when you kissed in the shed. And Alannah wants you as much as you do her."

"I'd hoped to make the announcement of our match tomorrow at Liam and Shelia's engagement party. But before returning to Oakland this week, I asked her to marry me. She said no."

"How did you do it?"

"Do what?"

"Propose."

He furrowed his brows. "What difference does it make?"

This time Zaira released a full laugh. "It makes a big difference, silly. You have to show her she's more important than anything else, that you'll sacrifice everything for her, and that you'll go to the ends of the earth to be with her." She sighed blissfully.

Kiernan slanted her a look. "You've clearly been reading too many romance novels."

With a quick shrug, her lips turned up into one of her impish smiles.

Even if Zaira was being overly romantic, what if there was more he could do?

The honest truth was that he would do *anything* and sacrifice *everything* to be with Alannah.

He sat up straighter. What if he really did sacrifice everything to go to the ends of the earth with her? He'd already started the process of selling his glass factory. And with the loss of his business, he'd proven that he didn't have what it took to become a savvy and prosperous businessman like Da.

It was time to admit he'd failed in his ventures. He wouldn't live up to his da's reputation and wouldn't make the Shanahan name successful in his own right.

His mind began to spin. He'd sell his portion of the brickyard to Liam, give him full ownership. He'd take any profits that were left after helping with the repairs and follow Torin and Alannah to California. He'd wait for Alannah to be ready for a relationship with him. He'd spend his life waiting if need be. And when she was finally willing to have him, he'd be there.

He scrambled to his feet. "I have to get her a message as soon as possible." Did he dare visit her tonight and tell her not to leave St. Louis with Torin, not until he had the chance to get his affairs in order?

Zaira stood. "I'm going into the city tomorrow morning. I can deliver a message to her."

He started to shake his head, needing to see Alannah and speak forthrightly for himself. But he stopped himself. With how he'd failed to convince her so far, maybe he had to prove himself first. "All right. I'll give you a note to deliver."

He smiled wryly. He'd been wondering why Bellamy had given Alannah his list of requirements for a wife that day at the pond. He'd been frustrated that Bellamy hadn't just destroyed it.

Now he knew why the wily matchmaker hadn't. Bellamy had saved it to spur Kiernan into confessing what he really needed—a new list of requirements for a wife.

It was time to do what Bellamy had wanted all along.

31

Alannah paced the length of Zaira's bedroom. With its lovely white furniture and soft yellow and white linens, the room was summery and bright and cheerful—just like Zaira's room at Oakland. Even so, Alannah felt trapped, and her heart was knocking against her chest with a need that was keenly desperate.

Kiernan hadn't returned to the city since the day earlier in the week when she'd rejected him. The longer he was gone, the more frantic she was becoming to tell him she was sorry for pushing him away. In fact, she wanted to see him so badly that today she'd even considered riding out to Oakland.

But she'd pushed aside the possibility because she couldn't risk Shaw finding out she was staying at the Shanahans' city home. If he came looking for her here, he'd find Torin and finish killing him.

After almost a week since the attack at the brickyard, Torin was walking around and getting restless. Donahue was visiting him again and had brought several pieces of machinery that they were working on together in Kiernan's bedroom.

Torin didn't need her tending to him anymore. And Winston shooed her away every time she tried to help him with the chores.

Of course, she'd had plenty of time to read the newest book Kiernan had given to her. But this time, reading hadn't brought her the usual satisfaction. She sensed that nothing would satisfy her until she had the opportunity to talk with Kiernan again.

"Alannah?" came a womanly voice outside the bedroom door. "'Tis me, Zaira."

Alannah raced to the door and threw it open, not caring that Zaira might discover Torin was alive and staying in Kiernan's bedroom just down the hallway. Alannah needed a friend, and Zaira had become one in spite of their social differences.

Zaira, as usual, looked windblown and flushed but radiant. In a riding gown of pale green, she had her hair tucked away under a matching bonnet with a wide brim and a large ribbon tied underneath her chin.

Before Alannah could brace herself, Zaira threw her arms around her, hugging her tightly.

Alannah couldn't hold back a laugh of surprise at the enthusiasm.

The young woman smelled of sunshine and wildflowers and brought with her the warmth of the late afternoon.

"I'm so happy to see you." Zaira pulled back, smiling widely.

"Oh aye, I'm happy to see you more."

"You'll be even happier when you see what I've brought you." Zaira's smile turned smug.

"What have you brought?" Another manuscript to edit perhaps?

Zaira closed the door behind her, then snapped open her reticule and dug through it. After several seconds, she pulled out a folded paper and held it out. "From Kiernan."

From Kiernan? Alannah's heart began to pound irregularly. A part of her wanted to grab it and rip it open. But another part was too afraid to find out that he was giving her what she'd said she wanted and was now telling her farewell.

"'Tis a good note, Alannah." Zaira squeezed her hand gently. "He isn't letting you go, so you may as well accept that you're stuck with him. With all of us."

Rapid tears stung Alannah's eyes. "Really?" She could hardly force the word out.

"Really." Zaira motioned toward the sheet. "Now read it."

Alannah unfolded the note, unable to control the shaking of her fingers. As she spread it open, her eyes took in the title: *Qualities Needed in a Wife.*

The list was numbered from one to twelve just as it had been previously. But next to each number was the same thing: *She has to be Alannah, the woman I love.*

At the bottom of the sheet was another short sentence: *I'm going to California with you because nothing else means as much as you.*

Overwhelming relief weakened her knees, and she grasped the chest of drawers beside her to keep from crumpling.

Kiernan still loved and wanted her.

In fact, he was willing to sacrifice everything for her,

including giving up his businesses and aspirations in St. Louis to travel west with her.

What kind of man would do that? It was beyond anything she'd ever believed possible, a love like she'd never known.

Kiernan Shanahan was a man worth keeping forever. He'd proven that to her already in so many small ways. Now with his willingness to sacrifice so much to be with her—his family, his wealth, his businesses, his plans—how could she doubt how much he loved her?

And how could she let him give it all up? She couldn't. She didn't belong in the West with Torin. She belonged here in St. Louis with Kiernan. Even if a part of her heart would always be in Tralee and Ireland, she had a new home now, and that was with Kiernan.

The pressure in her chest swelled. Torin had been right. She couldn't push Kiernan away any longer out of her fear of losing people she loved. There would be losses and hardships because of the brokenness of their world. But she couldn't forget that God was walking with her through them and would be with Kiernan and her no matter what they faced. They would have a wise and loving Companion for their journey ahead.

Was it possible she could find a way to show Kiernan how much she loved him, just like he'd shown her?

But what could she do? She glanced at Zaira to find the young woman was waiting expectantly. "I love him too."

Zaira smiled. "I know."

"Ach, I need to be showing him how much. But what can I do?"

Zaira's smile widened. "I have an idea." She stalked toward the closet and opened the door to reveal a dozen lovely gowns, the ones Kiernan had encouraged Alannah to wear but she hadn't been able to bring herself to do so.

She'd already felt strange using the beautiful room, much less wearing such fine clothing.

Zaira began pulling out gowns, holding them up, and then tossing them onto the bed.

Alannah didn't move. She never quite knew what to expect from the young woman, and now was no different. What was her plan?

Zaira dug deeper into her closet and emerged with a pale blue evening gown. "What do you think?"

"'Tis gorgeous, to be sure."

"My thoughts exactly." Zaira walked around the bed to the opposite side that wasn't full of gowns. She laid the blue one down and spread out the skirt made of gauzy tarlatan. "Then we're in agreement that this is the gown you'll wear tonight?"

Alannah took a rapid step back. "Me? No, I couldn't, not at all."

"Nonsense. It matches your eyes perfectly, almost as if it was made just for you."

The light blue was pretty, and Alannah couldn't imagine a dress more beautiful. "No—"

"You'll wear it to the party tonight."

"Party?"

"Shelia and Liam's engagement party."

Wasn't the party when Kiernan had wanted to announce their match? Alannah recoiled. She'd didn't belong there, would never fit in, couldn't go. Everyone would gossip about them, about her, and she'd end up embarrassing him.

Surely there was some other way she could show Kiernan

she was willing to do whatever it took to make their relationship work.

"Well?" Zaira arched a brow.

"I can't . . . I could never . . . 'Tis impossible."

Her thoughts tumbled to a stop. If Kiernan had been willing to go to such great lengths because he loved her, she had to be willing to do the same. She couldn't think of anything more difficult than attending an engagement party and mingling as a guest among the types of people she'd only ever served.

But she'd do it for Kiernan because he was worth all the discomfort and difficulty. She also had to do it for herself, to prove she could push past the barriers that had always been in place and learn to live without them, just like Zaira.

Zaira was still watching her.

"I'll go." Alannah forced the words out.

"You know Kiernan won't want you going out in public, not if there's a chance Shaw might still be searching for you."

"Rightly so." If she came out of hiding, she needed a plan for staying safe from Shaw. Maybe going to the party was a bad idea, after all, especially because Kiernan wouldn't approve. Maybe she would have to wait. . . .

But how could she? She had to do this tonight, had to make this step to show Kiernan she loved him enough to set aside everything that was holding her back. She swallowed her protest. "I'll do anything to go to that party tonight."

"Anything?" Zaira's eyes took on a mischievous glint.

"Aye. Anything."

"That's a good, lass." Zaira picked up the dress and spun around with it, looking much too satisfied with herself. "You leave it up to me. I know just what to do."

Had the young woman arrived with a whole plan already in place?

Alannah hesitated a moment longer. Then she nodded. She'd meant what she said—she would do anything to be with Kiernan, even give in to another of Zaira's dramatic adventures.

32

Kiernan leaned against the railing of the veranda, watching the road beyond the lane for Zaira. She should have been back by now.

He slipped a hand into his pocket, pulled out his watch, and flipped open the cover. It was half past seven. The party was already underway at the Douglas estate.

Liam had told him that he'd been instructed where, when, and how to propose to Shelia, which took some of the enjoyment out of the occasion. But Liam, as always, was a good sport. No doubt he'd do the deed with his usual finesse and charm, earning Shelia and her family's approval and entertaining all the guests.

If Zaira didn't return soon, they would have to leave for the party without her or miss Liam's special moment altogether.

Kiernan slid a glance toward the shade of the veranda where his parents were sitting, Da smoking a cigar and Mam working on her needlepoint, both attired in their fine evening wear. They didn't seem bothered that Zaira was late. Madigan and Quinlan didn't seem impatient to go either and were playing an improvised game of cricket in the backyard.

Something didn't feel quite right.

He straightened and stuffed his watch away. Then he crossed to the front steps.

"Going somewhere?" Da asked.

"To the city to find Zaira." He couldn't wait another minute without knowing how Alannah had responded to his list. He'd ride in and find Zaira. If she was positive about Alannah's reaction, then he'd go directly to her and propose. This time the right way.

"She'll be here in a wee minute." Da set his cigar down in his ashtray.

"Something must have happened."

"You know Zaira," Mam said a little too casually. "She's always such a good girl and will be back shortly."

Kiernan turned to face his parents. "What's going on?"

Mam continued to poke her needle through the fabric without giving him a glance, and his da twisted his cigar.

"It's Alannah." His muscles tensed. "What aren't you telling me?"

"Everything's fine." Da's tone was placating.

Kiernan could only stare at them—Da in his finest tailcoat and top hat and Mam looking so grand, almost regal, in her evening gown. They'd made a life for themselves with wealth and prestige and power. For so long, he'd thought that's what he wanted too—to follow in Da's footsteps and do even better.

But in comparison with having the woman he loved, nothing else mattered anymore. Even if he wasn't able to talk to

Zaira first, he had to go to Alannah and try one more time to win her over.

He shook his head curtly and started down the steps. "Go to the party without me. I'm riding into town." He couldn't worry about hurting Liam. In fact, Liam probably wouldn't notice his absence, at least not until hours had passed.

"Wait, Kiernan." Da rose now too.

"I have to go."

"I just wanted to let you know how proud I am of you."

Da's words halted Kiernan. Proud? Of him? "After the destruction of one business and having to sell the other? I'm a failure."

Da waved a dismissive hand. "So you've had a couple of setbacks. You'll recover."

Kiernan wasn't so sure about that, but he reined in the comment.

"I don't tell you enough," Da continued. "But I'm proud of the young man you're becoming, so I am. You defended the people working for you. You're standing up against the wrongs. And you're pursuing the woman you love. There's nothing more admirable than that."

The unexpected praise brought a sudden lump to Kiernan's throat. His da was sparing with praise, so to have his affirmation in the face of so many challenges softened the blow of losing so much lately.

"Thank you, Da," Kiernan managed through a tight throat.

At the faint jangling and rattling of a carriage, Da squinted in the distance. "Ach, there she is now."

At the bottom of the steps, Kiernan held himself back as the carriage came into view and then turned and rolled down the lane toward him. Hopefully, Zaira had good news for him.

As the carriage circled to the front of the house, the drawn window shades prevented him from seeing inside and gauging Zaira's expression and whether the mission had been a success.

He blew out a breath, one containing all his frustration and anxiety over the past twenty-four hours since making his decision and writing his revised list. Then he stepped up to open the door for Zaira. Before he could reach it, she pushed open the door and began to descend. He took her elbow and assisted her, all the while searching her expression.

She was somber, and her eyes were guarded.

"Did you deliver my note to Alannah?" He was being rude, skipping right over greeting her, but at the moment, his heart felt like it was about to fall out of his chest.

"I did." Zaira wrapped her arms around him in a hug.

"And?" He embraced her briefly, his pulse only beating more wildly with every passing second. "What did she say?"

Zaira stepped back and exchanged a glance with Da and Mam who'd risen from their seats and stood at the top of the stairs.

"Well?" Kiernan demanded.

A movement in the door of the carriage drew Kiernan's attention away from Zaira. Alannah stood in the doorway, one satin shoe on the carriage step, a gloved hand on the handle, and mounds of satiny blue material surrounding her and turning her into a princess. A portion of her blond hair was elegantly twisted up, and part hung down in delicate ringlets, with a crown of white roses only adding to her royal ensemble.

Speechless, he was at her side in the next instant, taking hold of her elbow and assisting her. Her eyes met his tentatively, her blue dress making the blue of her eyes brighter. With the gown off the shoulders, her shoulders were bare, her pale, unblemished skin so smooth, begging him to touch it. If he could, he'd start at her shoulder and draw a trail to her collarbone and then stop right in the dip at the base of her neck. That would be a perfect place to kiss her.

As if hearing his thoughts—or at the very least, reading the desire in his eyes—she lowered her gaze to the ground, watching each step as she made her descent. Once her feet were both firmly settled on the ground, she lifted her eyes again and met his, this time more boldly.

"Hello, Kiernan." Even though her gaze was direct, her voice was soft, almost uncertain. "I wanted to deliver the answer to your letter myself."

He didn't need her to say anything more to realize she'd come to Oakland because she wanted to be with him and was willing to give their match a try. As tempted as he was to gather her into his arms, he held himself back and let her speak what she'd come to say.

"I love you." She spoke the words loudly enough that everyone could hear them, even his parents. Her fingers trembled, but she clasped her hands together. "I hope you can forgive me for pushing you away—"

He dropped his mouth against hers the way he'd been dreaming about doing since the night he'd kissed her in the shed. He almost groaned at the taste and feel of her. He didn't care that his family was watching, didn't care that he was delaying their departure to the party even more, didn't care that he was declaring in front of his family how much he cared about her.

It was past time they all knew exactly how he felt about Alannah.

She melded her lips to his eagerly, clearly not worrying about their audience either. The passion, the wanting, the need . . . it was all there the way it had been during their last kiss. But it was stronger and more powerful, drawing their souls together and leaving him in no doubt that he'd lose a part of himself if he let her go without him.

"Save it for later." Zaira laughed and shoved him.

The movement was enough to make Alannah break the connection. She ducked her head, suddenly shy, as though remembering that his parents were there. Madigan and Quinlan had also come around the house, tousled and sweaty in their suits and staring at the two of them.

Alannah smoothed her gloved hands over her skirt, the slim waist and tight bodice revealing all her womanly curves. "I came tonight to accept your offer to attend the engagement party with you."

"You did?" He couldn't keep the surprise from his voice.

"Oh aye. I need to do it. For you and for myself."

He wasn't sure exactly what she meant, but he guessed she wanted to overcome the barriers and fears that had been holding her back the same way he'd needed to move beyond his. Even so, as much as she wanted to go, she couldn't. He didn't even like that she was standing out in the open where anyone could see her.

He reached for her hand. "You can't show yourself at the party. It's not safe—"

"It will be, to be sure."

"It's not worth the risk. I'll stay here with you, and everyone can go without us."

She turned and glanced into the carriage. A moment later, a man wearing a priest's robe poked his head out. He was one of the priests from the Cathedral. What was he doing here?

Before Kiernan could make sense of what was happening, Alannah lowered herself to one knee amidst the pooling of her beautiful gown and then took hold of his hand and peered up at him. "You've already done the asking more than once. Now it's my turn."

His heart began to race. Was she doing what he thought she was?

"Kiernan, you would make me the happiest woman alive if you agree to marry me."

"Tonight," Zaira hissed.

Alannah blushed. "Tonight."

Everyone around him seemed to be holding their breaths—his parents, his siblings, even the priest. But the answer was already obvious. At least to him. He lowered himself to his knee in front of her, pulled the box from his trouser pocket, then opened it to reveal the ring he'd purchased earlier in the week. It was a blue topaz with tiny diamonds surrounding it.

He slid it down her finger, claiming her for himself as he did so. This woman would forever and always be his and his alone.

When he finished, she held her hand out and examined it.

"I love you, Alannah. And I'd go to the ends of the earth to be with you."

Her eyes rose to his, and she seemed to be searching his soul.

He couldn't hide anything from her, didn't want to hide

anything. He wanted her to see all that was within him, including how deeply passionate he was about her. He'd meant what he said at the bottom of his new list—he'd intended to go to California with her.

She pressed a hand to his cheek. "I'll not be going anywhere, Kiernan, except to be wherever you are. That's all that matters to me."

Her eyes were bright and honest and true. And he knew she was telling him that she wanted to live in St. Louis with him and let Torin go on ahead to California.

The problem was, Kiernan wasn't sure if he needed to stay. He was done comparing himself to his da. He no longer needed to prove anything. He wasn't sure why he'd ever felt the need in the first place. If he never gained as much or made a name for himself, it wouldn't matter. He would be content having Alannah and their life together, whatever that entailed.

His da was grinning as though he'd been in on the plan all along—maybe he had been. And his mam wore a tender smile, one that said she wanted him to be happy, and that if Alannah brought him happiness, she'd be okay. His siblings crowded closer, and the priest descended and moved to stand in front of them.

Alannah smiled at Kiernan tentatively. Then she leaned toward him and touched her lips to his in an achingly soft kiss, one that said she saw him for who he really was and would always love him no matter what the future brought their way.

"Are we going to have a wedding or not?" Zaira asked with a laugh from beside Alannah.

Kiernan broke the gentle kiss and then stood, bringing

Alannah to her feet with him. "I can't think of anything better." As he wrapped his hand around Alannah's, her fingers tightened within his, and he knew that she couldn't think of anything better either.

33

"You don't have to be carrying me up the stairs," Alannah whispered against Kiernan's neck. "I can walk, you know."

She loved the feel of his arms underneath her and the solidness of his chest against her. She loved burrowing her nose near his jaw and breathing in the remains of his woodsy aftershave. She loved that her fingers were entwined in the longer strands of his hair at his collar.

She absolutely didn't want him to put her down. But since he'd carried her over the threshold after Winston opened the door for them a few minutes ago, he hadn't put her down. His arms had to be getting sore.

After a short wedding ceremony on the front veranda at Oakland, she and Kiernan had climbed into the carriage and gone to the Douglases' for Shelia and Liam's party. The rest of the Shanahan family had followed in another carriage.

The priest hadn't been in a hurry and had taken up the offer of a meal while he waited for a return ride back into the city.

Upon arriving at the party, Alannah couldn't deny how

afraid and intimidated she'd been as Kiernan had led her around and introduced her as his wife. Most of the guests had been kind, at least to her face. But she'd seen them whispering and casting slanted looks her way and knew they were talking about Kiernan and her and their hasty marriage.

All throughout the party, however, Kiernan had stayed by her side, held her hand, tugged her to his side, and stolen kisses whenever he could, mostly to her cheek and forehead, assuring her that she was more important than anything or anyone.

As much as she'd wanted to avoid Shelia and Liam, Kiernan had seemed to take delight in approaching the newly engaged couple, showing them the ring, and making a point of saying how he had no regrets in how things had turned out.

When Shelia's eyes widened at his statement, Alannah was fairly certain the young woman knew that Kiernan was referring to that day when she'd come to Oakland and said: *"I hope you don't regret not choosing me."*

In fact, Kiernan had kissed Alannah in front of Liam and Shelia, then wished the young couple well, saying, *"I hope you find as much love and happiness as we have."* After that, Kiernan led her away from the party, telling her he'd had enough and was ready to leave.

With the priest in their carriage for the ride back into the city, Kiernan had been on his best behavior and had done nothing but hold her hand. Once in a while when the priest wasn't looking, Kiernan had stroked a thumb over her palm, fanning the banked heat inside her each time he did.

By the time they'd reached the Cathedral and said goodbye to the priest, heat had been flowing through her veins, so when Kiernan had leaned in and kissed her, she'd been more than ready. They'd kissed the few blocks from the Cathedral to the house. It hadn't been long enough, and she hadn't been ready to stop.

But Kiernan had picked her up and carried her inside, and now she didn't want him to feel obligated to carry her all the way to Torin's room.

"Please, Kiernan," she whispered, even as she brushed a kiss on his jaw.

"No." The word came out as a growl as he reached the top of the stairs.

She could feel his muscles flex against her lips. And oh saints above, she loved it. "What will Torin think when I show up in your arms like this?"

"I don't care." Kiernan's voice was rumbly and did strange things to her stomach.

How was this even possible that Kiernan was her husband? She had to be dreaming, and any moment she'd wake up and find herself without him.

She tightened her arms around his neck.

The motion brought him to a halt in the center of the hallway. "What's wrong?"

She breathed him in again and ran her fingers through his hair. "I'm afraid this isn't real."

He pulled back so that she could see into his dark blue eyes. The intensity within them made her tremble. "You're mine now, Alannah." His tone was low and raw. "And I'll never leave you."

"I know you won't leave me." Her whisper came out with a little embarrassment. "And I don't ever want to be apart from you. If I could have my way, I'd spend my every waking and sleeping hour with you."

"Now you know why I don't want to put you down." His thick lashes fell to halfway, but not before she saw the fire in his eyes and knew he was feeling the same way she was.

She smiled. "But you have to put me down for a few minutes. I don't want to surprise Torin too terribly."

"He'll be happy."

"Oh aye, I think he will."

"Then he'll have to deal with me holding you."

She couldn't contain her laugh of delight as Kiernan finished crossing the distance and entered Torin's room without even a knock.

As he stepped inside with her in his arms, she flushed a wee bit knowing Torin would take one look at them and realize something was different . . . except that Torin wasn't in his bed. The covers were tossed back and rumpled, several pillows on the floor, and a blanket dangling off the side of the bed.

Her heart pinched with sudden worry. "Torin?" she called as she pushed against Kiernan to lower her to the ground.

The passion now forgotten, she landed on her feet and then flew to the bed, pulling back even more covers, bending and looking underneath, and then scanning the rest of the room. But he wasn't anywhere.

All that remained of his presence was the machine that he and Donahue had been working on earlier in the day. And there was a note attached to it.

With her heart thudding harder, she crossed to the contraption and picked up the folded piece of paper. "Do you think Shaw found him?"

Kiernan had tossed open the closet door and was shoving aside clothing. "I pray to God no."

She flipped open the paper to find Torin's handwriting and a few simple sentences: *Alannah, thank you for marrying Kiernan. I've left in peace, knowing you're happy. This invention is your dowry. The brick dryer will help Kiernan increase production of his bricks so that soon he'll be the biggest and best brickmaker in the country.*

Torin had obviously heard about the wedding plan—likely from Winston. Now he was gone, no longer needing to worry about her.

Her heart ached for her older brother. She hadn't wanted to lose him, but in some ways, her marriage to Kiernan had set him free to live his own life without having to take care of her any longer.

She handed the letter to Kiernan and let him read it. As he finished, his eyes widened with wonder, and he crouched and began to examine the brick dryer.

She bent beside him. Although she didn't know anything about the machine or bricks or how to dry them, she guessed that Torin's invention might possibly revolutionize the brickmaking industry. "What do you think?"

"It's nothing short of amazing." Kiernan's voice contained awe.

"Does this mean you don't need to sell the glass factory anymore?"

Kiernan ran a hand across the top of the complex contraption. "I don't know."

"Torin seems to think this will make you pretty successful."

"Maybe I've changed my definition of success." Kiernan smiled at her softly. He'd told her about the conversation he'd had with his da, how his da had said he was proud of him even after all the losses. What mattered most wasn't what he accomplished but the kind of man he was becoming.

She was proud of Kiernan too.

He hesitated. "Liam told me earlier today that the city council is still planning to require bricks for the rebuilding of St. Louis."

"So 'tis possible the need for bricks will resume. When it does, the demand will be incredibly high, and you'll be ready to meet the demand."

Kiernan didn't respond but instead examined the machine for another long moment. When he straightened, that familiar determination she loved was back in his eyes. "Torin never stopped believing in the brickyard. Liam hasn't. You haven't. I guess I shouldn't either."

She smiled. "I always knew you were a smart man."

"Do you know what else I am?" He reached for her, wrapped his arms behind her, and drew her against him.

"What else?" She peered up at him, loving the feel of his body, the beat of his heart against hers, and the solidness of his presence.

"I am also the luckiest man." He bent and rested his forehead against hers. "Because I have you."

"Luck has nothing to do with it," she whispered. "It has everything to do with my wager with the matchmaker."

"*Your* wager?" A grin quirked up the corners of Kiernan's lips. "What if it was *my* wager with the matchmaker that brought us together?"

She laughed lightly. "He made one with you too?"

"The wagers got us both exactly where he wanted us."

"Oh aye." Bellamy had somehow managed to bring them together against all odds. How had he done it?

Kiernan's grin cocked higher on one side. "And now, I've got you exactly where I want you."

"Is that so?" She nuzzled in closer. "Since you have me as your captive, whatever will you do with me?"

He swept down, captured her lips, and showed her what he intended to do all night and forever.

34

Another unsold painting.

Bellamy McKenna shoved the canvas back onto the shelf on top of the half dozen other landscapes no one wanted.

He had to remember he wasn't to blame for the lack of interest, and he couldn't take the rejection personally, not after how well he'd been doing all spring.

No, it was the cholera's fault. With the epidemic getting worse, more families were leaving St. Louis to escape the growing death toll. That meant fewer people were left to visit the art galleries and shops. Those who remained behind had other more pressing matters on their minds than purchasing paintings.

"It will pass." His whisper echoed in the shadowed shed that served as his art studio. But even as the words settled around him, so did a cloud of despair. If W. B. M.—William Bennett Moore—eventually began to sell art again, William Bellamy McKenna would still be just a nobody in Oscar's Pub.

Maybe Bellamy had been wrong to take a secret identity in order to sell his paintings. Maybe he'd been a coward. Maybe he'd relegated himself to living a lie.

"Bellamy!" Oscar's voice boomed across the alley from the back door of the pub. "Stop your dawdling and bring in more Guinness."

Bellamy exhaled a tight breath into the shed's stifling air. With the arrival of July, a fresh wave of heat and humidity had descended upon the city like a sticky, damp blanket. He could hardly move without sweat trickling down his back, plastering his shirt and vest to his body.

He ran a hand across the large trunk where he kept all his supplies. Maybe for the time being he needed to keep things locked up, give his painting a rest, focus on other things—like his matchmaking.

"What the wee devil are you doing in there, Bellamy?" came Oscar's voice again. "You better not be wasting time doing you-know-what."

Bellamy's muscles turned rigid.

Doing you-know-what was as close to describing the act of painting that Oscar ever got because saying the word *painting* was equivalent to using God's name in vain. Other than the derisive insinuations, Oscar never talked about it, never showed an interest in it, never acknowledged it.

It was almost as if by ignoring it, Oscar could make it go away. Just like he had with Mam's painting . . . And look how that had ended.

Bellamy had the urge to yell back and tell Oscar to get the Guinness himself before walking away and never glancing back.

But as strong as the urge was at times, Bellamy could never

do it. Instead, he forced himself to heft up the closest cask of the Irish beer, then kicked open the shed door.

Across the alley, Oscar stood in the back door of the two-story building that housed the pub, his thick, wavy gray hair damp with perspiration, his face and nose ruddier than usual. He'd shed his suit coat and had his shirtsleeves rolled up past his elbows, the armpits wet and yellowed.

"You know what you're needing?" Oscar called as his eyes narrowed on Bellamy.

Bellamy started to cross the alley, the Guinness sloshing with each step he took. "I'm sure you're going to be telling me whether I want you to or not."

Oscar's grin kicked up. "You know me well, that you do."

"Oh aye."

"Then you'll not be whining when I tell you that it's time for you to find a match of your own."

"You'll not be whining when I tell you that I'm not ready." Bellamy never would be ready, not when every matchmaker in his family that he could remember had been unlucky in love. Very unlucky. The matchmakers excelled at finding love for others but failed miserably when it came to finding love for themselves. Oscar knew that. In fact, he'd had a disastrous marriage.

"You keep saying you're not ready," Oscar said, waggling his brows, "but I saw the way you were looking at Zaira Shanahan."

Bellamy couldn't hold back a scoff. "I was looking at her like the annoying pest that she is."

Oscar guffawed. "You were looking at her like you wanted to annoy her right back . . . with a kiss."

With a kiss? Bellamy stumbled and then halted near the

door. Heat rose into his face that had nothing to do with the humid summer day. Aye, there was no denying that Zaira was attractive. She was a beautiful spitfire, one whom any man would want to kiss.

But even if he had been in the business of kissing beautiful women—which he wasn't—he still wouldn't kiss Zaira . . . because he didn't like her or the fact that she knew his secret identity as W. B. M. Somehow she'd figured it out, and now she lorded it over him, teased him about it, and made him squirm with the worry of who she was going to tell.

The truth was, he didn't want to have anything to do with her, wanted to stay as far from her as possible. And he certainly didn't need anyone hearing Oscar's declaration about kissing Zaira and the word getting around to her. She would only lord that over him too.

He checked both ways down the alley to see who was around. The back door of the adjacent store was wide open, but thankfully, no one seemed to be listening.

"Ach, it doesn't matter." Oscar scratched at his round belly. "James Shanahan may have accepted one working-class match with Kiernan, but he'll be looking farther up for his next child."

Bellamy shrugged. "'Tis not my concern."

"It might be your concern soon enough when he comes calling to find Zaira a match."

Protest pushed to the tip of Bellamy's tongue. Zaira was too young at nineteen to get married. Wasn't she?

With Oscar's keen gaze upon him, Bellamy schooled his features into passivity and gave another nonchalant shrug. "If Mr. Shanahan comes calling, I'll find Zaira an annoying husband to keep her company."

Oscar stepped out of the doorway to allow Bellamy to pass. "Your reputation as a matchmaker is growing, especially because word is getting around about the love matches you made."

"Naturally." Bellamy set the cask down on the floor inside the kitchen.

Jenny and Gavin were both at work preparing food for the noon and evening meals—although they didn't need large quantities of late, since they had fewer customers.

Jenny paused in her swift chopping of vegetables at the center work table. With her dark hair pulled up into a twisted knot, she was as elegant and pretty as always. At certain times, when she looked contemplative—like at the moment—she reminded him of Mam, and the usual pain stabbed his heart.

At the stove, Gavin was in the process of shredding chicken into a pot and didn't bother turning around. As a brother-in-law, he was quiet but had been a solid and kind presence in their family for the past ten years that he and Jenny had been married.

"It's good that everyone is hearing about your love matches." Oscar lumbered through the kitchen, swiping up a biscuit from a platter on the sideboard overflowing with dishes. "You need to build a name for yourself as an intuitive matchmaker who knows how to find good, solid matches that will last a lifetime."

Bellamy halted. Something wasn't right. Oscar never had anything positive to say about his unconventional methods. So why now?

Oscar paused in the doorway that led to the bar and dining room and gave an impatient wave. "Come on, then."

Bellamy arched a brow. "Doncha be prodding me along without telling me where you're pushing me."

"Senator Whitcomb is here." Oscar's eyes took on a glimmer that told Bellamy everything he needed to know—that the senator was important and that Oscar counted it a great honor to have him visit the pub. Also, the senator had clearly come to see Bellamy for matchmaking help, and that's why Oscar was being so nice.

"And . . . ?" Bellamy prompted.

"And the senator wants you to help him with a match for his daughter."

"Is that so?"

"Apparently, Miss Whitcomb heard about your love matches for the Shanahans, and she's hoping for the same." The older man chomped another bite of the biscuit, sweat rolling down his forehead.

Bellamy doubted any of that was true. The senator likely had a much stronger reason to seek out a matchmaker at midday in the midst of the worst cholera epidemic in decades. Bellamy studied Oscar for any clues.

The tenseness in Oscar's shoulders was the sign that he would have preferred to handle the match for himself, that he wasn't necessarily happy to hand it over to Bellamy. But at the moment, he had no choice but to humor the senator and bring Bellamy into the process.

Bellamy combed his damp hair off his forehead and then started toward the dining room. He'd just been telling himself to focus on matchmaking. He liked the challenges, liked analyzing people, liked giving couples the happily ever after that he'd never get for himself.

As he stepped out of the kitchen and into the front

room, the waft of old beer and cigar smoke greeted him. The shutters were pulled closed on the windows, keeping out the sunshine and the heat, but also closing in stale air.

The room was nearly empty. Georgie McGuire sat in his usual spot at the bar counter, his head down on his arms, loud snores rumbling around him. A group of older men congregated at their regular table and paused in their conversation at the sight of Bellamy.

He nodded a greeting in their direction, then turned his attention to Oscar's corner table where a well-dressed, middle-aged man was smoking a cigar and twisting at a glass of Bushmills whiskey. He'd taken off his hat to reveal slicked-back brown hair and long sideburns with a neatly trimmed mustache. His face had a youthfulness as well as an edge of frustration.

It was easy to deduce that the frustration was the reason the senator had come to form a match for his daughter. Now Bellamy just needed to figure out what was causing the frustration, then narrow down the best groom who could help alleviate the problem.

As Bellamy wound around the bar counter, the senator rose from his chair and examined Bellamy from his head to his toes, as if assessing whether he had what it took to solve the dilemma.

From behind, Oscar's voice was low and filled with warning. "The senator needs a match for his daughter in one week. If you can't do it, just say so."

Bellamy's steps didn't falter. He'd found a match for Enya Shanahan in less than an hour. Surely he could find a match for the senator's daughter in a week.

"There's no room for failing this match." Oscar spoke firmly. "If you do, it'll ruin you."

Bellamy hadn't failed yet. Of course, he'd only had three matches—the three for the Shanahans. But he'd done a fine job. And he'd do a fine job for the senator too. "I won't fail. Doncha be worrying about that."

Oscar didn't answer, not even with a snort or harrumph.

At the silence, Bellamy's pulse tripped. Oscar was rarely silent. And so the lack of response spoke louder than anything else, alerting him that the match would indeed be difficult, perhaps more difficult than any he'd done yet.

He might not be successful at painting . . . yet. And he definitely had no hope of being successful in finding love for himself. But there was one thing he was good at, and that was finding love for others. He'd do it again now. That's all there was to it.

If you enjoyed

A Wager with the Matchmaker,

read on for an excerpt from

A RELUCTANT BRIDE

Available now wherever books are sold.

one

LONDON, ENGLAND
MAY 1862

Hang on a little longer, my lamb." Mercy Wilkins shifted the listless infant in her arms without slowing her pace.

Clara had stopped responding on Chilton Street, but the slightly warm breath coming from between the little girl's colorless lips told Mercy she wasn't too late . . . so long as the Shoreditch Dispensary wasn't crowded and so long as Dr. Bates was available. He'd treat the infant even though Mercy had no way to pay for his services.

"Don't you fret," she murmured. "If Dr. Bates isn't there, I'll sell my shoes to pay the fee."

Mercy ignored the cold dampness between her toes, the puckered skin on feet that hadn't been dry since spring had chased away the chill of winter and invited a familiar tormentor in its place—rain.

The frequent showers not only soaked her half boots but also turned the streets into swamps of mud and horse manure. The mixture oozed through the holes where her toes had worn through the leather and threatened to suck the shoes off her feet.

She'd tied the frayed laces tight, causing them to break and forcing her to knot them yet again. Though the strings didn't reach the tops of her boots anymore, she was lucky to have them, lucky to have boots at all when so many wore nothing on their feet but rags.

"I'll gladly trade my boots for you to be seen to by a doctor, my sweet one." She brushed a kiss against Clara's cheek. The infant's face was as pale as the fog that hung over the rooftops, and as thin and hollow as the terraced houses that lined either side of the street.

Several boys bumped against Mercy, jostling her. Fingers darted in and out of her skirt pocket with the nimbleness of an expert thief. She had nothing for the boys to steal. The looks of her should have told them that. Except that with the sick infant, maybe they supposed she had a halfpenny tucked away to pay the doctor.

She caught sight of the face of one of the boys, recognizing him in spite of the layer of soot and filth. "Mr. Martins is looking for another boy to clean the streets. Go talk to him and earn your bread the honest way. D'ye hear me?"

The boy didn't acknowledge her comment except to hunch further into his man-sized greatcoat and tip his round cap down to shield his face.

Mercy shook her head but plodded forward. If Mr. Martins would only offer her the street-cleaner job, she'd take it in a snap. But no amount of her pleading had changed his mind about giving the work to a young woman.

"Heaven save us all," he'd exclaimed. "What's the world coming to with women thinking they can do a fellow's job?"

Mercy had wanted to retort that dodging betwixt horses and carriages to shovel up steaming piles of dung didn't take any special talent. Surely a woman could do the job just as well as a man. But Mr. Martins made it clear enough he wouldn't hire her, just like the dozen other people she'd approached that day.

"No matter," she whispered. "I'll find something. Just you wait and see."

Clara's head lolled, and Mercy shifted the infant again. Not quite two years old, the child didn't weigh much more than Twiggy's newborn babe. Even so, after carrying the girl for blocks, Mercy's arms burned from the burden.

Through the foggy mist hovering in the narrow street, she glimpsed the Shoreditch Dispensary. Like the surrounding businesses, it leaned outward and was propped up by beams to the building across the street. The beams were almost like canes, meant to keep the aged, tottering structures from collapsing into the filth below.

Between high windows hung strings of soggy garments, so threadbare and gray they resembled the rags Twiggy sorted at the factory. Their soaking from the recent rain would wash away the grime for a moment, but never for long. In this part of London, the filth was as constant a companion as the rats.

"Almost there, dear heart." If only she'd known how sick the girl was, she would have brought her earlier. At least in the late afternoon, the streets weren't as crowded. And at least the rain had decided to show some compassion.

Upon reaching the dispensary door, Mercy fumbled at the handle, kicking her boots against the brick step, attempting to dislodge the muck. As she entered, the dark gloom of the hallway greeted her.

An old man crouched in the corridor cradling his arm. A mother sat opposite him, holding a bundle of blankets with a tiny bare foot poking through the fabric. The babe's stillness, as well as the mother's vacant gaze, told a story Mercy had heard too many times.

"Doctor!" Mercy strode down the hallway, her footsteps squeaking and squishing with each step. "I'm in desperate need of help."

"Wait your turn, you young cur," growled the old man. "There be others needing the doctor first." He nodded to the mother and babe. The woman stared at the faded green wallpaper, the remnants of a time when the home had been fancy and belonged to a family of means. Such families had long since moved away and built larger homes in parts of London Mercy had only heard about but never seen.

Mercy regarded the babe's unmoving outline, then faced the older man. "The doctor may be able to save a life. Do you want two children dead instead of one?"

She held his angry gaze until finally he dropped his sights to the muddy footprints that caked the wood floor.

"Doctor," Mercy called again as she made her way to the room Dr. Bates used as his office. "Please, I need your help. Straightaway."

Seeing the door was ajar, she bumped it open with her hip. The massive desk positioned near a boarded window was cluttered with books and papers and inkpots. A lantern was lit and illuminated its dusty globe painted with delicate flowers. But Dr. Bates wasn't there.

The door of the adjacent room swung open, and a young man exited, his hand swathed in bandages. He didn't spare her or the others a glance, as if they didn't exist.

Mercy supposed it was easier for some people to pretend the problems weren't there. The heartache, the burdens, the needs . . . it was all so overwhelming at times.

Clara's weight dragged at Mercy. For an instant, she was tempted to slide down next to the mother with the dead babe and stare at the wallpaper too. But at a clank from the open doorway, Mercy forced herself to move, gathering the strength to fight for one more life.

"Doctor?" She entered the room unbidden. "Can you give a look at my little lamb?"

At the room's lone table, a young man stood in front of a basin of water where he was washing his hands. Beside the basin lay a scattering of instruments and supplies—a scalpel, small scissors, ligature thread, and needles. He'd discarded his coat over the back of a nearby chair to reveal a striped waistcoat and a finely tailored shirt, its sleeves rolled up to his elbows. His dark brown hair was tousled, likely the result of a long day of rushing from one urgent need to the next.

His face was unfamiliar, not one of the usual doctors who gave of their time at the dispensary. Since Clara needed immediate attention, this man would have to do.

He glanced up and paused in his scrubbing. Exhaustion crinkled the corners of his eyes and forehead. "I shall be with you in a moment." He didn't speak unkindly, just wearily.

"I don't have a moment, sir." Mercy crossed the room toward the cot. "This sweet child is failing fast, that she is."

Gently Mercy lowered the girl, whose limbs flopped about, her strength and life all but gone. Mercy dropped to her knees beside the cot and caressed Clara's cheek and forehead, brushing back strands of matted hair. The girl's dirty face was shriveled, her eyes shrunken, her lips cracked.

"Don't you leave me, dear heart. The kind doctor will fix you up. I promise."

Thankfully, the doctor didn't delay and instead crossed to them quickly. He knelt on the opposite side of the cot and checked the infant's pulse, an air of urgency emanating from every brisk movement he made. "What are your daughter's symptoms?" he asked as he lifted first one eyelid and then the other.

"She's not . . ." Clara wasn't Mercy's daughter. Yes, they shared the same blond hair. But couldn't the doctor see Mercy wasn't wearing a wedding band?

As soon as she asked the silent question, she chastised herself. A wedding band wasn't necessary to have children, especially not where she came from. This doctor apparently knew it too.

He placed an instrument against Clara's chest. "Her symptoms?"

"She can't keep anything down, sir. No liquids or solids. It all comes out one way or the other."

The doctor rose so suddenly that Mercy started. "How long has she had the vomiting and diarrhea?"

"It began last night—"

"And you are just now bringing her in?" Irritation edged his voice.

"I'd have brought her earlier if I'd known, sir," Mercy replied. If only Clara's mother had thought to call for her sooner.

"Fever?"

"Come and gone."

The doctor muttered something under his breath as he rummaged through supplies in a chest. He returned with a teaspoon and a small brown vial. "I would normally suggest having the child drink a mild solution of salt and warm water until the poison is eliminated and vomit runs clear."

"Poison, sir?"

"Her symptoms point to cholera infantum."

A chill crept up Mercy's spine. Most people called it summer diarrhea because it occurred in the summer months when the heat made the foulness of streets and ditches almost unbearable. She'd watched helplessly last August as a dozen little ones in her neighborhood had wasted away, including her own baby brother.

"That cannot be it, sir," Mercy said. "It's not summer yet."

"Cholera infantum can strike at any time of the year." The doctor unscrewed the lid on the brown bottle and poured a scant amount into the spoon. "The condition is related to tainted food, possibly spoiled milk."

Mercy used her fingers to comb back Clara's hair. Milk was rare in the slums. Had Clara's mother found some? If so, she'd have given the treat to the girl expecting it to nourish, not poison, her.

"Raise her head," he instructed.

Mercy lifted Clara's body.

He brought the spoon to the girl's mouth. "She's too dehydrated and won't rouse to drink. Our best hope is to administer the acetozone every ten to fifteen minutes."

With surprising tenderness, he tipped the contents between her lips. He watched the pale, unresponsive face for a long moment before holding out the spoon and brown bottle to Mercy.

She took the items hesitantly. "Sir?"

"You may administer the next dose when I tell you it is time. Meanwhile, I shall prepare an enema for her."

Mercy nodded.

He crossed the room and searched in the chest again. Then he laid out a syringe and catheter and began mixing a solution from a number of bottles. From the fine cut of his garments to the way he held himself, she could see he was a gentleman. But strangely his face and arms were as sun-bronzed as a dockhand's.

Perhaps he'd recently returned from India or Africa or one of the other tropical colonies. She'd heard such places were blissfully warm all the year long. Those were the kinds of places that occupied her dreams during the winter, when they had only enough coal to keep from freezing to death but never enough to be warm.

"You're new to the dispensary, sir?" she asked, letting her curiosity get the better of her as usual.

"No." His stir stick clanked against the glass container as he swirled the cloudy liquid. "I'm only helping Dr. Bates for a few days now and then while I'm in town."

"Oh, Dr. Bates. Now, he's a right fine gent." Not only didn't he charge her for his treatments, but he was always kind and offering her helpful advice.

She swished the contents of the brown bottle. How much would this new doctor charge her today? Would the offer of her shoes be enough? They were the last thing she owned of any value. She'd long since pawned the rest of her possessions. Would she, like some of the women she knew, have to start trading favors for what she needed?

The very idea repulsed her. But as she ran a finger along Clara's delicate nose and traced the outline of her face to her chin, she could begin to understand what drove some women to such desperate measures.

Mercy glanced at the doctor and caught him staring at her. She half expected he'd read her thoughts, that she'd see lewd calculation in his eyes the same that she'd seen in Tom Kilkenny's eyes when he'd told her she could be a serving wench in his pub. She knew as well as everybody else that Tom's wenches did more than hand out mugs of beer.

She'd told Tom she'd rather go to the workhouse.

He'd only laughed and warned her the workhouse would ruin her pretty features and turn her into a hag so that no one would ever want her.

Mercy had only to think about how much Patience had changed in the few months she'd lived at St. Matthew's Bethnal Green Workhouse. Before going in, Patience had been like a rare blade of green grass poking through the piles of garbage in a dark alley. But she'd withered so that whenever Mercy visited the workhouse, she hardly recognized her sister anymore.

All the more reason why Mercy needed to find a job, so Patience could live at home again.

The doctor shifted his attention to Clara, but not before Mercy glimpsed the compassion in his expression. He felt sorry for her because he thought Clara was her daughter. She ought to correct him, but what if his assumption motivated him to work harder to save the child?

"It's time for another spoonful of the acetozone," he said as he readied the catheter.

Mercy poured the medicine into the spoon, cradled Clara in her free arm, then slowly tipped the liquid into the girl's mouth the way the doctor had. "There you are, sweet one."

She envisioned Clara's adorable smile, the one she'd given Mercy yesterday morning when Mercy had delivered half rolls to the children who lived in her building. Occasionally Mr. Hughes, the old baker over on High Street, gave Mercy the rolls that had gone stale. It was a kind gesture. She supposed he did it because she'd once stopped a boy from thieving a basket of fresh bread from his shop.

Even if the rolls were harder than a pewter pot, they were nourishment all the same. And Clara was just one of the children Mercy made a point of helping whenever she could.

She bent and pressed a kiss against Clara's sunken cheek, waiting to feel the faint warmth of the little one's breath. Instead, there was stillness. Mercy sat up only to find the gray liquid dribbling from the corner of Clara's mouth.

Her stomach twisted with a deep knowing, one she wanted to ignore. She dragged the spoon under the leaking medicine and brought it back to the girl's lips. "Come now, lamb. You have to take this."

She attempted to pour it in, but it trickled back out. She tried again and again, murmuring, "Please sweet one, please . . ."

Finally she became aware of gentle fingers tugging at the spoon, attempting to pull it from her. She tore her gaze from Clara to find the doctor across from her. His brows slanted above eyes brimming with pity.

How dare he give up so easily? She wanted to shove his hand away, to scream her protest and cling to the spoon, as if by doing so she could cling to hope. But having seen death too many times in her eighteen years, she knew the fight would be futile.

She released her hold and let her hands fall to her lap.

The pain in her chest was not as easy to release. It gripped so tightly she struggled to suck in a breath. Then she fought to push away the ache just as she always did. She'd learned long ago to stuff it out of sight or she might just go mad from the sorrow.

"I'm sorry." The doctor sat back on his heels, haggardness grooving more lines into his face.

Mercy bent low and kissed the little girl's forehead, praying her kiss would anoint the child as she journeyed to a better place.

Surely anyplace in heaven or earth would be better than London.

Jody Hedlund is the bestselling author of over fifty novels and is the winner of numerous awards. Jody lives in Michigan with her husband, busy family, and five spoiled cats. She writes sweet historical romances with plenty of sizzle. Visit her at JodyHedlund.com

Sign Up for Jody's Newsletter

Keep up to date with Jody's latest news on book releases and events by signing up for her email list at the link below.

JodyHedlund.com

FOLLOW JODY ON SOCIAL MEDIA

Author Jody Hedlund

@JodyHedlund

@JodyHedlund

More from Jody Hedlund

When a St. Louis Irish matchmaker pairs a shy young woman who spends her time caring for immigrants with a wealthy, flirtatious man whose father wants him to settle down, they can't imagine a more opposite pairing. But as they work together to protect the neighborhood from an epidemic, all they know about love and sacrifice is tested.

Calling on the Matchmaker
A Shanahan Match #1

Enya Shanahan's ill-fated marriage has left her with an annulment and a child on the way. Her father's solution is for her to marry again, and the local matchmaker knows just the man: Captain Sullivan O'Brien. Enya's heart is closed off to love in this marriage of convenience, but a greater purpose draws them together.

Saved by the Matchmaker
A Shanahan Match #2